'IT' TAKES A WOMAN

J PIGOTT

© J Pigott

Published by PJ Publications

June 2010
Proofread by LIBRO proofreading & editing;
http://libroediting.wordpress.com

ISBN 978-0-9566761-0-8

DISCLAIMER

Cover Design by Clare Brayshaw

Prepared and printed by:

York Publishing Services Ltd
64 Hallfield Road
Layerthorpe
York YO31 7ZQ
Tel: 01904 431213
Website: www.yps-publishing.co.uk

DEDICATION

To Peter. As a Girl Guide, we used to say: "Make new friends, but keep the old; one is silver, the other gold." You are golden, and so will be our next wedding anniversary. God Bless you, and our wonderful family. With eternal love, Jan.

ABOUT THE AUTHOR

Janet Pigott was born in Yorkshire and brought up in York. She is currently a member of Pens of Erdington Creative Writing Group and had 4 short stories published in the group's *Little Book of Smells* published by the tutor/mentor, Jan Watts in 2009.

In 2010 she submitted a monologue and poems for inclusion in the writing group's next book, *Chores – The Truth About Housework* to be published on Lulu.com as a contribution to the City of Birmingham Artsfest celebrations in Autumn of the same year.

She has written three textbooks, two with co-authors: *Word Processing Experience Student's Edition (co-author Roger Atkins-Green); Word Processing Experience Teacher's Handbook*, and *Office Proofreading (co-author the late Marion Smith)* all published by Stanley Thornes Publishers, Cheltenham, England, in the 1980's.

ACKNOWLEDGEMENTS

To my dearest husband I give my sincere thanks for all his support, encouragement, help with researching historical facts, and personal knowledge that he has shared with me, and for answering all my questions tirelessly and willingly.

Although my mother and father are no longer alive, I would like to thank them for all the love, care, affection, encouragement and help they gave me. I think they would be proud of this book but shocked at the characters which I have created for Audrey Small's parents.

I would also like to thank Jan Watts, playwright, and tutor/mentor of Pens of Erdington Creative Writing Group, for reading several chapters of my script as I wrote the story, and offering helpful advice. My cousin, Mike Race, encouraged me to persevere, and have this novel published. Christine Coleman was extremely helpful with advice about publishing following her success with Paper Lanterns. Liz Broomfield provided a skilful proofreading and copy editing service. Pat Pedder at Erdington library, and staff at Mere Green library, kindly offered opinions on print styles and headings for the book.

Whilst the story was in its final production run I holidayed with my cousin Angela Hill, and her husband, who had lived in Belgium for over 20 years. Angela explained the tension which exists between Flemings and Walloons, and the Walloon dialect. Her husband, Dr J A Hill, thought it would be better had I said in Chapter 16 that the school trip went to Blankenberge where Flemings and a few Walloons lived. He also patiently showed me computing techniques about which I previously knew nothing, and I am extremely grateful to them both for their concern and advice.

Clare Brayshaw and staff at YPS were most helpful and professional at all times. Without all of these people, this novel would not have come to fruition in its present format. I give sincere thanks to everyone involved in this publication.

CONTENTS

CHAPTER 1

REFLECTIONS

'Da-a-ad, what's sex and what does sexy mean?'

Larry Small lowered his Sunday paper and peered over the top of it, confronting his innocent 12-year old daughter, Audrey.

'Wherever did you hear those words?'

'I didn't hear them. I just read them on the front of your newspaper.' Somewhat embarrassed, he replied:

'Well, they're not words you should concern yourself with. Don't ever let your mother hear you say them, or you'll be in real trouble. This paper's for adults, not children.'

He raised his Sunday newspaper and continued reading.

'I only asked because at school they said if we didn't know anything, we had to ask.'

'Don't you go asking about that at school! Tomorrow I'll get you a book from the library and you can read about it for yourself.'

The next day he brought a book home but when Audrey thumbed through it looking for pictures she only found what looked like a diagram of something resembling an animal's face with curled down horns, and an odd-looking tadpole with an extra-long tail. It was a medical book written in a style which was far too old for her to follow, and contained many unfamiliar words. She gathered it had something to do with babies, but wasn't interested in it, and put it to one side.

That was eight years ago. Now she mused about it, as a light aroma of fern fronds permeated the atmosphere in the isolated copse where she lay on a tract of mossy carpet in a state of exhilaration and pure escapism.

A chaffinch chirped in the shimmering foliage, outwitting the call of crows and the fluttering beat of her exposed breasts.

Audrey Small and her boyfriend, Rocky Driver, had cycled to Stockton on Forest on the outskirts of York. The sun shone brightly. Fluffy clouds floated across an azure sky as the couple folded their arms around each other passionately. A delicious, warm feeling ran through their bodies. This was something wonderful; something amazing; something which could last a lifetime.

A slight soughing of wind amongst the branches brought her mind back to reality. Rocky, aware of her change of attitude, interrupted her thoughts as they took a downward turn.

'Penny for them?'

'I was just thinking about my mother. What ever would she say if she could see us now?'

'Forget about her. She can't rule your life for ever. You'll be a legal adult soon and once you come of age, you'll be able to do as you please without any comment or interference from her. Just enjoy being with me.'

'Oh, Rocky, love, I'll try. But I can't help wondering what I've done to cause her such angst. There are times when she's almost like a mad woman.'

'Leave it, love, and put her out of your mind. It's personal experiences that mould people into what they are. You can't do much about what she's gone through in the past, so come here again, you delicious nubile thing.'

He drew her closer and caressed her breasts again.

In those precious moments Audrey adored him. His touch was gentle, tender and caring. It was the first time anyone had held her so closely. She closed her eyes and savoured the suckling sensations.

They lay in a passionate embrace, but had a mutual respect for each other's virginity.

When it was time to go home they pedalled their way through York's narrow city streets, taking short-cuts where they could to reduce their ten mile ride to Audrey's house. When they arrived, her armpits sweated and smelt of dank musk; Rocky's forehead was beaded with perspiration.

Audrey knew her father wouldn't be home until his shift was over and her mother would most likely be engrossed in her usual weekend baking session whilst listening to "Saturday Night Theatre" on the Home Service radio programme.

They trundled their bikes from the back-lane into the old air-raid shelter at the rear of the premises.

'Come in, love, What do you fancy for supper?'

'Another bite of you if I can get it', he joked.

They went through the back door into the kitchen. A mouth-watering aroma of freshly cooked cakes filled their nostrils. Suddenly they felt hungry for something other than love.

'Oh, yer come back sometime then! I'm busy. Yer'll have to get yer own supper ready.'

Audrey's mother had no compunction about being bossy. It was her stock in trade.

Rocky went into the immaculately clean dining room and sat down whilst Audrey made a pot of tea and some sandwiches. Her mother was irritated because when she was cooking she spread her ingredients and tins all over the worktops, and there was only room for one person to manoeuvre in the narrow kitchen.

Mrs Small opened the oven door and removed a hot baking tray of delicious-smelling golden-topped coconut macaroons. Rocky could see them from where he was sitting. As she removed them with a palette knife on to a wire cooling rack, he thought they looked as appetising as Audrey's breasts had been, each centrally placed cherry reminding him of the nipples he had drawn to prominence a few hours earlier.

'Where've yer been?' Mrs Small demanded, in a voice that provoked a steely atmosphere and implied 'tell me everything'. Before Audrey had time to blurt out anything he didn't want her mother to know, he responded quickly:

'We've only been out for a bit.'

'What've yer been doing?'

Audrey's palms sweated. The colour of her cheeks

rose. She bit her tongue and riveted her attention on Rocky.

'Comparing Yorkshire's broad acres with Mr Small's little allotment on Scarcroft Road,' he replied crisply.

Mrs Small was shocked by his sarcasm. No-one ever answered her back and got away with it. Her antipathy for him rose. Her mask of tolerance slipped to reveal a face malevolent with hatred for him.

'Why?' she snapped.

'For something to do on a bright sunny day,' he replied airily, hoping his reply would stop her from interrogating them further.

'I don't know why yer don't get a Saturday job and earn yerself some money. Young chap like you! Yer must need it. Can't be easy living on a college grant. Yer could clean windows, pull pints, wash beer glasses, deliver newspapers, there's lots of Saturday jobs to be had. In my day I had to work every day, Sat'd's and Sund'ys included. Hard work hurt no-one.' She glowered at Audrey.

'Can't stay in to help me with the baking, can yer?'

Before waiting for a reply she thumped the door shut between the kitchen and the dining room where they were sitting and banged baking tins down on the workbench, grumbling loudly, and obliterating the sound of the radio. She made vehement comments about how sorry she felt for herself being in the house alone, baking; being in a hot kitchen on a lovely warm sunny afternoon while they'd been out enjoying themselves. Audrey was embarrassed by the tension her mother was creating, and gripped Rocky's hand for comfort.

'We've upset her now.'

'I hardly think so! It's just a game she's playing with us to show that she's in control. She feels she must know everything, and be in charge. She feels annoyed because we didn't ask her permission to come back later than usual. Well, at our ages, we don't need to ask her. She's not going to tell me what to do and dominate my life the way she does yours. It's none of her concern. And if you'd any sense, you wouldn't let her treat you in this way either. She's not going to boss me around and, hopefully not you, for much longer.'

He increased his grip on her hand and looked at her with large brown velvety eyes.

'When I finish college next year I'd love to marry you. How about it? What do you think?'

Audrey was flabbergasted. So much had happened that day. That was the last thing she'd anticipated. The proposal was so unromantic. Had it come that afternoon she would've accepted it instantly, but she'd always expected someone to go down on bended knee, and he hadn't.

'Oh, Rocky, you know I'd love to, but don't you have to get dad's permission first?'

'There you go again, always thinking about other people before yourself! Life's what *we* make it. It's what *we* want that matters.'

She stroked his podgy fingers with her slender ones. Her exhilarated eyes gave him the answer he wanted to know.

CHAPTER 2

RECOLLECTIONS

After Rocky had gone home, Audrey helped her mother to wash the pots and baking tins.

Mrs Small was in a hostile mood and raised her voice acidly.

'I want yer to get rid of that lad. He's not yer type and never will be.' Audrey's blood boiled, but she tried to keep cool.

'What do you mean, mother?'

'He's not what I've got in mind for yer at all. I want yer to meet and marry a professional man – a lawyer, or a doctor, someone with standing in society, someone with letters after their name – not HIM!' Before Audrey could justify that when he qualified as a teacher he would be a professional man, Mrs Small screeched:

'Yer don't know anything about him. Yer don't know his stock. He hasn't got a car. He hasn't any money......'

'How do *you* know?' Audrey interrupted angrily. 'We haven't got a car or any money to speak of either.'

'Well, go on then,' Mrs Small challenged, 'tell me, how much money has he got?'

'Money has nothing to do with our friendship. He's kind and considerate and very patient with me, far more than you'll ever be, and I love him dearly.'

'Love him? Love him,' she shrieked, 'Yer don't know the meaning of the word. Yer far too young. Yer haven't been out with many other fellas, so just do as yer told and get rid of him.'

Audrey's heart sank, but she'd heard the bulk of this remonstration before. When she'd gone out with a previous boyfriend her mother had persuaded her to drop him and she'd succumbed to her influence. This time she realised that each time she brought a new male friend home, her mother was going to react in a similar manner. So, mustering every ounce of self-assertion, she retorted:

'Stop this, mother. I dropped Alistaire because you didn't find him acceptable, and now you don't like Rocky either. Well I do. I'm going to marry him. So I'll give you two choices. Either we'll get married in a Register Office without you, or you can help me to arrange a lovely white wedding, in Church, with all your relatives and friends there. The choice is up to you but I will marry him, believe me!'

It was the first time Audrey had stood up to her mother in this way and she couldn't believe how roused she felt. She expected her mother to lash out at her with her tongue, but she didn't. Instead, she was shocked into silence. With several most contemptible glowers, but nothing more said, Mrs Small stomped upstairs to her bedroom, slamming doors as she went.

Audrey remained downstairs amazed at how the altercation had ended but couldn't help wondering how things would work out now. She went into the kitchen and made herself a cup of tea. She sat down in a comfortable armchair and tried to relax. She glanced around the meticulously tidy room kept clean every day by her house-proud mother. She tossed questions around in her mind as to why her mother was so hostile to Rocky. He hadn't done or said anything to upset her; yet she'd taken an instant dislike to him but she refused to say why. Audrey sat and pondered the problems for a time, but couldn't come up with any real reason, other than that her mother might dislike any male friend she brought home, not just Rocky. She sat back and thought about her past.

Among her reflections she wished she'd had a pound for every time someone had said to her 'Small by name, Small by nature.' True, their surname was 'Small' and, indeed, her mother was diminutive. But it didn't apply to her father who was tall, rotund, and weighty.

Her mind was active, and she thought it odd that Grandma Ferry had named her daughter Suky. If she'd included the letter L it would have described her mother's personality more aptly – Sulky. Yet, to be fair, she wasn't always sulky. There were times when her mother was happy, considerate and caring. She'd always been possessive, wanting her own way, and never being wrong in any altercation with her sister, Dorcas, or her brother, Quilliam. But she was also very kind-hearted when anyone was ill. Someone once said it was as if she had an on/off switch. She could be absolutely charming when anyone came to the house even if she'd been in a frosty mood a few minutes prior to their arrival. And wasn't that the problem today? Her mother wasn't in charge, in addition to which Rocky didn't switch on smiles and ingratiate himself to her. He was just an honest, truthful, young man who didn't kowtow to anyone.

As she sipped her tea, she thought about the first time her mother had lost her cool and gone berserk. It was about eleven years ago, when she was nine years old. That was also on a Saturday. Her mother had told her to go to the pork butcher's on Ouse Bridge and buy a ring of polony and a large sized pork pie for dad's pack-up and she was to come straight home with her purchases. She didn't have enough small change so had given Audrey a blue £1 note to cover the cost, and put it in a little brown purse on a long thin leather strap which she put over Audrey's shoulder so that it lay diagonally across her body.

'Yer'll get some change so put it in the purse before yer leave the shop, then come straight home. Do yer understand?'

After confirming that she did, Audrey had set off with jaunty steps and arrived at her destination quite quickly. That had been a lovely sunny day, too, and she had enjoyed her freedom to be out on her own with not a care in the world.

When she arrived at the butcher's shop there was a long queue all the way round the shop. She joined its tail. She noticed a lady with an appealing bunch of flowers. Her eyes were drawn to the striking scarlet heads of the tulips, alongside some daffodils which had not yet broken their buds. She thought how lovely it would be if she could give her mother some flowers.

Eventually it was Audrey's turn to be served. She bought a ring of polony and a large pork pie which would be cut into portions and put in her father's 'pack-up' for several days. Funnily enough, she thought, the skin on the polony was exactly the same shade of red as the tulips.

The shop-assistant gave her a mass of change from her £1 note. She fitted the coins into her purse and fastened it tightly. She half ran, half skipped her way home, when she caught up with a little school friend, Polly Dickinson, who'd also been shopping as her 'Good Deed for the Day'.

Polly was a year younger than Audrey but they were both members of a local Brownie Pack so knew each other very well. Polly's father owned a Barber's shop on Bishopthorpe Road which was on Audrey's route, so they walked home together, chatting happily.

When they arrived at the shops Audrey saw some daffodils in full bloom in a bucket outside a green-grocer's.

'Oh, aren't they lovely?' she exclaimed 'And so cheap! I'm going to get a bunch for me mam because she never gets any flowers given.'

Polly went in to the shop with her and when they came out said:

'What are you going to give your dad?'

'Oh, I don't know! I hadn't thought about that.'

'Well, you can't give to one person without giving to the other – they're both your parents.'

'Oh dear!'

Audrey went puce with embarrassment.

'What ever can I get for him?'

'Why don't you buy him some fags? My dad sells them. We can get some at our shop.'

'Oh, I can't do that; he only smokes a pipe.'

'Well the only other thing dad sells are hairy-carrot covers. Ever so many men buy them when they've had their hair cut, so they must be useful.'

'Oh that's a brilliant idea! Dad has an allotment on the plot on Scarcroft Road opposite the school. I expect that's where the men use them. How much do they cost?'

'I don't know, but the price will be on the packet. They won't be much because they're only small, but at least it will be something to give him, and they'll have a present each.'

Proud and pleased with her purchases, Audrey had arrived home feeling buoyant but got the shock of her life at her mother's displeasure.

'What's all this?' she screamed. 'Where's me change? I didn't send yer to buy half-dead flowers with me money – and where on earth did yer get this French Letter? Who've yer been with? What've yer been doing?'

Audrey was petrified at the tone of her mother's voice.

'I haven't bought a French Letter. I don't know what you're talking about.'

'*This!* This thing for your father?'

'That's not a French Letter, it's a hairy-carrot cover! Polly Dickinson sold it to me out of her father's shop.'

'Well yer can just take it, and the flowers back, and get me ME money back. How on earth do yer think I'm going to feed us when yer spend me money on trash like this?'

She flung the flowers across the room. They hit the wall and slid down to the floor leaving a pollen mark trailing to the skirting board. Audrey was devastated. She'd only meant to be kind.

Suddenly she heard her father's key being pushed into the front door lock on returning from his shift-work. She froze. Much as he loved her, he loved his wife to extremes and always sided with her no matter what she said. Before he had opened the door and got into the vestibule she switched off the light and fled upstairs to her bedroom. She lay on the bed fully clothed. Her mind raced. What story would her mother tell him about tonight's confrontation? What twist would she put on it this time? What would the atmosphere between them be like the next time they were all together? Now Rocky had proposed to her, did she really care any more?

CHAPTER 3

ROCKY'S BACKGROUND

After leaving Audrey's house Rocky's aching legs automatically turned the pedals of his bike as he steered towards the teacher training college where he resided. His brain jangled. He talked to himself:

'Have I shot myself in the foot? I hadn't intended to propose in that manner. In fact, I hadn't intended to propose at all today. It was my intention to propose on my twenty-first birthday in a few weeks' time but it just seemed the protective thing to do when Audrey's mother slammed the door on us. Nasty woman! I hope Audrey never grows up to have a tongue like that. But she won't. I won't let her. I'll find a way round that vindictive woman.'

He stuck his legs out and freewheeled downhill for a pedal-free ride. He was determined Mrs Small wouldn't get under his skin – yet she already had. He never knew how he got back to college, but when he arrived he thrust his bike into the cycle rack, reached his room in a state of fatigue, flopped on top of the bed, and stretched out. He put his hands behind his head and closed his eyes.

He soon realised that he was saddle sore after his round trip of almost forty miles. He wasn't used to cycling; his sport was field events. As his mental state drifted into oblivion, clouds of recollections drifted to and fro in the whirling of his mind.

He remembered how he first met Audrey at a dance in the Assembly Rooms a year ago. She was wearing a pale blue dress which matched the colour of her eyes and her skin was soft and creamy. Her aroma was that of ripe honeysuckle which grew in his parents' garden at home. When he asked her for a dance and she rose from her seat to join him she was so small her head only reached the level of his heart. He remembered how clumsy he was, treading on her toes from time to time as they wandered around the dance floor to the tune of a waltz.

At the interval they went for a cup of coffee and he found her easy to talk to. She had a slight Yorkshire accent as opposed to his formal enunciation, which belied his rural upbringing, but more importantly in his opinion she had the excellent attribute of being a good listener. He liked that aspect of her. So many of the girls he'd met before were prattlebags, full of themselves, like empty barrels, and he'd been glad to get away from them as quickly as he could. But Audrey was different. There was something about her that made him feel wholesome. He didn't know why, but being with her gave him a warm glow. At the moment she was a shorthand typist but he felt sure she had qualities that would take her further in a future career, that is, if she wanted to continue working after they were married. It hadn't been that long ago that married women weren't allowed to work in the teaching profession, Civil Service, or nursing, but things had changed. Next year would be the start of the sixties and things were looking up. That was the last thing his memory recalled.

His sleep was broken by the sound of Church bells ringing. It was Sunday! Time to get up and go to Morning Service. He jumped off the bed and realised he was still dressed in yesterday's clothing. He'd have to move quickly if he was to shave, re-dress in clean clothes, have breakfast, and still get there in time. He forwent breakfast, grabbed his bike and made it just in time to padlock it to the Church railings before the service began. He knelt down on a lumpy tapestry hassock and amazed himself by hearing a silent prayer inside his head asking God to improve the tone of words produced by Mrs Small's sniping tongue.

'Whatever next? Why did I do that?' he asked himself silently, before sitting up in the pew.

The processional emerged up the Chancel aisle. The congregation rose. The service began, and finished, and he hadn't a clue as to the contents of the sermon; it had all passed over his head automatically.

When the service was over, he loosened the padlock on his bike and put it in his saddlebag, took out his cycle-clips and pushed them around the turn-ups on his trousers, before cycling to Audrey's house. He couldn't telephone her because there was no phone installed. He went to the back gate and put his bike in the shelter before knocking on the back door. Audrey's mother appeared.

'Oh, it's you!' she exclaimed with acidity in her voice.

'Hello, Mrs Small,' he responded crisply, 'I've come to take Audrey to my parents' home for tea today.'

'I suppose yer'd better come in then.'

Her tone was frosty, reluctant and resentful. He felt as if the atmosphere could be cut with a knife.

Audrey jumped up from her chair like a streak of lightening.

'Oh, Rocky, it's good to see you. Come in.'

She quickly adjusted her hair, put on a short blue coat and, leaving his bike in the shelter in the back yard, they caught a Sunday service bus to an outlying village called Bilborough.

Although they had been going out together for several months, this was the first time Rocky had taken Audrey home to meet his parents. On the journey he prepared her for what she would find.

He explained that his mother and father lived in an ancient rented cottage in the older part of the village. At one time it had been at the end of a row of farm workers' cottages, but the other four had been demolished long ago. His parents had the use of all the land which had been worked by the previous tenants. Now the building stood isolated in a well-tended acre of land on which they grew their own food. The odour of fresh vegetables when growing in rows was far more pungent than when cut and displayed in shops, and she needed to be aware that there might be a strong stench from a nearby pig farm, depending on which way the wind was blowing.

He also told her that no matter how hard his father worked on the land by day, and however tired he may be when he came home, he still tended his own garden in the evenings. If his dad didn't grow it, they didn't eat it. But there was always plenty to eat. Rocky was used to picking a pear off a tree when they were in season, or helping himself to a raw carrot or a pod of peas, as the fancy took him. Bread and milk deliveries took place daily and van men selling meat and fish frequented the village once a week.

When the couple alighted from the bus they walked some distance before reaching a gravel pathway. The smell of growing crops and new mown hay entered their nostrils, but it was the pong of slurry and pig-swill that moistened Audrey's eyeballs, even though she had been warned about it.

They stopped while she wiped her eyes, and Rocky dropped a kiss of comfort on her forehead before they moved on.

As they approached the cottage Audrey could see a weather-worn door on the right-hand side, and a window with tired net curtains to the left of it. Rocky didn't knock on the door, he just tapped it lightly and opened it simultaneously. He knew his parents, like most villagers, never locked their doors in the daytime. There was no need. Everyone in the village knew everyone else and the ethos of the community was complete trust. Also, there was no back door in the cottage, so if anyone came to the premises, they could be seen as they approached.

Rocky's parents had seen them coming, and his mother had already put the kettle on the hob.

'Come in, we're delighted to meet you. I'm so glad you've come.' Mrs Driver made Audrey feel most welcome.

18

'I couldn't have chosen better for him if I'd hand-picked her myself,' she was overheard to tell his father as she made a pot of tea.

'What a lovely lady Rocky's mother is,' thought Audrey as she gazed in the direction of his jovial mother's twinkling brown eyes.

'Mrs Driver?' ... Audrey's question was interrupted.

'Please call me Cora. I prefer it to being called Mrs Driver.'

'What an unusual name! Cora. I haven't heard that before.'

'Actually, it's Cora Angelina. My mother was called Angelina and I have a niece of the same name, but I haven't seen her for years since my sister and her family moved to live in Cornwall.'

Cora stroked her white hair which wrapped itself into a bob at the nape of her neck and ventured to peep around the base of her ears. But she wasn't a peroxide blonde; her hair had turned white overnight when she'd lost her first-born child on his third birthday. After that Rocky had been treated like Dresden China. He'd wanted for nothing in the way of love and appreciation. He wasn't a spoilt child, just one treasured and valued by his doting parents.

Cora's nourished, rounded figure and magnetic personality drew Audrey to her. Not particularly tall, she stood the same height as her husband who was as thin as she was round.

Unfortunately Edwynne had been born with an extra toe. Instead of having one, he had two big toes on his left foot.

His six toes didn't hurt him, but they reduced his mobility, so he'd found solace in working on the land where he could use his strong torso for lifting and carrying, and his right foot for pressing his spade into the ground when digging trenches and making holes in which to plant potatoes and seeds.

During the War Edwynne had been declared disabled for service because he couldn't march.

Audrey looked around the room. It was quite sizeable for a country cottage. At the window with ageing nets, there were navy-blue draw-curtains with loops, on a bamboo pole; and to the left of it, the front area had been partitioned off with a makeshift draught excluder made out of an old clotheshorse and some sacking to keep the cold out because the front door led straight into the room from the front garden. It looked an eyesore.

As she walked across the green linoleum she noticed that the dining chairs, painted white, had been 'touched up' recently and the smell of fresh paint lingered in the air. A huge fireplace with side-oven which had to be black-leaded occupied most of one wall and she shuddered at the thought of all the hard work which would be needed to keep it so bright and shiny.

On the opposite side of the room there were two white-painted cupboard doors with odd patches of raised paint obliterating old scuff marks. One door led into a pantry; the other cupboard stored their outdoor clothes. An oblong wooden table stood in the centre of the room and it was covered with a bright green and navy seersucker cloth which Cora didn't have to iron.

Two threadbare easy chairs with home-made covers rubbed arms together and three green cushions nestled into each of them. At the rear of the room there was a kitchen where there was an old stone sink with a pale blue curtain around it, and a well-scrubbed wooden table which Cora used for her baking. Apart from an old zinc bath hanging on the wall in the kitchen area, and a few well-tended plants on the windowsill there was nothing more to be seen downstairs.

Audrey didn't notice that there were no taps above the sink. All water had to be brought in from a well in the garden, stored indoors, and boiled as necessary.

From the front door there was a flight of stairs leading to two bedrooms, one in front of the other, accessed by a narrow landing, but there was no bathroom, and there was no inside toilet.

Rocky explained that the lavatory was outside in the back garden, in a shed beyond the well. It was nothing more than a wooden seat over a zinc container which emptied into a cesspit, and that was emptied regularly by workmen from the local council.

At first Audrey was horrified at her findings. She knew instantly that her mother wouldn't approve of this lifestyle – it smacked far too much of poverty. But, as Rocky had said earlier, life is what we make it – it's what we want that counts – and she silently asked herself:

'Do I love him for what he is, or for what he has? I've heard people say it's not where you've come from that's important, it's where you're going to that matters. He's already lifted himself up by taking elocution lessons to enhance his career opportunities. He speaks beautifully.'

She looked across the room to where he was seated and admired his large, masculine frame, his dark wavy hair with its widow's peak creating a V for victory sign on his forehead, and his long, sweeping eyelashes. She knew she loved him for what he was, not for any earthly possessions he may or may not have, and now she had seen his home and how he'd lived as a child, she felt protective towards him and wanted to give him some of the luxuries he'd missed out on in his earlier life. Yet, she realised that he'd had more motherly love and affection than she'd ever known. He was rich in Christian values, and her heartstrings tugged even more in his direction.

After tea, her offer to wash the pots with Rocky drying them was accepted. When she finished her chore, she emptied the bowl of washing-up water down the sink – and her feet got soaked. The bucket behind the blue curtain had been full of waste water and it overflowed. She felt incredibly embarrassed, but Cora and Edwynne saw the funny side of the situation and laughed like drains while Rocky helped her to clear up the mess.

Time passed quickly. They looked at photographs and Cora told her how Rocky had always been a knowledgeable boy. At the age of ten years he'd passed his scholarship examination and gone to the nearest grammar school. He'd taken, and passed his General Certificate of Education Ordinary levels a year earlier than most pupils, and had passed his Advanced levels when he was seventeen. He'd grown up at a time when youths, on reaching the age of eighteen, were conscripted into doing National Service. So, having attained the necessary entry qualifications to become a teacher, he'd opted to go as a medic in the Royal Air Force first, on leaving school at seventeen, rather than waiting until he was eighteen and possibly wasting a year, before going to teacher training college. He'd gained valuable experience in the RAF getting to know people, and their attitudes to life, which she hoped would put him in good stead for his chosen career. So he'd started his three-year teacher training course at the age of nineteen. He would be twenty-one in less than two weeks' time.

Audrey asked if he had any suggestions for a birthday present.

'I'd quite like a watch, or a radio, or a camera' he said, 'But I'd like to choose my own.'

'Oh, I think that can be arranged,' his mother replied, then changed the subject back again and continued:

'At first, the transition from school-leaver to compulsory serviceman was a shock for him. First and foremost he'd left us and his friends behind, but he was a good letter writer and sent letters home explaining how he wasn't used to the strict discipline, the square-bashing and the unforgiving shouting that occurred. He'd also had shocks in other respects. Sometimes sick conscripts in the wards couldn't read or write. Many times he'd been asked to read a letter to, or write one from, a sick recruit in the ward on which he worked. Some of them were physically well-developed men over the age of twenty-one and he found their lack of reading and writing skills a very disturbing factor.'

Audrey showed surprise at hearing about grown men who couldn't read or write. Cora noticed her disbelief and asked:

'How can children go through Infant, Junior and Secondary levels of education and not be able to read or write when they leave school? In this day and age it's beyond me!'

Before she could respond, Rocky's father cut in with more reminiscences:

'The day that most conscripts liked the best was when they joined the pay line. Each recruit received a weekly pay packet containing between £2 to £5 depending on personal circumstances and length of service. But Rocky didn't have to join the pay line. A staff officer took the medics' pay packets into the wards and distributed them so that they didn't have to leave their patients or their duties. Rocky was a good boy. He was always very careful with his pay packet. After checking it, he used to allocate a portion to be sent home, and asked us to deposit some into a bank account for him, so that by the time he left the services and went to college he would have a little nest-egg to call upon when needed.'

Audrey was impressed. His parents were very proud of him, and it showed.

On the way home Audrey thought if only her mother knew the half of this she may be proud of him too. But for some reason or other she had taken an immediate dislike to him, yet she refused to say why, and so far it had been very hard work to try and bring her round. But Rocky was nice, and worth fighting for, even if she did have to fight her own mother.

CHAPTER 4

DIVERSE HITCHES

Three days before Rocky's twenty-first birthday Audrey came home from work to find her mother had been taken into hospital with acute appendicitis. Her father was home, which was very unusual, and he cooked scrambled eggs on toast for their tea which, again, was unusual. His main tool of the kitchen was a frying pan. He often fried sausages, bacon and an egg at two, three, or four o'clock in the morning before going on a shift, and he would dip a doorstep of bread into the lardy fat after he'd tossed some of it at the egg to form a skin of cooked albumen over the yolk. But not today. He was anxious and on edge. Mrs Small would have had her operation by now and they'd be allowed to visit her for a short while after eight o'clock.

'Why didn't you phone me at work, dad? I'd have got permission to come, I'm sure I would.'

In his mild Yorkshire accent he responded:

'Couldn't get the thing to work, lass. When I got to the phone box I couldn't remember your work's number. I looked in the telephone directory and found it, then I hadn't anything to write it down with. I tried to turn the dial, with the book hanging off the edge of the shelf, but I didn't get through. When I pressed button "A" I lost the two pennies I'd put in and didn't have any more coppers left.'

'You should have pressed button "B" to get your money back, dad, or you could've put a sixpence in. You only press button "A" to be connected.'

'Too late now, lass. Anyway, there's nothing you could've done. Apparently the missus from next door came in this morning to have a cup-a-tea and a chat, and found mam having terrible pains in her stomach. They got worse and were so violent, that she asked the woman to go and telephone for the doctor. After he'd been, and mam had been rushed to hospital in an ambulance, the woman phoned the railway offices to let me know. Fortunately my train was still in the sidings so they let me come home.'

Audrey was surprised at the speed of the illness; her mother hadn't said anything about it at breakfast time.

They ate their tea before walking to the bus stop. They had to change buses at the railway station then walked the remainder of the journey to the hospital.

Mrs Small was back in the ward, but barely out of the anaesthetic. She looked a pathetic grey sight and hardly recognised them. She lifted her eyelids. Her eyes were dull and unresponsive. Her lips moved; she opened her mouth; her tongue wobbled, but not a sound came out. She closed her eyes and slumped into another deep sleep.

Audrey knew she couldn't contact Rocky other than by letter. When they got home she scribbled a note to him, got out her bike, and crazily cycled to the main post office at Leeman Road where she knew there was a collection at midnight. She caught the post with a few minutes to spare, then pedalled home at a more sedate pace.

Next day, when Rocky received the news, he murmured:

'Oh, God, I only prayed to you to stop her harsh words, not for you to mute her altogether. Don't let her die. Just stop her from speaking to me like dirt. I can't see Audrey before my birthday, so she'll just have to wait.'

* * * * *

Between going to work and visiting her mother, Audrey bought a camera which Rocky had admired in a camera shop the previous week. She took it home and wrapped it in ornate paper, ready to give to him on his birthday. But, being imaginative, she took a broadsheet newspaper, tore strips off it, and rolled them like spills, making wider strips each time. She built them into the shape of a rolled umbrella, and positioned his present inside it. She covered the whole object with glitzy gift-wrap, and a big bow ribbon. Her idea of camouflaging his present was because he was an avid reader. Every weekday he bought a quality daily broadsheet and practically read the print off it, so she hoped he would see the symbolism of giving him newsprint, and would enjoy finding her surprise gift inside.

Mrs Small, on the other hand, hated to see people reading. She considered that if they were sitting in a chair with a book in their hands it was because they had nothing else to do, so she would find, or create, a job for them. There was little point in arguing with her because she was so domineering, and inevitably got her own way. Taking a book or a magazine for her to read in hospital would be futile, so Audrey took a crocheting hook, some wool, and some needlework to keep her occupied. Rocky visited her, and gave her some grapes. She begrudgingly accepted them, with a comment that they would probably be sour if they came from him, so Rocky spent more time talking to Mr Small than to his wife.

The following evening while Mr Small was at work, Rocky arrived at Audrey's house wearing an array of colours. He sported a navy-blue blazer, green shirt, red tie, yellow pullover, grey flannel trousers, brown socks and black shoes.

'Oh, my goodness,' she laughed. 'You look like a rainbow.'

'Well I feel happy' came his reply. 'Today, now I'm 21, I'm a legal adult.'

She kissed him and gave him his present. He looked at the shape in dismay. But when he opened it and found the camera inside, he was delighted. He laughed, and drew her close to him.

Electrical impulses shot up her legs and body. Her heart pounded with joy at his touch. He kissed her tenderly, then avidly. They cuddled, and held each other tightly. His roaming fingers set her whole body alight, but when he tried to part her legs with his hand she put on the brakes.

'No, Rocky, it's wrong without protection. I can't take the risk. What if I get pregnant? What will my parents say if we bring shame on them, and what ever would they say if they knew we'd done it in their house, on their carpet? I'm sorry, Rocky, Let's stop now, before it's too late.'

Rocky's ardour was broken, his spirit was shattered, his manliness depleted. He felt devastated and rejected. How could she stop him from his craving for her when he was at such a high point of fervour? And on his 21st birthday of all days. For once he was lost for words. But he loved Audrey beyond reproach; he couldn't risk forcing her, otherwise he might lose her forever. He thought of the words in the marriage ceremony "with my body I thee honour" and he slumped into resignation and frustration.

When they had regained their equilibrium Rocky was the first to break the silence.

'Last night I had a long chat with your dad. He's quite a philosophical man when you get to know him. He loves you, and your mother, very much and he's extremely worried about her now that peritonitis has set in. He's afraid he might lose her. He realises life's too short for some people; too long for others. Each encounter difficult consequences. He copes with your mother's outbursts because he understands her past problems and to some extent has a guilt complex and wants to put things right.'

'But what are her past problems? Why does he have a guilt complex? Why does she switch on and off the way she does? It's not natural the way she scurrilously puts us down at times, yet is absolutely charming to other people – outsiders, friends and neighbours.'

'I don't know. He didn't say and I didn't like to pry. But what he did tell me is that he loves you very much and wants you to be happy. He has no objection to my asking you to marry me. It may be a long time before your mother gets better, if ever, and by that time hopefully you'll have given me your answer and we'll be engaged.'

Audrey's body shook. Her hands trembled.

'So you're not put off by my refusal to go all the way tonight?'

'Audrey, my darling, I love you, and I respect you. You're just not ready to commit yourself freely before marriage. There'll be lots of other times when it will be right for us. Once we're married, there won't be a problem at all.'

'Oh, Rocky, you're so kind and considerate, and I love you to bits, I'm sorry about what's happened just now, but I just couldn't ...'

'I know my darling. I do understand. But please will you be my wife? I'll go down on bended knee and propose to you as you want me to.'

When he did, she didn't refuse.

* * * * *

Day by day Mrs Small grew stronger. Various relatives and friends visited her. They took flowers and fruit, and she became more amenable because she liked being the centre of attention. After several weeks' convalescence, she was discharged but when she heard of Audrey and Rocky's engagement she showed no interest whatsoever in their wedding plans.

At first, all didn't go smoothly with their arrangements. They couldn't find a venue available for the reception on the date they wanted. It was the same with the wedding-taxi services; and the church they wanted had six ceremonies booked for that day. Everywhere was fully booked. They couldn't understand it until the Vicar explained that the date they'd chosen was the first day of the 'Wakes Weeks' holidays. All the major manufacturers of chocolates and sweets – and industrial organisations such as construction, glass, printing, and the wagon works, closed for the same two weeks every year and people had booked venues – some more than a year in advance – to get the date they wanted so that they could honeymoon during the two-week closedown. The only option available to them was to change their chosen date. So they planned to bring it forward a week.

Audrey realised that they were going to need a lot more money. The purchase of her engagement ring, bought with money saved from Rocky's RAF conscription days, had used up the equivalent of a whole term's local authority grant, so each night she scanned the local newspaper looking for a better job.

Rocky put his mind to his studies. It was important to him that he should be academically successful, but he was also athletic. He was a Class III soccer referee and was good at field events.

One evening, while scanning the daily paper, Audrey noticed an advertisement for a Personal Secretary to the Matron of one of the local hospitals.

She applied, and was appointed at a considerable increase in salary. The qualifications she'd attained at the local technical college when she left school had carried her through, together with her experience as a shorthand-typist in a large legal practice where her typing had to be accurate; her shorthand transcription the epitome of perfection; and her greeting and meeting of clients and business personnel, professional.

On Audrey's first day at her new job Matron laid down her ground rules.

'A nurse cannot walk out on her job, the patient always comes first, and you can't go home until the day's correspondence has been cleared.'

Audrey was surprised at Matron's statement. She'd always gone home on time. Matron continued:

'It's my policy that we never start a new day's work with the previous day's administration in abeyance. We always clear the decks before we go home. We don't pay overtime. This is dedication to duty. Nurses have a vocation, not a career. They're carers, and they care very much about their patients and their posts. If they want to get on, they have to get on with me.'

Audrey was shocked at Matron's attitude. She wanted to say that in her opinion the nurses were being taken for granted; being used; taken advantage of, and so on but, like them, she needed the money that the new job would pay, and she didn't want to rock the boat on her first day, so she carefully guarded her tongue and decided to wait for a more appropriate time to express her opinions.

Matron Doughty ran a tight ship. She was a very important person in the hospital service and let everyone know it. She stood no nonsense from anyone and was a strict disciplinarian. She was firm and fair where loyal staff were concerned, but if anyone stepped out of line or disobeyed hospital rules she remembered it and held it against them.

Having experienced a difficult mother, Audrey soon learned how to handle her employer. She realised that Miss Doughty was a very lonely person. When Matron had finished her duties, she went to an empty flat in the hospital and because of her position didn't fraternise with nursing staff. She held herself aloof from them, and isolated herself from social contact with them.

Sometimes after a particularly difficult day Audrey deliberately stayed over half an hour just to talk to Matron and through their discussions they developed a mutual respect; but there were times when Miss Doughty was stubborn, or had a viewpoint which differed totally from hers, such as the time when Matron received a glowing reference for a prospective nurse, and refused to offer the applicant a place in the Nurses' Training School.

The reference had been provided by a Lady Anona Pelucydd, and ended "I cannot speak too highly of her." In Audrey's opinion, from the tone of the recommendation, Lady Pelucydd meant she couldn't speak *highly enough* of the applicant; but Miss Doughty thought that there was a sting in the tail. Despite all the good things said, she considered that the referee couldn't speak *very highly* of her, and as she was a member of the aristocracy, her words carried weight. To Audrey's dismay, the girl's excellent application was rejected. That was one occasion when Audrey and her employer didn't see eye to eye on something.

* * * * *

For a time, things progressed smoothly. Rocky passed his examinations and became a Ministry qualified teacher and began to look for employment to start after their marriage, when the new school term commenced. Preparations for the wedding went into overdrive.

When Audrey had attended a technical college she'd met a girl called Annie and over the years they became good friends. Once a week they would meet after work, and go alternately to each other's houses for tea. On one particular day before the wedding it was Annie's turn to go to Audrey's and they were going to choose the colour and type of material for their dresses and decide on flowers for the bouquets. They looked through magazines and discussed how most bridesmaids wore blue or pink dresses, but Audrey wanted to have a different colour. She suggested the bridesmaids might wear a very pale apple-green brocade, if they could find a shop which sold it, and have the material made up by a local dressmaker. Mrs Small, who was within earshot, sounded aghast.

'Apple green?' she challenged. 'Yer can't have apple green dresses for yer bridesmaids.'

'Why ever not? Apple green is a beautiful colour.

In fact, green is Rocky's favourite colour. He loves the trees when they're just breaking into bloom in the Spring; when they're in full colour in the Summer, and when they're changing colour in the Autumn. There are so many different shades of green, and apple green is such a delicate shade, it's gorgeous.'

'Yes, I know it is, but it's a very unlucky colour for bridesmaids.'

'Well, I've never heard of that before. It must be a silly superstition.'

'No, it isn't! Look at Auntie Nelly. Her bridesmaids had Lincoln green dresses with pale mauve sashes and matching mauve carnations in their bouquets, and her mother was dead within a week of their wedding; and Georgina Palmer's bridesmaids wore sap green dresses and carried white roses and her father died at the wedding reception while he was giving the bridal toast to his daughter and .....'

Audrey cut in quickly.

'All right, mam, you've made your point, but I still think it's absolute coincidence that those things happened. I wouldn't wish death on anyone, let alone you or dad, so I'll think of something else.'

By this time she didn't care about standing up for a colour. There were so many beautiful colours to choose from. Annie smoothed things over by saying:

'I wish I had a Rocky to love me the way Audrey's Rocky loves her. It must be wonderful for people like you and your husband to know that your daughter is marrying the man she loves and that he will look after her and take care of her for the rest of her life. You must be very proud indeed.'

Mrs Small shrugged her shoulders.

'I don't know about that – we'll just have to wait and see. Only time will tell.'

CHAPTER 5

THE WEDDING

The day before the wedding was a busy one. Audrey had booked the day off work. She met Rocky's parents in Church. They didn't have a car so had hired a taxi and taken masses of flowers which they'd grown in their garden. There was one flower to represent every person in their village. They decorated the altar, the pillars and the window sills. The church looked magnificent.

They hired another taxi to go home and Audrey went with them in a round trip and collected the wedding cake and took it to the restaurant where the reception was to be held. She got it there intact and set up the three tiers. It had been a labour of love. Her mother had baked three very rich fruit cakes and her father had cut turrets into them to represent York City's bar walls. She had covered all three tiers with home-made almond paste and iced them to her own unique design. She felt incredibly happy that everything was going so well.

Next morning the wedding party's flowers arrived early. The bouquets and button-holes were beautiful and Audrey felt ecstatic. She had a bath and got ready. Her two bridesmaids looked gorgeous in their cream coloured brocade dresses with bouquets of lemon tea roses and she had a white brocade off-the-shoulder wedding dress with pink-tinged Peace roses in her trailing bouquet.

Her dad had a new suit, and so did her mother, but her mother had kept her outfit secret. Now she came down the stairs looking extremely smart. Her suit was neat and fitted her beautifully but, to Audrey's amazement, it was a vibrant shade of pea-green. Audrey was shocked at the colour.

'I thought you said green was unlucky at weddings' she gasped.

'Yes, it is for the bridesmaids, but not for the bride's mother. When I saw it, I thought it would outdo every other woman there, because it's so stunning. Just a minute .....'

She dived into the cupboard under the stairs and produced an enormous hat box.

'Now my pièce de résistance' she exclaimed. 'I just couldn't leave it; it's a perfect match for me suit' and she lifted out a gigantic beehive of tulle and waxed net in bright pea green with a huge artificial yellow orchid on one side.

'Oh, mother!' Audrey gasped in disbelief at the monstrosity.

'Wherever did you get it?'

Her mother avoided the question.

'Isn't it fantastic? I just had to have it.'

She lifted it high above her head, drew it down over her hair, and cocked it on to one side at a rakish angle.

'Don't tell yer father,' she whispered, 'It cost me ten guineas.'

'Oh, mother, you look stu ..... stup ..... stupendous.'

She changed her mind about her first choice of word. She didn't want any friction on her wedding day and had to think fast to avoid offending her mother.

'You'll really be noticed, not only at the wedding, but on all the photographs as well.'

Mrs Small was pleased at what she thought was praise being bestowed upon her.

The first taxi arrived and took her to the church. A second taxi arrived for the bridesmaids, and finally the first taxi returned to collect Audrey and her father. It was only when they reached their front door that Audrey realised it was raining.

'Oh dad, what a shame. We're going to get soaked.'

'That's too bad, lass, with that lovely dress you're wearing, you'll have to pick it up so that it doesn't get dirty around the hem. I'll help you to lift it up while you get in the car.'

The taxi driver produced a huge white umbrella to shelter them as they got into his limousine.

When they arrived at the church, her dad wished her well and hoped she was doing the right thing. Audrey was in no doubt whatsoever.

The organ struck up. Everyone stood, and the bride slowly progressed on her dad's arm towards her handsome groom. The service was simple and sincere. They made their vows and the vicar declared them man and wife together and took them to the high altar to address them privately.

'Never let the sun go down on your wrath. If you have a difference of opinion, sort it out before you go to bed. Be chums for life. Be positive in your attitudes,' were some of his words of wisdom; others just seemed to float over their heads.

After the final hymn was sung, they were directed into the vestry where they signed three copies of the Marriage Register and were given one certificate to keep. They walked down the aisle to the church door, and were greeted by guests waiting for them in torrential rain.

It was impossible for the photographer to use his camera so Rocky suggested that he took photos at the reception instead.

A policeman held up the traffic while the wedding party and guests dashed across the road to a restaurant opposite the church. Everyone was wet and cold and tried to dry themselves as quickly as they could.

'Never mind, dears,' said Auntie Dorcas 'At least you've got sunshine in your hearts.'

As a wedding present to the bride and groom, Audrey's parents had paid for twenty people to sit down to a ham salad tea, and Rocky paid for house wine at table, and sparkling wine for the toast.

After the speeches were over Audrey went to the ladies' room to change into her going away outfit. Mrs Small followed her in.

'Well, let's have a look at yer wedding ring? I haven't seen it yet.'

Audrey put her left hand forward and Mrs Small clasped it with curiosity and scrutinised the ring. In a shocked voice her mother declared:

'That's not a gold ring.'

'No, it's a platinum one.'

Mrs Small raised her voice in disapproval.

'I've never seen anything like it!' she shrieked.

She threw Audrey's left hand downwards in a fit of temper and raised her voice even more.

'Well! I never thought that I would ever live to see the day when a daughter of mine would have a bit of bent wire for a wedding ring. Yer just not married without a gold ring. How could yer do this to me after everything I've done for yer and everything I've paid for? Dad and I've tried to make this a happy day for yer. Yer know I don't like Rocky, never have and never will, but I've tried so hard over the past year to bite my tongue after what dad said to me in hospital. All this paraphernalia we've just gone through is absolutely meaningless without a gold wedding ring.'

Audrey could hardly believe her ears. On this day of all days to say something like that! A huge lump caught in her throat; her heart sank; and she felt sick. She felt hot tears rising to her eyes, and she went numb at the unexpected, unprovoked bombshell.

After initially reeling with shock, she heard her own agitated voice saying:

'Oh, mam, how could you say such a thing on my wedding day? I love Rocky, and my ring, It was *my* choice, and Rocky liked it too, otherwise he wouldn't have paid for it.'

'Perhaps yer do, but don't come running back to me when everything goes wrong and yer get divorced. I want nothing to do with him, ever!'

Audrey's anger rose to a point that she'd never known before. She wanted to throttle her mother with her bare hands and retaliated:

'That's it, mother. You've had your say. You've now hurt me once too often, but you'll be sorry. You're no longer my next of kin, Rocky is. We'll go away and live elsewhere out of the reach of your wicked tongue. I really can't understand you. We've gone a whole year without any harsh words; you've made three gorgeous fruitcakes for my wedding; you've paid for this wonderful meal and spent the earth on that outfit you're wearing, and yet something gets into you and you come out with these horrible words. It's almost as if you've got a split personality.'

Mrs Small didn't wait to hear any more. She tossed her head, stomped out of the ladies' room and returned to the guests in the dining room. Her eyes flashed with anger at Audrey as she did so, yet on meeting the guests in the dining room, she smiled sweetly.

Flushed with outrage at their unpredictable encounter, Audrey went into one of the lavatory cubicles. Tears flowed, and she felt distraught. Her emotions were indescribable.

After a while she heard one of her guests come and use the cubicle alongside hers, and knew she must pull herself together. She dried her eyes and took in several deep breaths.

As she removed her wedding dress, to change into her going-away outfit, a cascade of confetti released itself and fluttered colourfully to the floor.

A large cloud of it disappeared through the gap underneath the door and into the ladies' room beyond the lavatory cubicle. That made her smile and triggered her imagination.

She likened the ejected shower of particles to the fertilisation process of procreation and envisaged the joy she and Rocky would experience that night when their marriage was consummated without a "hairy-carrot cover". She recovered her composure, washed and made up her face, got changed, held her head up high and went out to thank all her guests, parents and new in-laws, before they went their various ways.

Once inside their own taxi, which took them to the railway station to start their honeymoon, Audrey sat back to relax. She exhaled breaths of air which sounded like the rustling of wind though the branches of trees, as it had on the day they first fell in love. With her Rock beside her, she knew her old life was over, and a new life was just beginning, and she couldn't help wondering what the future had in store for them both.

CHAPTER 6

MOVING ABOUT

After their return from honeymoon Rocky and Audrey rented a one-bedroomed flat in a Victorian villa in Bishopthorpe Road. Audrey was not impressed with Victoriana; she found it dull and depressing.

She gazed around the dismal room. The dark brown paintwork on the doors, deep skirting boards and window frames did nothing to enhance its gloomy appearance. The ceilings were so high that if they put any heating into the room it would rise upwards beyond their comfort zone and they wouldn't reap much benefit from it.

She fixed her eyes on the cobwebs hanging from the ceiling. These would have to be removed with the aid of a pair of steps and a duster on a long pole. She found the old-fashioned ceramic irises climbing up the tiles in the fireplace offensive to her modern tastes. How could people drool over such monstrosities and actually like these period features? They were not to her liking at all.

Oh, well, it's a good job we're not all the same, she thought, otherwise these old houses would never sell. There would be people who didn't like her idea of a modern, labour-saving home with low ceilings to keep in the warmth, and pale, colourful shades of baths and lavatories. The old-fashioned claw-footed white bath in their bathroom would have to be cleaned both inside and out, and it would have to be done before they could use it, as it looked grey with grime.

She itched to remove the age-worn wallpaper in the living room with its tight floral pattern of yellow potentillas on a fawn background but strangely enough, the chocolate-brown carpet with foot-sized fawn shields didn't look too dirty, it just smelt fusty. She eyed the well-trodden floor covering and observed some dark brown stains from previous tenants' wear and tear. She hated the flat, but it would have to do for the short time they would be there.

Rocky, on the other hand, seemed quite unconcerned. It was a roof over their heads and it would be their first home together. He also considered it came to them at a very cheap rental of only one guinea a week.

Rocky's mother, Cora, thought one pound and one shilling every week was an extortionate amount for them to pay. She said they paid exactly the same amount of rent on their cottage as she paid for a whole pound of butter.

Rocky gently reminded her, and made light of the fact, that she had no running water in the cottage; it had to be carried in from a nearby well. They had no gas, and up to a few years ago they'd no electricity either. They'd cooked a number of their meals on an oil stove; and as a child he'd done his homework by the light of an oil lamp.

She reminded him that despite all that, they'd always been incredibly happy, dressed him well, provided everything he needed in the way of school and sportswear, and saved enough money to get him to college so that he could enter the professional career of school teacher. It wasn't as good as some boys had, but it was the best they could do with the money Edwynne earned on the land.

Rocky had hoped to be appointed to a teaching post in York when he finished college but the only jobs he saw advertised once he'd qualified were outside his specialist area. He'd studied sciences so wasn't prepared to teach humanities or arts. He wanted a job where he would be confident in his subject area of chemistry.

Unaware that no positions would be available to apply for later in the year, they had put a deposit on a new three-bedroomed semi-detached house with gardens front, side and rear, to be built in the Malton Road area of the City at a total cost of £1,750. Audrey's idea was that it would not only be brand new with no inherited dirt from previous generations, but it would be labour saving, and a reasonably long way from her parents' house so that they couldn't just drop in uninvited like their neighbours did.

They had looked at several older properties but in York so many houses in their price range had porous bricks, cracked and broken slate roofs, rotted window frames and so on. Audrey loved the little semi-detached houses in Nunthorpe Crescent. They were neat and clean and would have been ideal, had they not been so close to her parents' house. Now they had increased in value considerably.

She'd seen one of those houses for sale a few years after the War ended. It had been regarded by their next-door neighbour as a snip for four hundred pounds and, young as she was, Audrey had tried to persuade her parents to buy it, but her father wouldn't consider buying a property of any description whatsoever, even if they could have raised a mortgage. When she asked why he was so adamant about not owning his own home, he'd said:

'Well, lass, you have to do all your own repairs whereas if you rent the landlord has to do them.'

'That's a poor excuse' she replied. 'If you buy a house you may have to do your own repairs but at least one day you'll own it. It's just like paying rent to yourself. I'd rather have my own roof over me and sit on an orange box for a seat to start with, than pay rent to a landlord. It's just dead money. You'll never get it back, but you can sell a house and make a profit when you do. In a rented property you could find yourself out in the street through no fault of your own.'

'Oh, that will never happen to us, lass. If you buy a house you're just putting a millstone round your neck for the next twenty-five years. You don't want to go down that route. If you stop and calculate all the interest you have to pay to a Building Society you'll find it comes to thousands of pounds, not hundreds. You'll never get that money back. Believe me, we've worked it out and it isn't worth it.'

Years later, when the landlord had offered to sell them their house for seven hundred pounds, as sitting tenants, he'd still produced exactly the same reasons for not buying it.

Mrs Small had been furious about his apathy. She wanted to have her own home but he wouldn't budge from his viewpoint. It was then that her tantrums had started with a vengeance.

Once Rocky realised he wasn't likely to find a suitable teaching post in York, he bought a copy of a national educational weekly paper and found several advertisements for science teachers, but only two were in his specialist area. The jobs were in Essex. He applied for both.

His first interview was in a Secondary Mixed school and the other in a Secondary Boys' school. He was impressed with the latter. It had an excellent reputation and on meeting him, the Head was welcoming and amenable.

There was a mixed staff of forty teachers and an intake of eight hundred boys ranging from the ages of eleven to sixteen.

There were two sports fields and the school was set in a wide open space well out of town. There was an incremental salary scale and he would start on the third rung because of serving two years' National Service and completing his third year of training. Most colleges at that time offered two-year training courses. More importantly, a grace and favour flat was available through a special arrangement for newly-qualified teachers moving into the area.

When the Head asked if he would accept the post in the event of it being offered Rocky confirmed in the affirmative. He couldn't get home quickly enough to tell Audrey his good news.

'Oh, Audrey, it's wonderful. We'll have a chance to start a new life together on our own terms, in a new environment, in our own home. And, do you realise, that by the time I'm thirty-six I'll be on a salary of a thousand pounds a year? There's not many people that reach a thousand pounds a year in their lifetime. I feel absolutely great.'

'Oh, Rocky, sincere congratulations darling. Very well done. I think we ought to celebrate right now.'

'I couldn't agree more' he said, as they held hands and gleefully dived into their bedroom.

When the letter came confirming the appointment Audrey realised they had several problems to cope with. First, the letter made it plain that all newly qualified teachers had to do one year's probationary service – but Rocky knew that anyway – and felt confident he would sail through it, so he didn't consider that to be a problem at all, it was just part of the normal routine of the educational system.

Then there was the problem of telling their parents. Audrey felt sure Rocky's parents would be okay about it because he hadn't lived with them for five years, having done two years' National Service and three years at teacher training college, but she daren't think what her own parents would have to say, especially her mother! However, she was a married woman now; they would have to take it on the chin.

As anticipated, Rocky's parents congratulated him, and asked if they would like to stay to tea.

Cora put a curly home-grown cucumber on the table together with a warm crusty loaf she'd made earlier that day. There was also some honey from a neighbour's bees and a dish of part-melted butter. It all looked very appetising. She also put a bowl of tomatoes on the table.

'You know I don't like tomatoes' declared Rocky.

'Oh good, all the more for them that do.'

Audrey could hardly believe her ears. What, no reprimand? No forcing food upon him? How differently they'd been brought up! She also disliked tomatoes. She remembered how she'd been made to eat them in the past, even though they were too acidic for her digestion, and made her feel sick.

'Everything all right, dear?' enquired Cora. 'You're very quiet.'

'Oh, sorry, Cora, I was miles away. Did you grow the tomatoes and cucumber yourselves?'

'Of course! We're self-sufficient here. Dive in. Help yourself.'

'Well, actually, I don't like tomatoes either.'

'Huh, you're a well-matched pair, aren't you? What about cucumber?'

'I'm afraid cucumber repeats on me when I've eaten it, I'll just have some bread and butter.'

'What about lettuce? Do you like that?'

'Yes, that's okay. I don't have problems with lettuce.'

Cora called to Edwynne to cut one from the garden. He brought in a large, hearty, soft variety, which she dipped in and out of a basinful of cold water to clean it, patted it dry, cut it in half, and put one portion on Audrey's plate and the other on Rocky's.

'Oh, Cora,' she laughed, 'I can't eat half a lettuce.'

'Well, eat what you can and leave what you can't.'

Audrey made a sandwich out of three of the leaves and put the remainder to one side. Edwynne took it, cut it into shreds, smothered it in salt and vinegar, and ate it with a knife and fork. He called it a salad, and enjoyed it. She could hardly believe how differently she and Rocky had been brought up.

The following weekend they went to tell Audrey's parents about Rocky's new job. On the corner of Scarcroft Road there was a Co-operative store which sold groceries, bread and cakes. Audrey chose a Yorkshire curd cheesecake for her mother, which she knew was one of her favourite "bought" cakes; and an ounce Walnut Plug tobacco for her father.

'What's your number?' the assistant enquired.

Audrey recalled her mother's dividend number and claimed the receipt to give with their peace offering. This would be stuck on to a foolscap sheet and saved until it was time to hand it in to collect the dividend due to be paid.

Her mother was a whizz where figures were concerned and could add up the amounts on the receipts within seconds to check that the correct amount of dividend would be paid. The divi never paid out very much, but all income was welcome in their household.

Over a cup of tea, the position regarding Rocky's new job was explained. At first Mr and Mrs Small listened almost in silence. Mrs Small was livid.

'Leave York? This beautiful Cathedral City, where yer've been brought up and educated, just to be with *him*? How will I be able to pop in and see what yer doing and what yer having for yer meals? What on earth am I going to do when me only child lives miles away? Who's going to look after me when I get old and grey?'

Larry put his arm around Mrs Small and consoled her.

'It's not all that bad, mam, I get passes and privilege tickets on the railway, so we can go and visit them regularly. Anyway, they've got to go to where the work is. I was brought up in Beverley and had a good job there, but when the shop I worked for closed down *I* had to move elsewhere.'

He turned to Audrey and continued:

'This was before you were born. I couldn't find work for months and had to cycle round the streets selling tea. After a long time I saw a better job in York and came here. Anyway, it's your duty to go with your husband, so you must go with him, whatever your mam says. We all have to ride the waves of life, and believe me, I've had my share of ups and downs.'

Audrey was relieved. She'd expected violent opposition and fortunately her dad had smoothed things over. Mrs Small went into the kitchen to make a another pot of tea, and went into one of her silent moods. Rocky suspected that she may have a medical problem for her mood swings, but kept his thoughts to himself.

The following Monday Audrey told Miss Doughty about Rocky's success at obtaining a teaching post in Essex and tentatively handed in her resignation in writing. She thought Matron may be displeased because she'd been in the job for a relatively short time.

'Well, actually, Mrs Driver, I've got some good news too. As you know, the job title of Matron is currently in the process of being changed by the authorities to that of Principal Nursing Officer to give men equal opportunities with women in the nursing profession and last month I applied for one of those new jobs with a much larger Hospital Management Committee than this one. I didn't tell you, but when I had a few days off last week it was because I had an interview along with four men and another woman. I really had to fight for the job, but last Friday it was confirmed that I've been offered the post, to lead the way forward as an example of the way things should be done in hospitals in the future. It will be a huge challenge for me, but I'll enjoy it, so things will be very different for both of us.'

Audrey congratulated her employer and they discussed what needed to be done in the immediate future. Matron's tone softened:

'You know, Mrs Driver, often it takes a woman to help a woman. I may be able to help you. In my desk drawer I have a handbook which lists all the Hospital Management Committees in Britain, together with their addresses and telephone numbers. If I lend it to you, perhaps you could look up hospitals in the area you will be moving to, and see if anyone has a vacancy for a secretary so that you could have your job transferred from this authority without losing your pension rights.'

'Oh, thank you, Matron, I'll take it now if I may, and give it back to you when I've had a look at it.'

Audrey's spirits rose. It looked as if her employment could possibly be continuing, albeit in another part of the country.

The last problem turned out to be even worse than they'd thought. They had paid £175 to the builder to reserve the new-build house which they'd originally planned to have, but when they tried to get their money back they found he'd gone bankrupt so they lost their deposit, and that didn't bode well for buying a property if they didn't like the grace-and-favour flat that went with Rocky's new job.

CHAPTER 7

SETTLING IN

Fond farewells to Cora and Edwynne on Wednesday and formal farewells to Mr and Mrs Small on Thursday evening were over. The removal van was booked to arrive at eight o'clock on Friday morning. It was due to come from the storage depot already part-loaded the previous day, because they were sharing the removal costs with a family moving to Harold Wood in Hornchurch. Audrey looked into the pantechnicon. Although well packed, there was plenty of room for their few items to be placed down one side.

'There's the double bed we bought for five pounds from Auntie Dorcas when she bought a new single bed after Uncle Ross died, the new little table and two kitchen chairs which Grandpa Small gave us for a wedding present, six tea chests with our personal clothing and other wedding presents, and our bikes. That's it! I hope they don't break the delicate China tea-service from Uncle Quilliam and Auntie Jen, or the superb dinner service from Auntie Dorcas. Even though we've paid removal insurance it probably wouldn't be possible to get exact replacements.'

Mesmerised, they watched the van trundle heavily down the hill before turning into Scarcroft Road where it disappeared from sight. They locked the door to the flat that they'd rented for a month and pushed the keys through the letter-box.

Without looking back they walked to the station. As they did so dewy precipitation formed beads of moisture in their hair. Audrey's chest felt heavy, as it did when the atmosphere was damp.

'I wonder how long it will be before we can buy a car?'

'Years, I imagine' replied Rocky. 'We've both got to learn how to drive first and as neither of our parents have had vehicles it will be more difficult for us because we're not used to road conditions, signs, and procedures, and so on and, it will cost a lot.'

The light rain got heavier. Eventually, soaking wet, they reached the railway station. Opposite it, the city walls had greeted many visitors with gladness over the centuries. Now, grey and cold, they seemed to greet with lament in the downpour. Tall grasses on the moat seemed to sway in swirls of sadness at their departure. Even leaves on nearby trees seemed to whisper agitated adieus.

After a final glance at the sombre backdrop, the couple walked into the station and joined a short queue at the ticket office.

The train to London was on time. Rocky and Audrey settled into their seats and watched the suburbs and green fields pass by. Telegraph lines danced up and down the windows, as the poles onto which they were fixed flashed by.

Rocky read his newspaper. Audrey fidgeted and occasionally flicked over the pages of a magazine, but she wasn't interested in its contents and long periods of silence between them elapsed. The chuddledy-chuh, chuddledy-chuh of wheels over rails reminded her of her mother's cloppety-clop, cloppety-clop, down the back lane when she walked smartly to the shops. It was good to be leaving old sores behind, but she wondered what she was going to, and what her new life would bring.

From King's Cross to Liverpool Street a boring hour passed, followed by another train ride to Romford station. Finally, a bus took them to the estate on which they'd be living. There was just time to pick up the keys to their new flat and pay one month's rent in advance before the housing office closed at half past five.

After their tedious journey they were tired and hungry. On their walk to the flat they passed a fish and chip shop. The aroma beckoned them in. Rocky asked for one of each twice and a bottle of lemonade. The server didn't understand him.

'Wotcha want, mate, rock or plaice?'

'I'd like two pieces of haddock and two portions of chips.'

'We don't do 'addock. We got rock, wot's dog-fish, or plaice wot's flat fish, or I could cook a couple of bits of cod if you're willing to wait.'

'I'll wait' came Rocky's reply.

The assistant didn't put the fried fish on to greaseproof sheets and wrap them in newspaper like they did in York. He put some chips in the bottom of a white polystyrene tray and positioned the fish on top. He was just about to lift a container of salt when Rocky stopped him.

'No vinegar either? Cor, blimey mate! Okay.'

A few minutes later the couple arrived at their new home. Rocky undid the latch and pushed the front door open. The flat smelt fresh and clean, as if someone had been in and sprayed it with aerosol, or left some potpourri in a room. He put the brown paper bag on the floor, picked up Audrey and lifted her over the threshold, leaving the door ajar.

'Good job you're not heavy' he laughed.

He put her down gently and kissed her fullsome, warm, expectant lips tenderly. They hugged each other passionately for a short while, whilst the sweet smell of flowers wafted over their heads, welcoming them to a fresh, clean start.

'What a difference to the musty stench of the last flat when you lifted me over that threshold,' she observed.

A whiff of fried fish reminded them that their supper was still outside the open front door. Rocky brought the packet in and put it on a worktop in the small square kitchen off the hallway. Audrey peered in. She liked the bland wall units, and there was space for a cooker. She walked towards the sink under the window and tried the taps. Cold water ran from them both. Rocky tried the light switches and found that the electricity was working.

Next to the kitchen there was a small but adequate bathroom with a pale pink bathroom suite. They both approved its condition and cleanliness.

'What a vast improvement to the last bathroom we had! This is fantastic in comparison.'

From the bathroom they walked down the entrance passage. The spacious room at the end of it echoed with their footsteps on the dark mastic tiles. The gaping expanse looked enormous with no furniture or fittings.

A shaft of light intruded its beam of glittering dust particles through the window and left a pool of sunlight splayed onto the immaculately clean floor. Audrey did a jig of joy around the circumference and grabbed Rocky in a war dance of exaltation.

Finally there was a room big enough for a double bed and a wardrobe, but little else.

'Oh, Rocky, this flat is fantastic. We've really fallen on our feet this time. It's so much better than the last flat we had.'

Rocky agreed.

'We'd better eat our fish and chips before they go stone cold, because we've got nothing to heat them up on,' Rocky observed, suddenly feeling extremely hungry. They leaned up against the work surface and ate the food with their fingers. It tasted delicious. It didn't have the same heaviness that they were used to, it was much lighter, cooked in oil rather than in lard, so it was less greasy and more healthy. They devoured it ravenously and drank their lemonade straight from the bottles.

When their appetites were sated, they wandered back into the bedroom and had another little war-dance. Their revelry was shattered by the sound of the doorbell. The removal van was parked outside, and the driver was pressing to get home. The men quickly unloaded, set up the bed, dumped the tea chests in the big room and left the bikes in the passage. Rocky paid the bill, obtained a receipt, and in less than twenty minutes the men were gone.

Audrey went into the big room and looked for the tea-chest labelled 'bedding'. They made up their bed, then she found the electric kettle which Annie had given them for a wedding present, and took it into the kitchen. There they sat on the only two chairs they possessed.

'Tomorrow we'll have to buy buckets, bowls and brushes as well as food, so we'd better make a list.'

But they had no paper to write on.

'Good job I've got a good memory' commented Audrey.

'I think we'd be more comfortable lying on the bed than sitting on these kitchen chairs. Come on. We'll leave the rest of the unpacking until tomorrow.'

The next day the morning sun streaming into their bedroom woke them bright and early. Their first priority was to buy an oven. There were no gas connections in the flat, so they went to their local electricity showroom and chose a model which could be delivered and installed that afternoon. The shopping centre was not too far away, and there was a block of shops just around the corner from their new home. Rocky bought his newspaper and a weekly tabloid to read about local events. Audrey concerned herself with household items and food. She went in to the bread shop.

'Can I have a breadcake please?'

'Wot cher want, ducks, bread or cake?' The assistant wiped her hands down her apron to remove flour from her last sale.

'One of those, please' affirmed Audrey, pointing to a soft baked loaf on the shelf behind the counter.

'Oh, you mean a batch, ducks.'

'Is that what you call it? What a funny name. Where I come from a batch is a group of something ..... er ....'

'Is that so? Well here bread's called batches, baps, bloomers, cobs, split-tins, wholemeal' – she was about to relate an endless list when Audrey cut in:

'No, that will do, thank you.' She paid for the bread and went to the butcher's next door. Peering in through the window, it appeared that meat was much cheaper here than in York. Her eyes were drawn to an attractive-looking piece of red flesh with white fat around, and a deep bone at one end. She thought it looked nice and fresh, with white, not creamy, coloured fat which would have aged it. She went into the shop and enquired:

'How much is that piece of rib, there?'

'Rib? Do you mean this bit of chine?'

'Yes, that's the one. What did you call it?'

'Are you being funny?'

'No. It's just that we moved here yesterday and you all speak with a different accent and you even have different names for things. But I'll learn.' She paid for the meat and went into the green-grocer's. Fortunately, potatoes were still called potatoes, and carrots remained as carrots, so she made her purchases and walked home.

In the hardware shop she'd been given some Green Shield stamps.

'What's these?' she queried.

'They're for you to get a free gift. The more money you spend in the shop, the more stamps you get. Save 'em up, stick 'em in one of these books, then when it's full, take it to the Green Shield shop in the shopping centre and choose what you want. You can get brushes, shovels, things like that with one book full. Or you can save more than one book and get higher priced gifts. It's up to you. They're always useful.'

'I've never heard of them before.'

'Oh, yeah, you can get lots of sorts round here. The Green Shield are the best, but you can get pink ones from Victor Value food shops, and some of the petrol stations give Blue Chip ones. It's best to try and stick to one sort though. They mount up quicker that way.'

Once home, and the unpacking done, Rocky sat on a kitchen chair and opened his broadsheet on the kitchen table. Audrey made some coffee then unfurled the local paper. She got the shock of her life. Houses prices were more than double here than in York. Her eyes went up and down the property pages, across, and back. She could see nothing under three thousand pounds; the majority of houses were four thousand or more.

'Oh, Rocky, I can't believe this. I had no idea housing was so expensive in this area. I don't want to live in this flat all my life, nice as it may be to start with. I was hoping it would just be a stop-gap for us, before we bought our own house. It looks as if we'll never be able to buy one at these prices.'

Rocky closed his paper and put it on the table. Before he could speak she continued:

'It's as if we've moved to a foreign country. You'd think we'd come three thousand miles rather than three hundred. The weather is hot and dry; the people talk differently; they even have different names for things; they give you stamps that you can't post, and house prices are out of this world. Even the rent is double what we paid for that flat in York. What ever are we going to do?'

'The first thing we're going to do is to keep calm. It's no good getting upset.'

'I'm not.' Audrey's mouth winced in such a manner that he knew she was bothered.

'Look, love, although we lost money on the York house, we've enough money to tied us over until I get my first pay cheque in about four or five weeks' time. I'll give you five pounds a week food money, that should be plenty for the two of us, and I'll pay the insurances and the bills. I suggest that whatever we pay in rent, we save the equivalent amount towards a deposit on a house. For every pound we save, we'll call it a brick. By the time we've saved five hundred bricks we'll have enough to pay the ten per cent deposit, legal fees, and the stamp duty. Don't worry. We'll have our own house one day.'

'But it will take years.'

'Not necessarily. I'll be starting work on Monday and you'll be going for an interview for a job transfer next week, and if you don't get it, you can always go temping down here. We'll just have to be careful with what we've got, and not overdo things.'

After the cooker had been delivered and installed, they caught a bus to Romford town centre. There was an excellent market in progress. A fishmonger was selling enormous pairs of kippers for nine pence a pair. Rocky couldn't resist treating himself for his Sunday morning breakfast.

After they'd had a good browse around the bustling market they wandered in to North Street and came across a shop that sold oddments, seconds, and bankrupt stock. They peered through the window at the array of odd items and cast their eyes on a brand-new bed-settee at a mark-down price of five pounds.

'That has to be the bargain of the century' declared Audrey, 'and look at that those cheap ready-made curtains. I'll have some of them for our bedroom. And look at the price of that little fridge.'

'We can't afford all three items, but the settee would be very useful, and the curtains are essential, I must admit.'

They went in the shop and the assistant showed them how the back of the settee could be lowered to make a double bed, or it could be separated to make two single beds. They couldn't resist it, and paid an extra five shillings to have it delivered the following week.

CHAPTER 8

ROCKY'S FIRST JOB

There was no special induction course for newly qualified personnel into the teaching profession at Chestnut Grove Boys' School; it was assumed that qualified teachers knew what they were doing and would get on with it.

No new school term ever started on a Monday. It was considered that pupils were too animated when they returned after the holidays, so either they started on a Tuesday, or a Thursday, to give them time to settle in before getting down to the hard work of learning.

Rocky wasn't the type of person who could walk into a classroom not knowing where light switches were, what equipment was available, what stock was in cupboards, where the chalk was kept, and what escape routes were available in the event of fire. He needed to know everything.

The new academic year was due to start on the first Tuesday in September, but Rocky intended to spend the previous day finding out as much as he could and meeting any members of staff who had the same inclination as himself.

He got up early and pedalled his bicycle to the school, put the cycle into one of the racks provided, and padlocked the frame to it. He entered the school through a pair of large oak-framed glass doors.

Immediately opposite the entrance there was a varnished hardwood door labelled HEADMASTER. Standing in front of it was a newly qualified graduate looking lost and insignificant with his hands in his pockets and his head bent low over his chest. Strands of fair hair had fallen out of place and obscured his right eye.

'Good morning' greeted Rocky. 'You new here too?'

The slender boyish figure looked up, took his hands out of his pockets and proffered his right one to shake Rocky's.

'Hi. Yeah. I'm Victor Morris, Vic for short. I've come here to teach science,' he said in a slightly southern sounding accent.

'I'm Rockford Driver, but most folks call me Rock or Rocky. I've been appointed to teach chemistry.'

Vic flicked his hair back into place with a nervous reaction and said:

'Oh, we've a common interest then. Shall we find our labs? There's no-one in this room, the door's locked.'

'Good idea,' Rocky responded and led the way up the stairs.

In their search they were greeted with a strong smell of cigarette smoke and pipe tobacco coming from a room along a corridor. They headed towards it, opened the door, and could hardly see through the fug. There were a number of men and women sitting at desks and standing around, the atmosphere buzzed and hummed with the sound of animated voices.

'Morning, everyone, we're a couple of new bods starting tomorrow. We've been appointed to teach science subjects. I'm doing chemistry, and Vic here's going to teach general science.'

'Oh, you want Mr Beeston. He's Head of Department and you'll find him in the staff room further down the corridor' said a plump, short, bearded man.

'My name's Den Barbey. Let me introduce you to my wife, Lil.'

They shook hands and he called to a young fresh-faced, blue-eyed woman with blonde hair scraped back into a pony-tail. She looked thirty years younger than her husband.

After Vic and Rocky had been introduced to everyone in the room they made their way towards the next staff room where more senior members of staff had desks. As they walked along, Rocky enquired:

'Do *you* smoke, Vic?'

'Never' came the reply. 'Complete waste of money, and I'm saving up to get married next Easter. The cost of a wedding isn't cheap these days and Candy wants all the mod cons. Doesn't realise that it's taken her mother thirty years to get everything that she's got today. Candy wants everything to start with.'

'She'll learn. I've only recently married Audrey. Once we'd paid for church fees, taxis, flowers, dresses, licences, etc, our money ran down quite considerably. We've only got a little table and two kitchen chairs, a bed and an oven, but next week we're getting a bed-settee, so that'll help.

Audrey's hoping to get her job transferred so if she's successful we'll soon be able to start saving with two wages coming in. She's still got a bit tucked away in a Save As You Earn scheme that we haven't used yet, so we're not quite on our uppers!'

They ambled into the other staff room where there were fewer people and far less smoke. Mr Beeston rose from his chair near a window. He was not only Head of the Science Department but also third in charge of the school. He introduced the two new recruits to people in the room, showed them around his department, gave them appropriate syllabuses for their work, and their timetables which had been prepared by the Deputy Head. Rocky was glad they'd got things sorted satisfactorily and made a mental note that if ever he became a Headmaster he would always have induction periods for new staff. He would make it mandatory in his school.

By half past two everything they needed to prepare for the week ahead had been covered. Vic took his leave and went to the car park where he'd left his ancient, but trustworthy, Austin Seven. Rocky went to the cycle rack, only to find that his bike had gone. On the ground the damaged padlock and its chain looked like a curled up snake. He picked it up in disbelief. The lock had been severed with a hacksaw.

No-one admitted to having seen or heard anything. Rocky was devastated. Several members of staff helped to look for the bike but it was no-where to be found. He walked back to the flat in total disbelief.

'That's a good omen, I don't think,' he complained to Audrey, who'd never seen him angry before. He was always very placid.

'I've only been at the school for half a day, and some B. has pinched my bike. I'll have to be up very early in the morning if I've got to walk.'

'Borrow mine.'

'What if they pinch that too?'

'They won't. There'll be too many people around tomorrow. There's still time to go and buy an extra-strong lock before the shops close tonight.'

He retorted 'Thanks, but no thanks. I'd prefer to walk. Bloody tea leaves! I'll show 'em. They're not going to get the better of *me.*'

* * * * *

Word had gone round the staff room like wildfire that one of the new bloke's bike had been stolen the previous day. Somehow, it seemed to help. There was an empathy for his loss. Staff went out of their way to befriend him and he got to know them all quickly.

The following morning, as he walked to school, a car pulled up beside him. The nearside window rolled down. The untidy, hairy, face of Den Barbey poked across his wife's comely physique.

'Would you like a lift? We met briefly yesterday in the staff room,'

Den breathed heavily, and spoke with a prominent Cornish brogue.

'Thanks,' Rocky replied, and gratefully climbed into the back of the marine-blue limousine. The stale smell of worn leather upholstery and sweaty socks smothered the delicate hint of Lil's perfume and registered the fact that this old Jaguar was Den's pride and joy. The vehicle purred along smoothly. Den focussed on the inside mirror and saw an image of disbelief on his passenger's face.

'Yes! I've always liked big cars,' he commented. 'This one I inherited from my dad. Had it over ten years now, and it's still as good as the day I got it.'

'I wasn't going to say anything, but I was wondering how you could afford to run a Jaguar on a teacher's salary.'

'Nice one, Rock. Most people on first meeting us look at me, and look at Lil, and think we're father and daughter rather than man and wife. Live on the estate then?'

'Yes, we moved in a week ago.'

Den took one hand off the driving wheel and pulled on his untidy whiskers as he proffered free information.

'We moved in four years ago. Lillemore, Lil, as we call her, was our au pair. She came across from Sweden to look after our two little boys. But then my wonderful wife, *I don't think*, ran off with a builder that was doing some work for us and took the boys with her. Eventually I got divorced and married Lil.'

Rocky was lost for words. His mouth gaped open then closed again. Just at that moment Den peered into his rear view mirror and caught a glimpse of a hangdog look on his passenger's face.

'Yes, I can see you wondering. Most people do. Lil's twenty-six and I'm fifty-six. Quite a difference in our ages, I know, but she teaches basic English and I teach 'O' and 'A' level English so between us we make a good team. I'm hoping that when I retire we'll be able to set up our own little private languages school somewhere on the South coast where ships bring in boatloads of foreigners wanting to settle here. We can all have pipe dreams can't we?'

The car slunk into the car park almost soundlessly. They got out and Lil gave a sweet smile but said nothing. Rocky thought it very unusual for a woman not to enter into conversation or ask any questions, but at least she wasn't hostile like Audrey's mother.

New first-year students were not due to enter the school until Thursday when the school timetable would be running smoothly and the older boys had settled into known routines. Those gathered in the playground were well disciplined. When the Deputy Head, Mr Oliver, blew his whistle, it was magic. There was absolute silence. All the boys became glued to the spot. At a double blast they dispersed and formed into a dozen queues; and on a triple signal, the lines of boys moved decorously forwards, into the school building. Rocky was impressed. He'd been on six different school teaching practices in his three years of teacher-training and he'd never seen composure quite like it. He surmised that the Head must be very much in charge of his school, and he was pleased about that.

Rocky hadn't been allocated a class of his own in his first year but he still had to mark a register at the start of every lesson. This was a legal requirement and the documents could be used in evidence in a Court of Law, if necessary, to provide proof of a pupil's attendance or non-attendance at a particular time on any school day.

All the staff were required to attend morning Assembly, where a short religious service was held. On the first day of the new academic year Assembly was taken by the Head. After that, each member of staff was, at some time in the term, required to conduct the service. Rocky's name was well down the rota.

Throughout the day, five classes of thirty boys came, did their lessons and went. Rocky had been trained to be in charge from the first moment. He stood no nonsense from anyone and the morning had passed satisfactorily for him.

At lunchtime some of the pupils went home for lunch. Rocky went to the hall, part of which was set out for meals for those who stayed for school dinners. The food was adequate, but not exceptional, and he returned to his lab determined to bring a couple of yoghurts and an apple with him in future.

In the first session after lunch he could hear thumping, banging, shrieks of laughter, and much movement coming from the lab next to his. He succeeded in keeping his own class quiet, but everyone was intrigued to know what was happening in the room next door. Rocky daren't leave his pupils unattended because someone might turn on a bunsen burner in his absence, or the pupils might riot, so he and the class worked on through the turmoil.

Going home after his first day was over, he bumped into Vic.

'How'd you get on today, Vic? Get on okay with the lads?'

'Don't arsk! It was a nightmare.'

'Oh?'

'I hope we didn't disturb you, but this afternoon one of the kids who'd gone home for lunch came back with a shoe box. We'd just nicely got the lesson started when he lifted the lid to show his mate the contents. There was pandemonium! One of his pet gerbils had produced eight babies during the holidays and his mother refused to have them in the house any longer, so he'd brought them to school to see if any of his friends would have one. The lad sitting next to him jostled his arm, the lid came off, and the bloody things were running everywhere. The kids thought it was hilarious. They chased after them and tried to grab them, and I couldn't stop them. The awful thing was, Kevin hadn't brought anything for the lads to take them home in. So even if one of the lads caught a creature, it wouldn't stay in his pocket, and as soon as they lifted the lid off the box to put one in, a retrieved one came out again, so it was absolute bedlam.'

'Oh, so that's what was going on? We could hear something happening in the lab next to ours, but I couldn't leave my class to investigate.'

'Oh Gawd! I hope the Head never finds out.'

'Did you catch them all in the end?'

'No. Eventually we got all but two. I had to find and empty eight containers and put air-holes in the lids to put the rats in individually. Then the kids were arguing as to who was going to have them. I pray to Gawd that the missing two don't meet up and mate, otherwise I'll never hear the end of it. If the cleaners find them tonight, there'll be right ructions, and you know how much damage gerbils can do when they gnaw into things. I'm petrified of the repercussions. How about you, Rocky, how did you get on?'

'Generally speaking, I got on okay today, but I was surprised at some of the spelling mistakes the 14-year olds made. We did a distillation experiment and when they were writing up their notes I walked around the benches keeping an eye on what they were doing, and I saw the word thermometer spelled in so many different ways, it was unbelievable. I actually wrote the correct spelling on the blackboard before they started writing and either they didn't take any notice, or they can't read, or copy correctly. I can understand it being called a ferumita, or a furomitter – but a firmomminitre beggars belief – especially when it was written on the board in front of their eyes!'

'Cor, blimey, mate, you'll have to have a word with Lillemore Barbey to see if she can help.'

Vic offered to give Rocky a lift home in his little Austin Seven, Rocky accepted, and the pair of them had much to talk about regarding their first day's teaching experiences at Chestnut Grove School.

CHAPTER 9

AUDREY'S JOB

On the morning of her interview, Audrey rose early, bathed, dressed, set her hair, and caught a bus to Harold Wood Station to join the early morning rush hour.

The platform was crowded with masses of commuters. After buying her ticket, she joined them, and was pushed, shoved and jostled forward as the electric slam-door train eased its way into the station. This wasn't just rush hour; it was crush hour! The hustling, pushing, shoving, elbowing, shouldering, crowd surged towards the open doors, as every man, woman and teenager fended for themselves. She raised her foot to step into the train, but someone behind her wrenched her right shoe off with theirs. She couldn't turn round to get it. More people forced their way in. She could hardly breathe. The doors slammed closed and she was on her way to her all-important interview – shoeless. She had to think quickly. What was she going to do? Would there be a shoe shop nearby when she got off the train at Ilford? If so, would they have anything in stock suitable to go with her outfit? Even if there was, did she have enough money with her to buy another pair? She decided to get off at the next stop and go back to Harold Wood. She had allowed a good hour to spare in case there were problems with connections, but she never imagined something like this would happen.

When she arrived back at the station she went to the ticket office.

'I don't suppose anyone's handed in a lady's shoe this morning, have they? Brown leather, with a Cuban heel.'

An elderly man looked up and peered at her through the bottom of his spectacles.

'You'll 'ave to go to lost property and ask im,' he replied, pointing to a youth sitting at a desk near the next window along.

'It got forced off my foot as I got on the train to go to Ilford. I had to get off at Gidea Park and come back to look for it. I can't see it on the platform. I wonder if it fell on to the tracks below?'

'No good telling me. I'm 'ere to sell tickets. Did you get a ticket to come back 'ere?'

'No. I didn't think. I just got the next train back.'

'Do you want to go back to Ilford today?'

'Yes.'

'Then in that case you'll 'ave to pay for a return ticket from Gidea Park. You can pay the money with your lost property fee.'

'Lost property fee? I didn't know I'd have to pay to get my shoe back when it wasn't my fault!'

'Aw yeah, you do, mate,' he confirmed. 'Jack. Bring over the lost property book and this young woman's shoe what you found this morning.'

The youth brought a huge black-covered book to the ticket seller's window.

Although the writing was upside down to her, she could work out that the last large hand-written entry was:

1 brown ladys shoe heal broke. £1 to pay.

If losing a shoe hadn't been so serious to her, Audrey could have laughed out loud at the English mistakes. She couldn't help commenting out loud:

'Brown lady indeed!'

The lad just gawped. He had no idea that he'd made spelling and grammar mistakes. She felt tense and agitated, and examined the shoe.

When he handed it over, the heel was hanging off, and she hadn't expected that. She was in too much of a shock to laugh, and it was no further laughing matter when she was charged one pound three shillings and sixpence to pay for its return, to include the additional fare for coming back to collect it.

'You'll 'ave to 'urry if you want to catch the next train to Ilford. It'll be 'ere in about four minutes,' the old chap said.

Audrey paid cash and got a receipt. She looked at the shoe. It was useless to walk on. The heel was bent backwards and was hanging off. She twisted it and pulled it off, but she put the shoe on, anyway. She hobbled across to the opposite platform and managed to get on the next up-train with less crushing than before.

When she got off the train she caught another bus to her destination and walked like a Hop-along Cassidy, one shoe down, one sole down, until she reached the hospital entrance. What a good job she'd left plenty of time to get there, she thought.

The interview panel comprised three people. They welcomed her and invited her to sit on a chair in front of their large table. She re-positioned the chair slightly to one side to avoid being seated in a confrontational position.

The panel introduced themselves as Mr Longdon, the Chief Executive Administrator, Dr Biró, the Medical Officer in Charge, and Doctor Khan Gettuelle, a Specialist in tropical diseases.

The interview team had made a list of questions to ask her, but Dr Biró started by asking about her heel-less shoe. It broke the tension. She smiled and tried to make light of the incident, and they were impressed that she had started out early enough to cope with the situation and still be on time for her interview.

They asked three questions each from their list and were satisfied with all of her answers. Finally, they asked if she had any questions for them. Her first question was about the job itself, what did it entail?

She was told that she would be a personal assistant to Dr Biró, and would carry out all the routine tasks of a PA but he was a very sick man. He was due to go in to hospital in three weeks' time for a major operation and he urgently needed someone who could manage in his absence. Audrey pointed out that she was not a medical secretary and didn't have a command of medical terminology. Her forté was administration.

Mr Longdon's eyes lit up. Dr Biró's looked down, but he seemed pleased with her honesty and mumbled something about that's where Dr Gettuelle would be able to help.

Her second question was, that if the job was offered, when would her services be required to start.

'Immediately' shot back the reply from Mr Longdon. 'Can you start on Monday? Our need is urgent.'

He told her that Dr Biró's former PA had died suddenly a month ago and they had been struggling with an agency temp who wasn't really up to the job. Her references had already come through from Principal Nursing Officer Doughty, but they needed to see her original qualifications, not copies. From her shopping bag, she proffered a foolscap sized package. They perused her certificates with interest, and commented that she was, indeed, very well qualified on paper.

After a low tone discussion between the doctors and himself, Mr Longdon finally said that because of the additional responsibility she would be taking on, they felt able to offer her the position on the relevant PA scale an increment higher than her salary with the York Hospital Management Committee, plus London weighting. They wished her well, and looked forward to seeing her again on Monday.

Going home, Audrey felt light headed. She was going to earn much more money than Rocky, and he'd a total of five years' experience in the RAF and at training college, that she hadn't had. Somehow it didn't seem right that a woman younger than him was going to earn more than him, the breadwinner. On the other hand, she justified to herself that she'd had five years' work experience and that must have counted for something. She wondered what he would say when she told him she was going to have a gross salary of sixty pounds a month compared with his monthly gross of thirty-seven pounds.

In fact, Rocky was amazed when he heard her news. He took her into his arms and kissed her as they'd never kissed before. They made passionate love, and he told her what a clever girl she was, and how proud he was to have her as his wife. Audrey lapped up all the extra-special attention and was so pleased she'd rejected her mother's pleas not to marry him. Rocky was absolutely wonderful.

The next day Audrey wrote two letters, one to Cora and Edwynne, and one to her own parents. She told them how she and Rocky were getting on since their move to Romford, and of her new offer of appointment, but not of her new salary. She thought if she told Cora and Edwynne, they may discuss it with her parents when they next met together and if she told her own parents, it would probably cause problems of jealousy and envy as far as her mother was concerned, and that was the last thing she wanted. So she just told them about losing her shoe and having to walk almost a mile with one foot up and one foot down on the pavement. It wasn't funny at the time, but it amused her now and she hoped the incident it might amuse them, too.

* * * * *

Blighted by her first experience of rush hour in Essex, Audrey decided to cycle to work. It was a long journey which would take over an hour each way but she was fit, and a good cyclist. She set off at 7.20 am, having planned the route the previous evening. Her journey took her to Gallows Corner, down the main road through Romford town centre, past Chadwell Heath and beyond. She arrived in good time for her nine o'clock start.

The hospital was old and sprawled out over a large area. Her office was near the front gate. She asked a porter where she could leave her bike. He directed her to a decrepit bike-shed and she padlocked her transport securely after Rocky's experience at school.

She found her way into the building and was greeted by Dr Gettuelle who was already on duty, and guided her to her room. He opened the door and allowed her to go in first. Her eyes met with a dark, dingy, musty, soulless square. Under a window immediately opposite the door, she could see, and smell, an ancient fusty leather-topped desk, on which stood an antique Imperial typewriter coated in dust and breadcrumbs. In the kneehole of the desk, a pale grey well-worn typing chair rested. Her eyes ran around the room, noting there were two tables, both littered with loose papers, four hardbacked chairs and three rusting filing cabinets. Apart from a clock on the wall, that was it. She couldn't believe what she'd come to. At least she'd had a modern Olympia typewriter at her last job, but this was beyond belief. She wondered how was she expected to type quickly on that thing!

Almost simultaneously with her arrival, Dr. Biró came into the room, but was breathless and exhausted. He looked as grey as the old worn chair. She greeted him pleasantly, but couldn't resist passing comment at the age and condition of the typewriter on which she was expected to work. He didn't think it was that old; it just needed a bit of dusting! He said that his former personal assistant, Miss Plonkitt, had only used two fingers to type his letters. Her style of typing was search and stab, and if she hit the wrong keys she either rubbed her mistakes out, or she typed over them. Audrey was horrified. She couldn't believe her ears.

At times she found it difficult to understand Dr Biró's Magyar dialect, but gathered that he wanted her to compose his letters for him and when she typed them, to take two carbon copies. One copy was to be placed in the case study file, the other was to be put in a cattle tray.

'What's a cattle tray?' she enquired. 'I've never heard of one.'

'Top secretary like you, and you've never heard of a cattle tray?' He pronounced the word out loud: 'Kay Tee El,' then in baby-language, 'Kah Tuh Luh. It means Keep Till Later.'

'I've never heard of that before. It's a new one on me. I suppose it's what we call a pending tray.'

Doctor Biró's lips quivered and he raised his hand to his chest. 'Oh, the pain! The pain! I'll have to take a tablet.'

He sat down and took a white pill out of a small box in his pocket. Doctor Gettuelle went and got him a glass of water from somewhere, and showed great concern for his senior medical officer.

After a while Dr Biró appeared to recover slightly and instructed Audrey to compose his letters in his absence, and to get Dr Gettuelle to sign them on his behalf. He said it was his intention to take sick leave until further notice, but he would call in to the office on Monday mornings and go through Audrey's carbon copies to see if any follow-up would be required. If she needed to know anything, she should ask one of the doctors on duty. He mumbled pathetically:

'I'm too sick to be troubled with mundane things, it's up to you to get on with the job.'

Dr Gettuelle accompanied him out of the room and left Audrey alone in the musty environment.

Being curious, she opened the drawers in the desk. There was a selection of paper and envelopes in the top one, carbon paper, a supply of new typewriter ribbons, and paperclips in the second, and all kinds of oddments in the third, including screwdrivers, a typewriter cleaning kit and two long handled brushes. At least she would be able to get the breadcrumbs out of the typewriter!

She clicked down the two holding catches and removed the platen. Using the longest handled brush, she carefully brushed the crumbs outwards so that they wouldn't fall further into the well, and discovered they weren't the remnants of someone's lunch, they were actually morsels of rubber dust.

When she'd finished cleaning the typewriter to a healthier state of use and replaced the roller, she inserted a sheet of plain paper and did her fingering exercises up and down the keyboard to judge the weight of her touch and the quality of the print produced. She stopped typing and looked at the print. The a, s, o, and top of the e characters were infilled with typewriter-ribbon ink. She found a small stiff brush in the pack and cleaned all the type-faces. Then she typed the alphabet, forwards and backwards several times to check that the print was clearer.

Suddenly the office door opened. A man in a white coat with a stethoscope around his neck lolled in. In a clipped tongue he said:

'My goodness me, you type fast. How can you type like that? I never heard anything like it all the time I verked here.'

'I suppose, like you, Doctor, I'm well trained and experienced in my skills. Pleased to meet you. I'm Audrey Driver, Dr Biro's new personal assistant.'

He gave a long drawn-out 'A h h h,' before adding:

'I'm Dr Bannalurgee. I do infectious diseases and notify the Medical Officer of Health about all new I D cases admitted. I also assist Dr. Biró with post mortems. We usually meet in here on Mondays. Is he about?'

'He's been, and gone, but I can phone him for you ....'

Her voice trailed off as Dr Biró returned, looking slightly less grey. Obviously the severe pain had passed. The two doctors sat at a desk together, ignoring the high pile of papers, and Audrey was aware of vague mumblings beyond her earshot; then they called her over and explained some of their procedures and how she was to carry them out. They asked her to bring them the file of latest Smallpox admissions.

She soon discovered why the temp hadn't been very satisfactory. She hadn't filed to retrieve, she'd filed to hide. Audrey expected to find the folder under S for Smallpox, but it wasn't there. There were no alphabetical, subject, or numerical indexes in any of the cabinets, and no OUT/IN booking cards in the drawers. When she looked through the cabinets there was a conglomeration of dog-eared papers, dishevelled and in a state of disarray in their folders. She looked under I for Infectious diseases; T for Tropical Diseases; D for Doctor, or Diseases of any sort; B for Biró in case it had been filed under her boss's or Dr Bannalurgee's name; G for Gettuelle, K for Khan Gettuelle, and M for Miscellaneous, but the file was no-where to be found. Then she had a brainwave. Perhaps the folder had been mis-filed and put in the R section, which was just one letter in front of the S's. She found the missing folder under R for Research.

'Ah, here it is! I was beginning to think it must be hidden under that pile of papers on your desks.'

She handed the file to them with a sense of achievement at having discovered it at last, and thought to herself that if she hadn't found it, the doctors would have assumed it was her that was inefficient, not the previous PA. The doctors referred to the file for less than five minutes, then left.

At about ten o'clock, the morning's post was pushed through the letterbox in her office door. The porters didn't come into her room and hand it to her personally or say 'Good Morning'. She rushed to the door and opened it, but there was no-one in sight.

An hour later Mr Longdon came to her room to see if she was settling in. She told him of her shock at the disarray of the papers in the room and the antiquity of the equipment, plus the fact that the mail had been pushed through the letter-box without anyone coming in, or any word of greeting. He explained that the porters had probably come from the wards so they were less likely to spread infection by not coming into the room, but he said he would see what he could do about getting a new typewriter for her.

After he'd gone, she felt isolated and distanced and wondered whether she'd done the right thing in getting transferred to this job from her previous one with Matron Doughty and her spanking clean hospital. If Matron could see this room, she'd have a fit!

When she left the building at five o'clock Audrey couldn't get home quickly enough. But evening rush hour traffic was much more dense, and eventually it was quarter to seven before she got home. Rocky was worried about her. He'd had his tea hours ago and to her dismay, he'd eaten a whole coffee cake which she had hoped would provide a dessert for them for at least two or three days.

Audrey didn't see Dr Biró for the rest of the week. She had to cope on her own with little experience in medical matters, but managed to liaise with Dr Gettuelle from time to time, and he signed all the letters which she'd composed.

By the end of the week, Audrey felt exhausted. She'd done her best but hadn't found it easy. She wasn't used to using an old, antiquated typewriter, and she didn't like being isolated from other members of staff for long hours on end. She wished she hadn't been so keen to take on the job in the first place, but the money was good, and she'd been able to keep her pension; so she decided to battle on and try and learn new coping skills. She also had her doubts about cycling to work and back in such horrendous traffic, but she couldn't face the prospect of two train journeys a day in the rush hours plus two mile-long walks each way – it would take hours – so she decided to give it a go for a month, and if things didn't improve in that time, her best ploy would be to find work elsewhere, even if it meant losing her pension after all.

CHAPTER 10

MIXED EMOTIONS

After a relaxing weekend at home, the following Monday morning Audrey set off for work with a heavy heart, wondering what the week would bring.

About eleven o'clock Dr Biró went to her room and checked the contents of the "Cattle" tray. He was pleased with the letters she'd written, so he signed fifty sheets of letterhead paper in different positions – some in the centre, some at the bottom of each page – and told her she would have to compose his letters and type them to fit around his signature, so that they looked as if they'd been genuinely signed by him, instead of getting Dr Gettuelle to sign them, as in the previous week.

That was the last time she saw him.

Dr Biró never got his operation. The following Thursday night he died at home in bed.

On Friday morning when word got round, the medical staff were subdued. The work of the hospital continued but in sombreness and disbelief.

When Audrey got home that night, Rocky wasn't in. The Head had put up notices, and gone round the school, encouraging more staff to assist with unpaid out-of-school activities and Rocky had volunteered to help with circuit training and to referee soccer matches after school on weekdays because he refereed league matches on Saturdays. His colleague, Vic, offered to help with swimming lessons once a week.

Den offered to run a chess club after school on Wednesdays and Lil said she would also stay for an hour on Wednesdays but her contribution would be to teach the boys the intricacies of solving cryptic crossword puzzles. Rob Magistrate, Head of PE, said he would run a Junior Evening Institute provided there were sufficient children interested and he could get approval from the local authority to pay for specialist subject areas where none of the school staff could help.

The Head was pleased with the outcome of his efforts and said he would 'drop in' from time to time to keep an eye on the extra-curricular activities.

Audrey thought that it would have to be this night, of all nights, that Rocky wouldn't be home until ten o'clock. Her body ached for him to be there at that very moment, but that was part of his job, and she couldn't blame him for being out. He wasn't to know of the sorrow that had struck that day. When he did come home he showed empathy for the doctor's demise, and comforted Audrey, yet remained realistic about the loss of a very sick man she hardly knew.

The next day, being Saturday, they both had a long lie in. Audrey was roused by the sound of the letterbox opening and closing. Two letters had arrived, both with familiar handwriting. One was addressed to her, the other to Mr & Mrs R

Driver. The former was from her mother, the other was from Cora and Edwynne. Audrey opened her mother's letter while Rocky opened the one from his parents. Mrs Small's long, backhanded spidery scrawl read:

Dear Audrey,

Thanks for your letter. This is just to let you know that the wedding photos you ordered have been sent here. Do you want to come and get them, or shall we post them to you. If so, you'll have to send a poster l'order because the album and box they're in is heavy to post, and will cost quite a bit. Sorry to hear about your shoes but as your both going to have jobs with two wages coming in no doubt you can afford to buy another pear soon.

Mam (and Dad.)

In complete contrast, Cora's large, bold, upright round style read:

Our darling Rocky and Audrey

We were delighted to receive your letter and hear everything is well with you, despite losing the heel off your shoe, Audrey. We were so pleased to know that you weren't hurt in the crush. It could have been much worse.

We were also pleased to know that you have managed to get your job transferred, so that you won't lose your pension rights.

*Here, everything is all right with us. Edwynne
has had a glut of runner beans so I've had to
pickle some of them in salt water as there far
too many for us to eat every day. Auntie Matilda
has very kindly invited us to go and stay with
her at Christmas, so we wondered whether we
could come and see you at half-term? DV. We
could get a train to Romford but you'd have to
meet us at the station. Can you, Audrey, get
the time off with just starting a new job?*

*Take care, and continue to look after each
other,*

God Bless,

All our love to you both,

Cora and Edwynne.

x x x x

'What a difference in the two communications'
Audrey thought, 'but what does Cora mean by
DV?'

Rocky explained that DV meant Deo volente, the
Latin expression meaning 'God Willing'. It was one
of the things his mother had frequently used when
she had written to him in the RAF.

They worked out that half term would be the last
full week of October. If Cora and Edwynne could
come Saturday to Saturday it would be wonderful.
They could give them their bedroom and they would
sleep on the bed-settee in the lounge, and they
could take them to Southend to walk along the

mile-long pier, and go to London to see a show. The possibilities were endless. Now they really did have something to look forward to.

As the weeks moved on, Audrey hated her job more and more each day. Dr Gettuelle was appointed Acting Medical Officer in Charge until Dr Biró's job was advertised and an official appointment made. She didn't always understand his clipped English, and abhorred the smell of curry which emanated from the roots of his hair, and was on his breath when he spoke.

The cycle ride to work seemed to get longer every day and she tried riding down the Arterial Road, but the traffic there was even worse. She hated working alone, and became despondent, but felt she must snap out of the mood before Cora and Edwynne came.

One Saturday morning when Rocky had set out early to referee a soccer match that afternoon, she thought a bit of shopping might help to lift her spirits, so she went to the shop at North Street and bought a carpet square and two fireside chairs which would make the flat much more comfortable for themselves, and for her in-laws' arrival. The items were delivered that afternoon and by the time Rocky got in from his soccer match that evening, the lounge looked much more comfortable and homely.

Den and Lil had been upset to hear of Audrey's despondency with her job, so to try and cheer her a bit, they'd invited Rocky and her to a meal at Den's golf club the following weekend.

'Oh, that'll be lovely,' she exclaimed when she

heard of the invitation. 'We don't go out much because we can't afford it. Probably that's another of the reasons why I feel so down. Lack of people in the day, only us two in the evenings and at weekends, when you're not out on out-of-school activities or refereeing, and no relatives or life-long friends to turn to here. Perhaps we could invite them back here for a meal after Cora and Edwynne have gone back?'

Rocky agreed:

'Good idea. We'll put it to them and see what they say.'

The following Saturday Audrey sorted through her dresses which were stored in a case under the bed. She chose her prettiest one to wear that evening and ironed it. The material was a bright turquoise colour, printed with tea-plate sized purple and lemon dahlias. It was still fashionable with its full circular skirt and broad elasticated waist belt.

Den and Lil arrived at their flat at the pre-arranged time, and drove them to the golf club.

Whilst waiting for the lunch to be served, they sat at a small table and had a glass of wine. Lil twisted the broad gold wedding ring on her finger and smoothed the front of her cream coloured dress which was embroidered with delicate shades of tiny flowers around the collar, cuffs and hemline.

'That's a very pretty dress,' remarked Audrey.

'Actually, it's my wedding dress' Lil purred.

'Really?'

'Yes. You see, my parents didn't want me to marry Den because of our age difference. They said he was old enough to be my father. But he was my choice. They'd had their choices when they were younger, so why couldn't I choose for myself? We had many argy-bargies over the telephone and when they came over from Sweden they tried to make me go back with them, but I wouldn't. You see, although I love looking after other people's children, and teaching them, I have a dreadful fear of bearing children myself. I never ever want to become pregnant, and Den doesn't want to have any more, so we're ideally suited. We both love teaching, and we have a chemistry which attracts us to each other,' she explained in a soft Scandanavian accent.

She smoothed the front of her hair, and pulled her pony tail tighter.

'We never told anybody, but we arranged to get married in a Register Office. When the day came I put on this dress and we went together to the office where they marry people, but when we got there they asked about witnesses and we didn't have any, so we went out into the street and asked a couple of passers-by if they would come in and be witnesses for us. The first couple we asked said they didn't have the time, but the next couple we asked agreed. They came in to the office, witnessed our marriage, signed the papers, and left. We've never seen them again. I can't even remember their names.'

Rocky leaned forward over the table.

'So didn't you have a reception, or a wedding breakfast, or a cake?'

Lil's moist fingers twitched as she attempted to dry them on her handkerchief.

'Nooooh. We went to a nearby pub and had beer

and bags of potato crisps.'

'Oh, Lil, that's really sad' sympathised Audrey.

'Noooh it isn't. It's the way we wanted it. The wedding didn't cost much, and within ten minutes we were lawfully married. What more could we want?' she lilted. 'We're very happy together.'

She smiled sweetly at Den who sat back in his chair and allowed her to relate her story while he ran his fingers through his greying untidy beard.

Rocky was surprised to hear her story and realised that here were two women who'd both had mother troubles over their marriages, but Lillemore had sorted out her wedding problems without her parents knowing. At least she didn't have a confrontation on her wedding day like Audrey did with her mother.

After a delicious meal, Rocky offered to chip in with the bill. Den objected profusely.

'Wouldn't dream of it. You're our guests,' he replied as he took out his wallet. 'It will do you both good to have a little treat once in a while.'

With prolific thanks, they left the golf club to make their way home in Den's car.

'You've really settled in well haven't you?' commented Den as he took one hand off the driving wheel to scratch his whiskery face.

'Yes, school life's been good to me so far, but Audrey's not very happy since her boss died. It's a long journey for her to cycle there and back every day and .....'

Den interrupted in his delightful Cornish tone:

'Why don't you give it up then?' He smiled at her

through his rear mirror. 'There are plenty of jobs in this area. A person like you, Aud, should be able to pick one up in no time at all.'

Lil intervened:

'Why don't you go temping? I've a friend who's a temp and she loves it. She gets good money. I'm sure you would, too.'

Audrey responded positively:

'It's certainly worth thinking about. Doing temporary work is something I haven't seriously considered, because of losing my pension, but perhaps I should, because I absolutely hate, loathe, and detest the work I'm doing now, the equipment, my room, and the journey.'

Den quickly changed the subject. After paying well-earned money for a delightful evening out, the last thing he wanted was for Audrey to start whingeing about her job.

CHAPTER 11

WELCOME VISITORS

The next day Audrey and Rocky sorted their washing into light and dark colours, and Rocky took the two bags of laundry to the Washeteria. He'd been gone about half an hour when there was a knock on the front door. 'Wonder who that is?' thought Audrey as she walked down the corridor. When she opened the door she was amazed to see her father standing there.

'Good Heavens! Dad! What are you doing here? Come in. Is everything all right?'

Mr Small grinned as he stepped into the flat, carrying a small parcel.

'Yes, lass, everything's fine. But as I had a free railway pass, your mother wanted me to come and bring you your wedding photographs. Then she can put the money you sent her into her Post Office Savings bank book, plus the fact that we'll know that you've got them safely without being damaged.'

'Oh, thank you, dad. Come in. Welcome. Take your coat off. Sit down. Why didn't you let us know you were coming, we might have been out? Do you want a cup of tea, or coffee? How did you get here?'

The words tumbled out as she opened both arms to hug him, before leading him into the lounge. Larry put the package on the bed-settee while he took off his coat and handed it to her. He surveyed the room before sitting down.

'Nice little flat you've got here. No doubt you'll show me round in due course?'

'Actually, there's not much for you to see, but I'll be pleased to show you.'

'Where's Rocky?'

'He's taken our soiled washing to the local Washeteria. He'll be back in about an hour.'

She hung his coat on a coat peg near the front door.

'How are you? How's mam?'

'Funnily enough, lass, since you left home she's been much better in health and temper. She's got over her appendicitis and peritonitis, but recently her feet have been playing up.'

'Oh dear, I'm sorry to hear that. What's wrong with her feet?'

'Well, you know she's had bunions for years! Anyway, recently she's been walking quite badly, and says her feet hurt, so she went to see the doctor about them and he referred her to a specialist. She's been put on a waiting list to go into hospital early in the New Year to have both bunions removed. She didn't know how much walking she'd have to do to get here, so thought it best if I found out first before she comes to see the flat.'

'To see the flat, not us?'

'Well, you know what your mother's like. Only interested in material wealth and what you've got financially, and I also think she was a bit reticent about meeting Rocky.'

'Well, that's her problem! I really don't know what he's done to upset her, but she took an instant dislike to him from the first moment she met him, and she won't say why. I just don't understand it.'

'As you say, lass, that's her problem. If she won't tell us, we can't force her, no matter how hard we try. We just have to leave her to come round as and when she's ready. Now! Let's have a look around your flat.'

'We haven't got much for you to look at here. We're frantically saving up to buy a place of our own so only have the barest of essentials at the moment.'

Audrey moved forward to open the door into the hallway and show him the bedroom, kitchen and bathroom. As she did so he advised her in a fatherly manner:

'Don't you be putting a millstone round your neck! Please lass don't get into debt. I know what it's like. I've had some. Just take your time, and take one step at a time. Remember what Mr MaCawber said. Charles Dickens was very astute and what he said was true. Keep within your means, happiness. Overspend, misery. I'd hate you to go down that route.'

'I don't think we'll do that, dad.'

By the time Rocky returned with the laundry the pot of tea she'd made had been used so she made another pot and some sandwiches. They sat and chatted and caught up with each other's news. Larry was pleased that Rocky had settled in well at his job; but Audrey was guarded about her unhappiness and merely told him that Dr Biró had died, things had changed, and she was thinking about giving it up and going to work as a temp.

'You be careful, lass. You've got a good job with a pension. Try and put up with it for as long as you can. You haven't been there five minutes yet. You'll be all right when the new guy's appointed.'

'Can you sleep on the bed-settee tonight, dad, or would you rather have our bed? It'll be much more comfortable for you. I've just put clean sheets on it this morning.'

'Oh, I'm not stopping over, lass. There's a restricted train service on Sundays but I've checked and there's a train back early this evening so I'll catch that and get back to your mother. With a bit of luck I can be home by eleven o'clock tonight.'

'That's an awful lot of travelling in one day. Surely you can stay overnight?'

'No. I've got to go to work tomorrow and your mother's expecting me back tonight. It's only a flying visit. We'll come and see you when she's had her feet done and she's walking better.'

They caught up with each other's news, commented on the photographs, and after a cooked meal, in the evening went to Romford Station where Mr Small caught the first of his trains home.

On their way home Audrey made a decision. It had been lovely seeing her dad, but she told Rocky that in her opinion, in the past he'd been wrong about so many things, especially about house purchase, that she'd decided not to take his advice about not trying to buy their own home, or about resigning from her job. She was determined to do both things.

When they got back to the flat, she wrote a letter of resignation.

As anticipated, the following Monday morning when she handed it in, Mr Longdon was not pleased. He tried to persuade her to continue working until they could get a replacement personal assistant. But she was adamant. She thought that if she gave in to his request he wouldn't try to get another person quickly and, having made up her mind, she was determined to go.

* * * * *

When Cora and Edwynne alighted from the train at Romford station, he was carrying a large, battered, tan-coloured, leather suitcase and a heavy shopping bag. Cora was struggling with a large wicker basket.

Rocky greeted his parents with open arms and kissed them before taking the case from his dad. The pong from it gave the impression it had either been stored in a cupboard for a long time, or it had been bought in a jumble sale for sixpence.

Audrey kissed them both and took the wicker basket from Cora. That had an earthy smell, and she confirmed it contained fresh vegetables from their garden.

'Did you have a good journey, Cora?'

'Yes, it was quite pleasant. We got a taxi to York station and had seats in the train but the time has passed slowly. We've been on the go for five hours.

I'll be glad to get to your place and sit on a seat that isn't moving and have a nice cup of tea.'

'I'll second that' Edwynne endorsed, as he straightened his round-framed wire spectacles on his nose.

Cora moved a strand of hair that had fallen in front of her eyes. Audrey studied her and drew the conclusion that she'd put on quite a bit of weight since their wedding, but Edwynne remained as thin as ever.

'We'll soon be home and get you settled in. We've got two nice fireside chairs, so you'll be able to sit back and have your cup of tea in comfort.'

'Oh, good.' Cora retorted. 'I'm just about all in.'

On arrival at the flat Cora's first port of call was the bathroom. When she joined them in the lounge she enquired:

'Where's your mirror?'

'I'm afraid we haven't got a long one' replied Rocky. 'I use a shaving mirror and Audrey shares mine or uses the mirror in her powder compact.'

'However do you manage to see what your clothes look like?'

'We don't! We only see our faces in the flat. We have to rely on shop windows to reflect our full-length images.'

'Oh, we can't have that. While we're here we'll buy you one as a thank you for having us.'

'That really isn't necessary, mum. We don't want to be paid to have you. You know you'll always be very welcome to come here when ever you like. It's just that you'll have to fend for yourselves if you come in term time. Fortunately, we're both off this week as Audrey has booked it off as the last of her holiday entitlement before leaving her job at the hospital at the end of the month.'

In the evening they looked at the wedding photographs.

'Oh, that's a nice one' commented Edwynne.

'I like that' said Cora, followed by 'Just look at your mother's hat on this one. It's enormous.'

Audrey related the debate they'd had on the topic of wearing green at a wedding, and how it was the last thing she'd expected of her mother, not only to dress in green, but also to have paid ten guineas for her hat.

'Goodness me!' exclaimed Cora. 'I only paid fourteeen and six pence for mine and I thought I'd paid over the odds.'

'Well, everyone looked very nice. Some people pay a lot, and can look frumpy. Others spend far less and look fantastic. It's not what you pay for clothes, it's how you wear them that matters. You and Edwynne always look good.'

The following morning, after going to Church at Cora's insistence, they walked slowly back to the flat. Cora's walking seemed to be a problem to her. Audrey wondered whether she ought to suggest buying a walking stick tomorrow, but thought better of it.

The next day Cora wanted to go in to Romford. She walked round and round the counters of Woolworth's until Rocky felt dizzy.

'I haven't seen anything I want yet' she said and they came back empty-handed.

On Tuesday, they went by train to Southend. After leaving the station they walked towards the front, and down a slope to the mouth of the river Thames. How glorious it looked with the longest pier in the world extruding its way through the shallow water which sparkled, as gleaming stars of light danced on a gently undulating swell of waves. The water looked like a bejewelled carpet of magnificent diamonds and pearls. The smell of the sea was salty and atmospheric, and despite the loud squawking of seabirds they could hear the sound of a fun fair in the distance. In some respects it reminded Cora of their beloved Scarborough, the nearest seaside resort to their home. There, too, barrel organ music could be heard in the amusement arcades along the sea front and, near the harbour the smell of fishing boats, seaweed and fish and chips were familiar aromas. But this place was different. It was a calmer atmosphere. There weren't so many people about and the miniature train ran, not along the cliffs to Scalby Mills, but one and a quarter miles to the end of the jetty where an occasional pleasure boat tied up.

They bought return tickets and boarded the tiny train. As they travelled along the wind blew gently through their hair and small drops of moisture wetted their faces. They observed people walking the boards to the end of the pier, some pushing prams, others eating ice-creams, ice lollies, chocolate or candy floss. Some visitors were eating bags of potato crisps, or fish and chips; some pushed bicycles, or walked dogs. Yet despite all the activities, the ambience was calm and carefree.

They alighted from the train and walked to the jetty. Groups of fishermen and youths were casting their rods into the deeper water. Some had wriggling bait in tins; some had small fish in keep-nets. The sun, and salt, and sea were a refreshing change from the damp and earthy ground of their Yorkshire village and Cora and Edwynne lapped it up.

The following day they rested and just visited the local shops, but Thursday and Friday were full of activity. They went to London to see the long-running play, The Mouse Trap and thoroughly enjoyed the Agatha Christie "whodunnit", and on Friday morning Cora bought a full-length mirror in Romford market. Rocky put it up that afternoon and in the evening Cora and Edwynne packed their suitcase in preparation for their homeward journey.

On Saturday Audrey and Rocky went with them as far as Kings Cross station and saw them on to the right train for York.

'Hope you have a good journey home, and have a truly lovely Christmas with Aunt Matilda' they called as they waved farewell from the platform.

'See you next half-term.'

Rocky and Audrey spent the rest of the day in London and came home late that evening, happy that the visit had been so successful. Cora was such a cheerful soul, full of fun, and it had been a joy to have them stay for a whole week.

CHAPTER 12

SURPRISES

After the half-term break Audrey was glad that she only had two more weeks left to complete working her notice.

As her feet wound the pedals of her bike along the Arterial Road, she mused about how mislead she'd been about the hospital's name when she had first seen it in Matron Doughty's handbook. "Goodways Infirmary, Ilford", had impressed her. She had thought of 'good ways' being a good omen of what she might be going to. Now she knew better! As far as "Ilford" was concerned, it could have referred to 'ill', as people were in the infirmary itself – not only the patients – but also her boss. She thought, not only of Dr. Biró, but also of the previous PA who must have been really sick to leave the office so untidy, piled high with medical papers all over the doctors' desks. It had taken her hours to file everything away and make an index for the filing system. She realised that the new medical officer would want to sweep clean, and would soon have new desks, chairs, filing cabinets, and the promised typewriter which had never materialised; but that would be for his benefit and the new PA. What he did would be an improvement, but he could never shorten her journey each day or lessen the traffic, or regulate the weather. She put her head down low to combat the wind that caught her sideways at times, and with legs whirring the wheels, she turned her thoughts to the lovely week she'd just had, entertaining her delightful in-laws.

That evening when she got home, Rocky had some surprising news for her. Den and Lil were organising a school trip to Belgium for the Summer of next year and had invited them both to accompany them.

Pupils would pay for their own transportation and hotel accommodation but, because there had to be one adult to every ten children, there would be two free places for staff. Den would have one of the free places for organising it, and Rocky could have the other for the responsibilities he would have to undertake. Rocky was elated.

'I've never been to Belgium before. It's a wonderful opportunity. I know we'll have to pay for you but how about coming with us, Audrey?'

'Can we afford it?'

'Why not? We don't have to put every penny into saving for a house. We do have to have a life as well.'

'Okay, if you're sure, but why Belgium?'

'Well, Brussels, the Capital, is an up-and-coming City since the Economic Community set up there a few years ago. They had an International World Trade Fair there in 1958 and they had a structure built for it called an Atomium. Den was reading an article about it in a magazine and he was so impressed by it he thought it would be great for pupils to see it before it is taken down. Apparently it was only intended to be there for six months but it's still standing, three years later, so it would be really good to see it before it's demolished.'

'I've never heard of it!'

'Neither had I, but Den explained that it's not a building, it's a feature designed in the shape of an atom. There are six large spheres made out of aluminium, connected by enormous tubes that people can walk right through to exhibition halls and things. There's nothing else in the world like it, and it will be a real education for our pupils to experience it.'

Audrey removed her glasses, breathed on the lenses, cleaned them with her handkerchief and put them back on.

'Sounds great. Yes, I'll come. I'd like to see it, but we won't rob our housing fund. If the visit isn't until next Spring we've time to put some money away each week and I'll just have to cut down spending money on clothes and whatever else I can.'

'Don't overdo it, love.'

'No, but we need to be practical.'

They cuddled up together, melted into each other's arms; went into their bedroom and made passionate love. Everything in their lives was wonderful.

Next morning Rocky went to school and confirmed that Audrey would join them on the trip. He and Den talked about famous Belgian people like Georges Simenon who wrote the Maigret stories and how Lil thought that might encourage her pupils to read more if she could get them interested in the detective genre.

That afternoon Rocky came home on a high note. He picked up a letter and turned it over. He looked at the handwriting on the envelope, and the postmark. It was from Yorkshire. A thank-you letter no doubt. 'That's quick,' he thought. 'Funny Edwynne's written the envelope. Usually Cora does all the writing.' He opened the envelope and removed the single sheet of paper. His gills turned white. His hands trembled. His temples sweated. His body shook. His mouth ran dry. His eyes welled up. His beloved mother was dead.

He read the terse communication again in total disbelief. It was exactly a week since they'd all had such a wonderful day at Southend. It was only Saturday that she'd gone home. How sudden was that? He read the words out loud, trying to digest their message:

'Cora died 3.15 am Sunday. Please come. Love Edwynne.'

Rocky wiped the cuff of his right sleeve across his forehead, went into the lounge and sat down. He dropped the paper on the floor and for the first time in his life, lost his composure and sobbed his heart out. He was agitated and anxious because Audrey was still at work. He wondered whether to find a phone box and tell her now, or wait for her to get home. He decided it would be better to tell her face-to-face when she arrived. rather than upset her prior to her dicey journey along the Arterial Road where traffic was bad, even at the best of times.

Audrey got home about seven o'clock and couldn't believe her ears and eyes. She read the note over and over again. Salty tears scalded her face as they ran down her cheeks and dropped off her chin. She took a clean handkerchief to wipe them away but within seconds it was soaked and she went into their bedroom to get another one.

She sorrowfully returned, and gave Rocky a huge hug.

'Oh, darling, I can't believe it. Have we caused this to happen? Have we contributed to her death by walking her too far? Has the travelling been too much for her? Should we have realised that she wasn't well when she arrived?' She brushed more tears away with her handkerchief. 'Whatever are we going to do?'

Rocky swallowed a big lump in his throat and peered at his watch.

'First thing I'll do is go to see Den and Lil. They've a got 'phone. They may know the Head's home telephone number. If so, I'll ring him and see what he suggests. Last week we were all so happy together. Who would believe this news would come exactly one week after we had such a lovely day at Southend?'

'It must have been an awful shock for Edwynne, too.'

Oh, I wish he was on the phone so that I could ring him right now.'

'It's such a brief note, it gives no details.'

'Well, Edwynne's no scholar. He's done his best to let us know as soon as he can. I'll go and see Den.'

He left Audrey stressed and tearful. Her third handkerchief was as sodden as the first. She went into the kitchen and took some paper towels off the roll. She blew her nose into them. She binned the tissues and took more.

'It's not fair,' she sobbed to herself. 'Cora was such a lovely lady.'

When Rocky returned, Den was with him. They had contacted the Head who gave permission for Rocky to travel to York the next day. He would delegate other staff to cover Rocky's lessons and asked him to provide Den with a sheet of aims and objectives for his classes, which could be followed by substitute teachers. He also gave him his phone number and asked Rocky to keep in touch regarding his date of return to duty.

The next morning Rocky and Audrey walked to the nearest telephone box. He cancelled his refereeing match for the following two weekends, and Audrey telephoned the hospital to tell Mr Longdon what had happened, and she asked for immediate compassionate leave. His response was not what she'd expected. He wasn't sympathetic, he was taken aback by her request to have more time off. He said that she'd only been back for two days after having had a whole week off as her final claim to holiday entitlement, and the work of the hospital had to go on. His displeasure came through the earpiece of the phone loudly and clearly. He said he thought she was self-centred and thoughtless and if she didn't go to work it would have to be counted as leave without pay.

Audrey retaliated by saying that if she was sick she wouldn't be able to go to work – but she knew that she'd never registered with a GP in this area so she wouldn't be able to get a medical certificate from a local doctor to support her and, she wasn't medically sick – she was just sick with despair and horror at Cora's sudden and unexpected demise, and Mr Longdon's attitude. She told him she was going to York with her husband, whatever he said, and the call ended on a sour note. Distressed and agitated, they went to the station and caught a train to York.

Edwynne was grief-stricken and cried unceasingly. Through his tears he explained that when they got home Cora didn't feel well. She had a cup of tea and decided to lie on the bed for a while rather than sit in a chair. About ten minutes later he heard a thump and went to investigate. She was lying on the floor with blood coming out of her left ear. She was too heavy for him to lift back on to the bed. He ran to a neighbour's cottage and the people there called an ambulance. She'd had a stroke. Her mouth was twisted and she couldn't speak. The doctor said she was failing fast, and he was right. She died a few hours later.

Audrey couldn't hold back her tears. Rocky tried to fight back his grief but was angry that such a good woman had lost her life at a relatively young age. When they said farewell at the station a week ago, it never entered his head that he was saying goodbye for ever.

The funeral was a simple, yet kindly, ceremony. The Church was packed with villagers and people from the Women's Institute. Edwynne fought back his tears during the ceremony. Outside, at the internment, as the mahogany coloured box was lowered into the grave he heard a loud splash. He took a handful of earth to throw over her casket and as he leaned forward he could see brown muddy water in the bottom of her resting place. He shuddered violently at the sight of his beloved wife's coffin lying in it. He howled as he let the handful of dirt fall from his fingers. This was the worst day of his life. He wailed for himself as well as for Cora. His lamentations were infectious; hardly anyone around the grave could prevent themselves from weeping. Thunder rolled from behind ominous clouds. The day darkened as the entourage drifted back to the Church Hall for the wake.

Some mourners talked about what a good person she was; how sad it was to lose a good woman in the prime of her life; some ate heartily and drank tea or coffee; but the thought of food at such a time sickened the family. None of them could eat a bite. They merely mingled with the grieving group, thanked them for coming, and for their condolences.

Rocky had limited time off work for compassionate leave. He did as much as he could to help Edwynne with paperwork regarding Probate and asked him if he would like to accompany them back to Romford so that he wasn't alone. But Edwynne wanted to give himself time to decide what he was going to do. Initially he intended to stay in the cottage and tend his garden, and his sister would stay for a couple of weeks. After that he would take things a day at a time.

Travelling home, Rocky and Audrey were despondent. They reproached themselves for not spotting how ill Cora was. Their hearts were heavy. It was as if a vibrant light had gone out in their lives and the bulb could never be replaced.

CHAPTER 13

CHRISTMAS THOUGHTS

After Audrey and Rocky arrived home, there was only one week of her notice left to serve. She dreaded meeting Mr Longdon and mentally prepared herself for a battle of words. She set out earlier than at any time previously, and arrived an hour before he was expected. Dr Gettuelle came into the office and offered his condolences, which she accepted with thanks.

'What you do to people?' he asked. 'First Dr Biró, then your mother-in-law. Do be careful, usually things come in threes.'

'It's buses that come in threes,' she responded, then as an afterthought added:

'Probably Cora *is* the third. Didn't Dr Biró say his secretary, Miss Plonkitt, had died the month before I came here?'

'Oh, yes, that's right, she did die. So perhaps you don't put jinx on people after all.'

'I hope not,' she asserted.

'I keep copy of medical notes for typing. When you away, we have temp. She type some, but not quick, and some not right. These for you.'

He handed over a folder containing loose papers scribbled in almost unreadable handwriting.

'Thanks. So Mr Longdon got a temp to come in while I was away?'

'Yes. She coming back this week to learn to take over from you. You meet her soon. She start at nine o'clock. I have to go now,' and he left the room in the hope that by the end of the day all of his case notes would be typed up accurately.

Audrey got on immediately, typing as fast as her reading of his handwriting would allow.

At nine o'clock precisely an elderly lady with short, straight, grey hair arrived and introduced herself as Mrs Silver. Audrey thought she looked well over seventy years of age. Her face was lined with wrinkles and her hands were misshapen with arthritis. In her left ear she wore a neat looking National Health hearing aid which was hardly visible at first sight. On her left wrinkled arm she wore a huge-faced wrist watch, and on her left hand a broad, well-worn, wedding ring. She looked as if she might be going to a dance rather than to work. Her black cotton dress was ankle-length and just revealed her 1920's style black strap-over shoes. The deep, yellow metal bracelet on her right arm looked more like a manacle from slave days than an expensive piece of gold jewellery.

She proffered her right hand to shake Audrey's. She introduced herself in a rich BBC-type tone, but over-enunciated her words. Her false teeth moved slightly, and she chomped them back into place. She said she'd been sent by a secretarial agency to take over Audrey's job at very short notice and the Hospital Secretary wanted her to stay until a permanent replacement was employed.

Audrey introduced herself in a manner that she hoped would make the woman feel comfortable and explained the short notice had been because her mother-in-law had died very suddenly and she'd had to rush off to York with her husband, to be with his father. Mrs Silver was understanding and sympathetic. They discussed various aspects of work which still needed to be covered, and Audrey showed her where everything was kept, that she hadn't already found out for herself the previous week.

Mrs Silver's personality was eccentric. When Audrey opened a filing cabinet drawer to show how she'd made index cards and kept everything neat and tidy, the temp theatrically leaned forward to peer in, and her ankle-length skirt swept the floor.

Then the time came when Mrs Silver answered the telephone.

'There's a corl four your,' she pronounced.

'Who is it?'

'Eye doughn't know. You'll have to arsk. Eye doughn't always hear what they say.'

She handed the receiver to Audrey, who heard the caller quite clearly, and dealt with the communication effectively.

Dr Bannalurgee came in with an audio tape to be transcribed and also dictated two sets of case notes to the new temp. She kept asking him to repeat things because he spoke far too quickly for her.

Audrey thought that there would be a lot of fun and games when she left; what with the two doctors' clipped English, and Mrs Silver's cut-glass pronunciation, they'd hardly be able to understand each other.

She couldn't help noticing that when Mrs Silver typed, she kept raising her left hand high up above her head as if she was going to query something, then changed her mind and continued typing.

After a while Audrey's curiosity got the better of her and she asked if there was any reason for the eye-catching movements.

'It's a typing style Eye've developed over the yahs, and Eye carn't change it now. Eye've typed like this for over twenty yahs. When there was a war effort for married women to go to work, Mr Silver didn't want me to – but Eye felt that Eye ort to make a contribution to what ah men were doing to save ah country – so Eye went to work in the War Orfice. There were several men working there, and to show them that Eye was married, Eye kept raising my left hand to indicate Eye was wearing a wedding ring. Eye thought it would discourage them from any carnal thoughts that they might have about me, or for arsking me out for a date.'

Audrey was flabbergasted at the explanation.

Suddenly the door opened and Mr Longdon came in to the room.

'You two getting along all right? I heard voices.'

His tone was not offensive or hurtful, as she'd expected, and it took the wind out of her sails.

'Yes, we're getting along like a house on fire. I'm sorry I had to rush off so suddenly ....'

'It's done now. Fortunately the staffing agency was able to send us Mrs Silver within an hour of our calling them, and she'd been a great help, haven't you Mrs Silver?'

The old lady's chest swelled with pride and she acknowledged the compliment graciously.

Later that afternoon when Audrey checked the case notes before they were given back to Dr Bannalurgee she couldn't believe the number of spelling mistakes that Mrs Silver had made. Despite having advised her that morning to refer to medical, English and thesaurus dictionaries, the temp hadn't bothered to do so.

In addition to spelling mistakes, she had obviously mis-heard words on the audio tape. Audrey smiled inwardly to read that one patient had suffered from 'Simon Ella' instead of Salmonella and another had died from 'Gone for Ever' instead of Gonorrhoea. Despite her amusement, she had to enlighten Mrs Silver and ask her to correct her work, but the little old lady didn't seem to mind.

'Oh dear,' she admitted, 'This isn't the first time Eye've misheard a word or two. Eye've worked in a horspital before and Eye once said that a child suffered from a spiny beef eater instead of saying he suffered from spina bifider. Eye've never been so embarrassed in all my life!'

'Well, as I've already said, please check everything. You can't afford to make mistakes in a hospital.'

'Oh, Eye will from now on,' Mrs Silver agreed, as she put more letterhead paper into her typewriter and retyped the two letters correctly.

Audrey made a list of all the duties she'd undertaken, and another indicating where things were to be found in cupboards and cabinets, in preparation for the new PA that was appointed, because she couldn't believe that Mr Longdon would employ Mrs Silver on a permanent basis.

As she pedalled home from the hospital for the very last time she experienced a feeling of sheer relief, light-headedness, exhilaration and joy that her work there was over. She knew in her heart she would never return. Not ever! It was as if a dark veil had been lifted from her head. She smiled to herself then laughed out loud at some of the errors Mrs Silver had made that week. Perhaps she could get a decent job as a temp if the best they could send to replace her, was a person like Mrs Silver! At last she was free. Free to do her own thing; to go her own way. What did it matter about a pension at her age? Rocky had one and she could probably claim part of his State Pension when the time came. Her legs pedalled even faster and she got home in record time that evening.

* * * * *

As Christmas was approaching, Audrey wrote two letters, one asking Edwynne about his Christmas arrangements, and the other to her parents, asking about theirs. Edwynne replied quickly. He was bearing up better now, but had not changed his plans. He would still be going away, as previously arranged.

Mrs Small wrote a much longer, more rambling letter. It wasn't possible for Audrey and Rocky to go to their house for Christmas as they were having

Grandpa Small to stay with them and they didn't have another bed available. Audrey perused the last sentence again, and read the words out loud:

'You told me on your wedding day that Rocky was your next of kin so he'll have to look after you now, we've got enough to do looking after grandpa.'

The words hurt. They shouldn't have, but they did. It wasn't a case of being looked after! She assumed it was because her mother didn't want to have Rocky in her home after what she'd said about him at the wedding reception.

Audrey's eyes smarted at the thought of missing out on a family Christmas. She'd just have to buy presents that were unbreakable and light to post.

In her reply, Audrey asked for some suggestions as to what her parents might like for Christmas presents. Mrs Small's answer came that she would like a petticoat, or a cardigan, for herself and a pair of pyjamas for dad, but would she be sure to buy them at Wise & Goodbrand's and enclose the receipts so that if they didn't fit they could be changed at the York branch.

'I know why she wants me to buy things there and send the receipts,' Audrey told Rocky.

'I've seen her do it before with items that grandpa has given her in the past. She has the joy of opening her parcels on Christmas morning, then takes the goods, and receipts, to her local branch; tells them they don't fit, or are the wrong colour, and gets *her* money back.'

Well, that's up to her, love. Once you've given someone a present, it's up to them what they do with it. I don't suppose she's the only one that does that.'

'Perhaps not, but it isn't the sort of thing that I would do.'

'I know. But if you don't want her to get *her* money back, don't enclose the receipts. Just post her the presents, or buy them somewhere else.'

'If I buy them somewhere else and they don't fit, she can't change them, and if I don't put a receipt in she'll just take them back and get a credit note or a gift voucher. Oh, I'll just put the receipts in anyway. I'll see what I can get first.'

The following week Audrey went Christmas shopping. She wondered what she could buy for Rocky. Her problem was solved when she saw a neat portable radio on a half-price special offer. It worked on mains or batteries so he could move it from room to room. She wrapped it in Christmas wrapping paper and hid it under the bed. He wouldn't dream of looking under there!

At the start of the school's Christmas holidays Rocky helped to choose a small Christmas tree and some baubles and they enjoyed dressing it and putting up decorations.

On Christmas morning they exchanged presents. Rocky was delighted with his radio and she was equally pleased with a pretty pink-faced mantel clock. To date, they'd only had their watches and an alarm clock to rely on. The mantel clock was unusual and very feminine. She loved it, and gave it pride of place in the lounge.

They opened their presents from Rocky's dad, who had sent a plastic-coated apron for Audrey and a five-year diary for his son.

Then they opened the presents from Audrey's mam and dad, who had sent four gold-coloured brocade cushion covers and hoped Audrey could afford to buy the pads to go inside them.

Friend Annie, sent a long letter updating them with her news and enclosed a postal order for £2 to treat themselves to something they needed for their home, and Vic and Candy had sent a stylish card and letter telling them that they were going to stay with Candy's parents over the Christmas season. Den and Lil had gone to Sweden for Christmas and the New Year to visit Lil's parents so Audrey and Rocky were on their own all over Christmas.

Rocky experimented with his radio, finding different channels and listening to various programmes, whilst Audrey cooked a small chicken and prepared their Christmas dinner.

During the evening they listened to a Review of the Year programme.

'I didn't realise that the contraceptive pill went on sale last January' observed Rocky, raising his eyebrows.

'Nor did I' flushed Audrey. 'But don't ask me to use it. I hate taking medicines of any description and until it's been tested and tried over a number of years I don't think it's safe to use, even if it is licensed now. You don't know what after-effects there may be. If I get pregnant, now that I've left work, then I do.'

'Fair enough, love, but I'm glad I don't have to use condoms any more! They were like eating chocolate through the silver wrapping paper.'

'Oh, Rocky!' Audrey laughed, 'If a family comes along, it does. If I conceived a child today it wouldn't be born for another nine months – and that's two months after our first wedding anniversary – so no-one could say we *had* to get married.'

Rocky took an apple out of the fruit bowl and bit into it before continuing:

'What a lot of things have happened this year. The building of the Berlin Wall was bad enough last August – and then there were all those arrests in Trafalgar Square when one and a half thousand CND demonstrators were arrested when they had that Campaign for Nuclear Disarmament sit-down.'

'But there were nice things happening too,' Audrey reminded him.

'Of course. It was a real triumph for Russia to put the first man into space. Yuri Gagarin orbited the world for over an hour. It was a truly magnificent achievement. Then there was Alan Shephard that did a fifteen minute sub-orbital flight a month later. The Americans and Russians must have spent billions of pounds in their efforts to win the space race, mustn't they?'

'I suppose they have,' Audrey responded, 'But it's all in the name of progress. I wonder whether we'll ever see a man land on the moon in our lifetime?'

'Don't know. I suppose it could happen!'

'Anyway, it's been a fairly good year for us, too.

Despite all the problems I had with my mother, we got married; you got a job; and a flat here. And despite the fact that I transferred my job to one I couldn't abide, it's given us a chance to save quite a bit of money towards a place of our own.'

Audrey's eyes misted over as she continued:

'The only things we didn't expect were to lose your wonderful mother, Cora, and the doctor I worked for.'

The lower rims of Rocky's eyes filled with warm moisture.

'Yes, losing my mum was truly awful,' he gulped, and bit into his last portion of fruit like an automaton.

He went into the kitchen to put the core into the bin and came back with a bottle of sherry and two glasses.

'Let's drink to absent friends. Let's say a special goodbye to my dearest mum who loved me with all her heart and soul and did everything she could to help and encourage me on my way, and to your mum and dad and grandpa Small.'

Rocky filled the glasses; they raised them to their lips.

'God Bless you, Cora. May your spirit rest peacefully in Heaven with the stars that Yuri and Alan encircled.'

'I'll drink to that.' Audrey replied.

'Happy Christmas darling,' they said in unison as they finally toasted each other.

'And a very Happy New Year, too,' Audrey added. 'I wonder what changes the next phase of our lives will bring?'

CHAPTER 14

HOLIDAYS

Larry Small's handwriting was calligraphic. His upright strokes were thin; downward strokes broad; style compact and neat; it was a pleasure to read his writing, but not such a pleasure for the message it related. Mrs Small had been notified that she would have both bunions removed in a couple of weeks' time.

Audrey thought it wasn't a very good start to the new year, on the other hand her mother had suffered with her feet for years so perhaps when her feet were better she'd be less crabby. She made preparations to leave enough tinned food in the pantry for Rocky to cope whilst she was away and travelled the three hundred miles to York.

She visited her mother in hospital every day for five days, taking her fruit, drinks, talc, and other necessities. On the sixth day when she visited, a new patient had been admitted to the bed next to her mother's. When Audrey arrived in the ward, the curtains were drawn around the new patient's bed, so that she was obscured from view but the conversation could be heard very clearly. Audrey was amused to hear how it progressed:

Nurse: 'Hello, there. My name's Nurse Berkeley. I've been told to ask you a few questions. Do you mind answering them for me?'

Patient: 'I'll try.'

Nurse: 'Right, dear, what's your full name?'

Patient: 'Hetty Hackett.'

Nurse: 'And are you married, Hetty?'

Patient: 'I was, but I'm widowed now.'

Nurse: 'And what was your surname before you were married?'

Hetty: 'Oh, before I was married I was pretty.'

Nurse: 'You were pretty?'

Hetty: 'Yes, that's spelt P r i t t i e.'

Nurse: 'Prittie. Okay. And how old are you, Hetty?'

Patient: 'I'm not sure. I think I've had my 80th birthday. If I remember rightly, I think they had a party for me.'

Nurse: 'So what's your date of birth? Can you remember?'

Patient: 'Oh, yes. It's 5th April 1876.'

Nurse: 'So you're – 85 then – coming up to 86 this year?'

Patient: 'Am I?'

Nurse: 'Well, you must be if you're born in 1876 and you haven't had your birthday yet this year.'

Patient: 'I'm sorry if I can't remember very well. It's more difficult when you get older.'

Nurse: 'It's perfectly all right, Hetty. Now another question. Can you remember what your mother's maiden name was?'

Patient: 'Oh, goodness! What a question to ask. Many? Mary?

Oh, yes, I remember, she was called Mummy.'

Nurse: 'No, I don't mean what you called her, I mean what was her MAIDEN name.'

Patient: 'What's a maiden name? I don't understand.'

Nurse: 'It's the surname she had before she got married.'

Patient: 'My goodness me! I can't remember that. She died donkey's years ago.'

Nurse: 'It's all right, Hetty, don't worry about it. I don't suppose you can remember your telephone number either?'

Patient: 'I don't need to. I've got it written down in my purse.'

Nurse. 'What a good idea. Where's your purse?'

Patient: 'I don't know. I think it's in my handbag.'

Nurse: 'And where's your handbag?'

Patient: 'I'm not sure. It's probably in my bedroom.'

Nurse: 'Right. I'll leave the space for the telephone number blank at the moment.

Now, Hetty, who is your next of kin?
Have you got anyone close to you, like a
son, or a daughter?'

Patient: 'No thank you, nurse. I don't want
a drink of water, but I'm absolutely
bursting to have a wee-wee. Oo, oo. Ooo,
ooo. Oooo, oooo.'

Nurse: 'Hang on a minute, Hetty. I'll be back in
a minute.'

Suddenly there was a flurry of activity and the
nurse rushed off and came back with a bed pan.
Audrey was tickled pink by the cameo episode and,
in shorthand, quickly jotted down the gist of it on
the back of a used envelope.

'Poor old soul,' her mother observed. 'I hope I
never get like that.'

Between visiting her mother in hospital, keeping
the house clean and tidy, going to see what she
could do to help Edwynne, and seeing friends and
relatives, she had plenty to do for the next two
weeks. Her mother made excellent progress and was
discharged from hospital, pleased that she'd had the
operation done. She was diligent in performing foot
exercises, encircling her feet in the air, first to the
left, then to the right. Feet up and down alternately,
pedalling in the air, keeping the circulation moving
without touching the ground, and resting her legs
in a raised position when seated.

One afternoon when she'd been home about four
days, Mrs Small wandered into the kitchen where
Audrey was preparing the evening meal.

'You don't cut potatoes like that' she scolded. 'You've never seen me slice potatoes across. You cut them downwards.'

'Who's doing the potatoes, mother?' Audrey replied in an irritated tone. 'They boil much quicker when cut horizontally because there's a bigger surface area, and they don't taste any different do they?'

'Oh yes they do. I can tell. I like mine done my way, not yours.'

Mrs Small looked at the pieces of steak laid out on the chopping board. She picked one up, fingered it, smelt it, and disapprovingly commented:

'How much did you pay for this steak? It looks tough. I hope you didn't pay a lot for it. It's more like stewing steak than braising steak. Your father's not used to this type of meat.'

'Nor am I. We can't afford steak at home. It's the best I could get for the money.'

Audrey avoided mentioning the price she'd paid and asked whether Mrs Small should be standing in the kitchen and why it was that for some reason she always wanted to pick a fight with her.

'I'm not telling you. I've kept it from you all these years and I'm certainly not telling you now.'

'You must, then we can clear the air and start afresh.'

'Well, I'm not telling you and that's that. Just mind your own business and get on with your jobs.'

Mrs Small set her face in a way that Audrey had seen so many times before, and went back into the middle room of their tunnel-back house, put her feet up and sunk into silence.

Audrey put the kettle onto the gas ring, made a cup of tea for them both and proffered a cup to her mother.

'I do wish you would tell me what's wrong. Have I done something to offend you? You can be such a difficult person to get on with. Sometimes I don't know why I bother! Why can't you tell me what the problem is?'

Mrs Small sipped her tea in silence.

Audrey's frustration arose. She knew from past experience she couldn't argue with a person who wouldn't answer back.

'If you're going into one of your moods and are not prepared to talk to me, then I'm going home at the weekend now that you're on your feet again and the worst is over.'

Again there was no response.

That evening Audrey asked her father about her mother's attitudes.

'I've no idea what causes her to be like that, lass. She's been like it ever since you were born. The doctor thought it might be post-natal depression and gave her some tablets, but they only helped for a short while.'

Larry drew in deeply from the pipe he was smoking. The ashes glowed scarlet and he puffed out billows of smoke into the room.

'What beats me is that she's not like it all the time. Sometimes she's the exact opposite; caring, congenial, carefree, it depends whom she's with.

Most people around here think she's a wonderful person and get on with her very well. It's only you that seems to trigger her off.'

Audrey blinked and wafted the smoke out of her eyes as a cloud of Larry's polluted emissions travelled in her direction.

'Do you think she suffers from schizophrenia from time to time?'

'Don't know, lass. Daren't mention it. She once jumped down my throat when I suggested that she saw the doctor about it. That's why I escape to my allotment whenever I can. I like to have the freedom to get out, smoke my pipe and have a bit of peace and quiet as well as tend my crops.'

The fug in the room got heavier and Audrey found it very unpleasant. It reached her chest and she started coughing. She flapped the offensive murk away with her hands, as he continued puffing at his pipe.

'I've asked to bring my holidays forward to next week so if you want to go home at the weekend that's all right. I'll be here to look after her for the next fortnight. Surely a month after her operation she'll be able to walk reasonably well again even if she has to take it slowly. She's already walking around the house.'

'Well, if you're sure it's all right, I'd be glad. I told Rocky I'd probably be here for two weeks and that was up last week.'

'Yes, lass. You go home to your husband and look after him. We'll be all right here.'

'Perhaps Auntie Dorcas will come and do some shopping?'

'Perhaps she will. We'll see.'

The next day Audrey went to see Edwynne to say 'cheerio' to him. She looked around the cottage. It was clean, neat and tidy, but somehow the atmosphere felt destitute. She looked at Cora's empty chair. A big lump rose in her throat.

'Would you like to come back to Romford with me, Edwynne?'

'Thanks, but no. I've been away all over Christmas and the New Year with Aunt Matilda and there'll soon be lots for me to do in the garden. Weeds don't clear themselves, they just take over. Give my love to Rocky and take care of each other.'

Back at the flat Rocky welcomed her with open arms. He had much to tell her, most of all how much he loved and had missed her. They went into their bedroom and made up for lost time. The weather outside was cold and fresh. The atmosphere in their bedroom was hot and steamy. They kissed ardently; the bed rocked and swayed; the neighbours in the flat below were in no doubt that they were back together again.

The following weekend Den and Lil were due to arrive mid-day for Sunday dinner. Rocky had invited them to come as a thank-you for the excellent meal which Den had treated them to at his golf club, and for them all to complete all the relevant papers for their forthcoming summer holiday to Belgium. They only had a kitchen table and two kitchen chairs so Rocky put them in the lounge and drew the two fireside chairs close to the table and put cushions on them to make them higher. He searched for a radio station where soft music could be left on in the background. At first he found loud music where a group called the Rolling Stones, were performing. There was also singing by an American boy, Elvis Presley. He thought neither of those sounds were appropriate and eventually selected a station which was more suitable for the occasion.

The dinner party was successful. Audrey pushed the boat out, by serving celery soup, porc-en-croute with root vegetables, trifle, cheese and biscuits and coffee, whilst Rocky provided a bottle of red and a bottle of white wine recommended by the Manager of their local wine shop.

After they'd finished eating, Den sat back and played with his grey, bushy beard and pulled on his grey straggly eyebrows.

'That was a fine traditional meal. I enjoyed that. We don't have much plain food. We like curries.'

Lil offered to help wash the dishes.

'No, leave it for now. We'll just put them in the kitchen and get on with completing the forms.'

They cleared the crockery into the kitchen and stacked the items by the side of the sink. Rocky removed the table cloth and Den picked up a folder and laid the forms on top of the table.

'Ever taken a school party abroad before, Rocky?'

'Never. I've taken groups of lads on day trips, especially to soccer matches, but I've never been abroad, not even when I did my National Service.'

'Well there's all this paperwork to be done first – local authority forms, application forms, booking forms, insurance forms, etc, we'd better get on.'

Unnoticed, Audrey slipped into the kitchen, closed the door, and started to wash the pots. She had a drainer full of clean plates and cutlery before Rocky came to find her.

'Come on, Audrey, Den needs some personal information from you.'

She went into the lounge to be greeted by a mass of paperwork spread all over the floor.

'Mind where you put your feet' requested Den. 'They're not stepping stones to put your feet on.'

They laughed. She sat on the bed-settee.

Den finished completing the forms and said that he would hand them in to the Head the following day.

'You'll need to have eyes in the back of your head' he warned. 'You'll earn every penny of your "free" trip, Rocky, believe me.'

Lil intervened:

'I hope we don't experience anything like we did three years ago when we took a school party to Lake Garda.'

'Oh, no. That was very bad,' Den responded.

He related the story of how they had accompanied two party leaders on a school trip to Italy, together with another couple of teachers. One of the boys didn't want to go but his mother insisted. His father had died before he was born and he'd been brought up by his mother and grandmother for the past twelve years. He had no brothers or sisters and had become somewhat effeminate and clung to his mother's apron strings. She thought it would do him good to see a bit of the world and have some male company with his peer group, so she'd saved enough money to pay for his trip and have quite a bit extra for him to have fun whilst he was on holiday.

They had flown from Heathrow to Milan airport and caught a coach from there to Limone. There was much excitement on the journey but this little chap didn't join in with the ethos of the group. Lil noticed that on the coach he was sitting by himself, looking rather sullen. She went and sat with him and asked if he was all right. He told her that he wasn't.

He was unhappy because he felt his mummy didn't want him any more, otherwise she wouldn't have forced him to come when he didn't want to. Lil explained that wasn't true. It was because his mummy loved him so very much that she wanted him to have a happy, normal life and see a bit of the world. She couldn't afford for both of them to go on holiday somewhere, so she had done her best to save up for him to go and enjoy himself with his school friends. She sat with him for the rest of the journey and he seemed to be comforted by the attention she gave him. They had only been in the hotel for twenty minutes when two of the boys rushed to the team leader and told him that the lad had committed suicide by jumping off a balcony. It ruined the holiday for everyone. The police came. There were questions to be answered. Did he jump? Did he fall? Was he pushed? Had he been goaded or bullied? Who had seen it happen? What were the names of the witnesses? There were statements to be taken, forms to be completed, a post mortem to be held, his body to be returned to England, his mother and grandmother to be notified, comforted and de-traumatised. The tragedy had gone on for months. It had been horrendous.

'Now you tell us!' Rocky was gob-smacked.

'We said at the time we'd never go on another school trip abroad – but that was three years ago – and hopefully that sort of thing won't happen again.'

'I certainly hope not,' responded Rocky.

'Well, we're not going to an hotel with a balcony this time so we hope and pray everything will be all right.'

The lounge unexpectedly appeared to be dimly lit. Rocky switched on the light. He hoped the thought of a trip to Brussels wouldn't lose its appeal to Audrey after hearing that story. He definitely wanted to go abroad, and being in charge of a small group of ten children should be a piece of cake after teaching class sizes of thirty or forty pupils.

Audrey didn't seem to notice his furrowed brow.

'I'll go and finish the washing up and put the kettle on. Would you prefer tea or coffee?'

There was a mixed response from the trio.

'Right, I'll do both – tea and coffee.'

'I'll help' offered Lil. This time her help was accepted.

Whilst they drank their beverages they looked at the photographs taken at Christmas in Sweden.

'Oh, that's a nice one of your mam and dad' observed Audrey. 'But you're not like them in appearance at all.'

'Noo?'

'No, they're much shorter than you. I expected they would be taller.'

'Ah, well, that's the way it is.'

She shook her head from side to side. Her fair hair, scraped back into a pony-tail rustled with the movements.

'Are you sure you still want to come with us to Belgium?'

'Wouldn't miss it for worlds,' they chorused.

CHAPTER 15

TEMPORARY WORK

After visiting her parents, and Edwynne, each weekend for four weeks, to keep an eye on their progress, Audrey felt the time had come when she was able to register with a secretarial agency in Romford.

The pay offered was four shillings and sixpence an hour for typists, five shillings an hour for shorthand-typists, and seven shillings and sixpence for secretaries. Audrey took her packet of qualifications with her and quoted Principal Nursing Officer Doughty as a referee. She explained that Dr Biró had died, and gave Mr Longdon, the Hospital Administrator, as a second referee.

The lady at the agency seemed impressed with her qualifications and asked if she was available to start immediately at Mastermind & Planners Ltd, Mechanical Engineers, on the Farringdon Avenue Industrial Estate. She was told to ask for Sam Highly, Head of the drawing office.

She caught a bus from Romford town centre to Straight Road, and walked up Farringdon Avenue, looking at the names of factories and buildings.

When she found the engineering company, she presented herself at Reception and asked for the Head of the drawing office. The receptionist directed her along a lengthy corridor to the third door along on the right.

She knocked on the door. Someone called 'Come in.' She pushed open the door and saw row upon row of technical drawing desks and boards, set squares, and about a dozen men working in a large room.

'I'm looking for Mr Highly, Head of technical drawing,' she said to the nearest man.

'Oh, Sam's over there' he said pointing to the most beautiful woman Audrey'd ever seen. 'Sam's short for Samantha.'

Audrey was shocked. She'd never imagined a woman being Head of a drawing office, especially one as chic as this. She approached the "film-star" vision and felt belittled. The woman had a magnificent head of long, thick, dark-brown, wavy hair, immaculate make-up and brown mascara which enriched the depth of her burnt sienna eyes.

'Good morning. I'm Audrey Driver, from the secretarial agency. They said you needed a shorthand writer urgently.'

The magnificent looking creature eyed Audrey up and down. She smiled sweetly as she alighted from her perched position at her drawing board to reveal that she was wearing an immaculate tailor-made coffee-coloured suit and cream blouse. Her stiletto shoes were in matching brown and cream leather, and the hand which she extended had been manicured to perfection with long, well-shaped, polished fingernails which gleamed under the office spotlight.

'That's right. Good morning, Audrey. I'm Samantha Highly but everyone here calls me Sam. I hope you can write shorthand at a hundred and thirty words a minute because on Wednesday we have a specialist engineer coming here from America for six weeks to teach our engineers a new technique which they've developed over there, and we'll need you to prepare for his arrival and tie up loose ends when he's gone. He speaks extremely quickly and he'll be doing a lot of dictation. He wants you to create instruction sheets, handouts, lecture notes, and make a technical manual for our engineers to refer to.'

'I hope I can still write at that speed but it's a long time since I passed my exams and I haven't had much speed practice lately, but I'll give it my best shot. I'm surprised he doesn't want to use an audio machine.'

'He doesn't like them. He much prefers to have a person around him. Audio machines don't make coffee and bring him files when he needs them. He needs a professional PA who will look after him, and his specialist work. Your hours will be nine to five with three quarters of an hour break at lunch time and two ten minute breaks, one in the morning for coffee and one in the afternoon for tea. The job will start today, if you can stay now, so that you can get used to the equipment you'll be using. We have a lot here and some of it's quite technical.'

'That's fine by me' Audrey replied. 'No doubt someone will take me to the office where I'll be working and I'll be able to get started.'

'Of course. I'll take you to his suite of rooms and allocate a locker for you to put your coat and handbag away safely.'

Audrey followed her to another room, locked her coat in the narrow steel locker, and put the key in her skirt pocket. Sam tutted and pursed her lips.

'Tell me, Audrey, are those your best clothes? The image of a skirt and jumper is all right for a shorthand-typist but this job is very special and needs someone to really look the part at the level of work you'll be doing and the position you'll be holding.'

Audrey's heart jumped. She was taken aback by the last question and comment.

'I've got some suits at home' she reacted in a hurt voice as if she'd been slapped on the wrists. 'But I thought I was just going to the agency to enrol today. I've never done temporary work before and I didn't know what to expect. I never thought they would send me out the same day as enrolling, but they didn't have any other high-speed shorthand writers on their books and urged me to come here straight away.'

'Oh, it's not a problem today, we're delighted to have you.'

Sam's voice softened into a well-meaning tone.

'But when Mr Kartewter comes on Wednesday, please would you wear a really smart outfit, as first impressions are so important in our line of business. Perhaps you've noticed that I've nurtured my team to wear suits, impeccable shirts and ties, and I'm proud of each and every one of them. I wouldn't like you to feel overshadowed by any one, and just hope you'll enjoy working with us all.'

Audrey breathed a sigh of relief and followed Sam into the suite. Mr Kartewter's room was also large. The suite included a small lecture theatre, and a reprographics room. Audrey's eyes boggled at the quality of the equipment and furniture. In her office there was a huge desk and typing chair, cupboards in matching teak wood, modern filing cabinets, and the very latest electric typewriter.

In the reprographics room she was drawn towards a large ink duplicator. It was very similar to the smaller model she'd used at technical college several years earlier. There was a small offset litho machine for producing top quality prints. She knew that would be all right for her to use, too, because she'd learnt how to make paper and metal plates and produce prints from a similar model when she'd been training for her secretarial qualifications.

There was also a small thermal photocopier, a laminator, a binding machine, but the largest piece of equipment was a dyeline machine for making blueprints. She had seen a demonstration of one several years ago, but had never used one herself. She knew that someone would have to help her if she had to use it.

After Sam had gone, Audrey put some paper in the roller and typed her fingering exercises. The touch was sensitive and she unintentionally obtained some double letters. She practised her alphabet until she was satisfied that she could master the new-fangled machine. She spent the rest of the day, and the following one, preparing for the American's arrival.

Hank Kartewter was a dapper little man with greying hair parted down the centre. He was probably in his late forties or early fifties. Audrey wore her going-away outfit and he seemed to be impressed by her smart appearance. Sam introduced him to Audrey. He proffered his hand to shake hers.

'*Audrey* Driver? Can't have that' he gushed. 'Far too confusing.'

Audrey stared at him in disbelief.

'Don't say he doesn't want me after all the preparations I did yesterday.' He read her thoughts.

'I can't have a person called Audrey working for me because my son's name is Aubrey It's quite a common name for men in the States. But I think over the phone the names will sound too similar, so I'll call you Odj.'

Audrey was taken aback. She'd never been called Odj before, not even as a nickname at school. Den tended to call her Aud, but never Odj. Her brain whirled. Should she object, or accept it? Better than being called Odd perhaps but her new employer rattled on as if a whirlwind was spouting out of his mouth, and the time to object had passed.

Her first duties were to take dictation and prepare instruction handouts. She called a meeting of all the engineers he was to instruct, went into the conference room with them, and took notes. She had a job to keep up with him at times because he rushed his words at breakneck speed. It seemed as if he couldn't get them out of his mouth fast enough, but she managed to get an outline down for everything he said.

The day was full of activity, and at the end of it he thanked her and said he looked forward to working with her again the next day. It was the first time in the business world that anyone had thanked her before going home, and she appreciated his acknowledgement of her skills. She felt he was a real gentleman.

Mr Kartewter proved to be easier to work for than the doctors. In spite of spoken English tumbling out of his mouth with great gusto, he was always available when needed. She was sorry when he had to return to the States and her temporary job was over.

* * * * *

Audrey wrote to her parents and didn't ask, but told them that as it would be Easter the following week and Rocky had a school holiday, they would be going to stay with them for a week. To her surprise, her mother didn't object to her taking the lead, but when they arrived, she could feel an apprehension towards Rocky.

To avoid a scene brewing, they went to see Edwynne, and he was in good health. He gave them a lot of fresh vegetables to take to Mrs Small and that helped to ease the tension.

Easter Monday was a gloriously sunny day and as Mrs Small's bunion operation had healed satisfactorily and she was walking much better, they all went for a day out to the Museum Gardens and were amazed to bump into Vic and Candy.

'What are you doing here?' Rocky asked.

Vic shuffled in an embarrassed jiggle.

'We're on our honeymoon, actually.'

Candy's eyes were bright. She was an ebulient character with lots of sparkle and charisma. Vic moved his arm from around her shoulder but she drew up even closer to him and slid her hand into his.

'We got married on Saturday. I'd heard you talk about York so much over the past year, I thought I'd like to come and see it for myself.'

Candy giggled.

'We haven't seen much of it yet, though. This is our first day out.'

'You should have told us,' Rocky replied. 'We'd have bought you a little wedding present. Didn't you tell anyone at school? No-one said anything. I'm sure they would have had a whip-round and wished you well.'

'No, we didn't tell anyone. But I thought I mentioned it to you when we met at school on our first day there.'

'Oh, probably,' admitted Rocky, 'but I'm afraid I'd forgotten.'

Candy explained how they hadn't told anyone outside the family because they'd wanted a simple, private wedding which didn't cost a lot. They'd been married in a church service with her sister as a bridesmaid, and they'd held their wedding reception at Vic's house, where a few relatives had gone for sandwiches which they'd prepared the previous day and wrapped in foil to keep them fresh.

On Saturday evening they'd driven to York in Vic's little car.

Charmingly, Mrs Small enquired where they were staying.

'At an hotel in Petergate. It's not very upmarket, but it's as much as we could afford,' replied Candy.

'You must come and see us while you're in York,' urged Mrs Small. Please come to tea.'

'That's very kind of you,' replied Vic 'but we're only here for another couple of days. We go back on Wednesday.'

'Oh, that's a shame' said Mrs Small, moving from one foot to the other. 'Would you like to come and stay with us for the rest of the week? We have a spare bed now that Audrey doesn't live with us any more. You'd be more than welcome.'

Candy gazed into Vic's eyes. He could see the question marks in hers. He squeezed her hand tightly but declined in a gentle tone which didn't cause offence to anyone. After exchanging a few more words the group separated and as they walked away Candy was heard to say:

'What a lovely lady. Wasn't she kind to offer to let us stay with her until the weekend?'

'Yes. Absolutely charming,' Vic agreed.

They had no idea from their meeting that Mrs Small could be domineering, opinionated and self-centred at times. They only saw the really nice side of her that friends and neighbours witnessed.

Easter week passed quickly. Rocky offered to help Edwynne with his gardening, but he preferred to do things his own way. He hadn't even liked Cora to help him. When she was alive they had an arrangement that she did everything inside the house and he did all the outside work. Now he had everything to do, but he was getting used to it. He didn't bake. The milkman delivered bread and a small selection of cakes and biscuits and a butcher and fishmonger came round the village regularly, so he didn't go to the shops. He had a couple of hens in a pen in the garden and they were good layers. They provided him with more eggs than he needed so sometimes he gave some to well-meaning women from the WI who occasionally called in to visit him. He regarded his plants as his family now. They were his motivation for staying at the cottage and he had decided he would never leave them.

Every week he went to Cora's grave, tidied away dying flowers and put new ones in their place. He knew Cora loved flowers. Now he grew them specially to keep her memory alive.

* * * * *

After the Easter holiday, Audrey went back to the secretarial agency. They didn't have another secretarial job within easy travelling distance available but offered her work as a temporary shorthand-typist at Spenditt & Drew, a finance company, which was accessible by bus. She found the office without too much difficulty and at Reception was directed to a typing pool. She'd never worked in one before, so it was a new experience to find a room with twenty-five desks set out in five rows and columns, just like a classroom. She observed that on each desk there was a typewriter. Some were manuals of differing ages and manufacture, and at the back of the room there were some brand new electric models, plugged into sockets at the rear edge of the desks.

Audrey's stomach turned over at the sight of a huge oblong platform with three steps up to it. At a desk on it, facing the workers' desks, sat a miserable-looking middle-aged woman. She was as thin as a lath, with straight, mousy, lank hair hanging down to her shoulders like rats' tails. It looked from the lack of style as if she cut it herself using a knife and fork rather than a pair of scissors. Mentally, Audrey compared her with the beautiful, well-groomed Sam Highly for whom she had last worked. This person was in complete contrast.

'Brought your own shorthand notebook and pencil?' queried the supervisor as she climbed down from her exalted position on the podium.

'I've brought a notepad, but I prefer to use a proper shorthand pen. Outlines get thicker as the pencil-lead rounds with use.'

The supervisor sniffed.

'Oh, a clever clogs, I see.'

Audrey prickled at the overseer's attitude. She was patronising and her comment wasn't necessary. She was filled with distaste for the woman, but wasn't quick enough to come out with an appropriate reply.

'Do you want a manual or an electric typewriter?'

'I'll have an electric, I've been using one in my last job and the touch was much lighter than striking keys on a manual.'

'Good. That means you'll type quicker and get more work done.'

Audrey couldn't fail to miss the undertone of another snipe at her, and her guard went up. She bridled as she thought to herself that speaking down to people and sneering at them in order to prove their authority, was a bad management ploy. It didn't get the best out of people, and it certainly wouldn't get the best out of her.

Miss Drabbal took Audrey to a desk on which there was an electric typewriter and explained their house-style for outgoing mail. All references had to be displayed on the left side of the paper underneath the letterhead. These should contain the dictator's and typist's initials, and the consecutive number of items typed in one working day, followed by a reference and the date. While she was explaining, a bell rang, a light-bulb lit up above the supervisor's desk, and Miss Drabbal called out a person's name. A young woman got up from her desk and went into an adjoining room.

'That's where the managers work. When the bell goes again, take your pad and PEN, and go in.'

Miss Drabbal rolled her eyes to the ceiling, and moved to the next desk along the row. Within minutes the bell sounded, the bulb lit up, and Audrey obeyed their commands.

When she entered the room there was no sign of the girl that had gone in a few minutes earlier. She was surprised because she hadn't seen her come out. There were four desks, arranged in a star-shaped cluster, with comfortable high-backed leather chairs on casters at each desk, and a hard wooden chair for typists at the outer ends of the desks. But there was only one manager in the room. He got up and extended his hand to greet her. His hand was much softer than hers, smooth, and warm. At his touch, an electrical impulse shot up her arm. He was handsome – an Adonis in a pin-striped suit! His searching eyes were as black as ink and penetrated deeply into hers. His eye-lashes were so long and thick they could have been false ones. He fluttered them at her, and beamed. She smiled as they shook hands but daren't look him in the eye for too long, otherwise she felt as if she would melt. He stroked his coal-black hair with his left-hand, then lowered it to his collar and straightened his tie.

'Haven't seen you before. What's your name?'

'I'm Audrey Driver. I've come as a temp.'

'Delighted to meet you, my dearie. And where have you been all my life?'

Taken aback, Audrey wriggled her hand out of his clinging grasp.

'Getting married, amongst other things!' she said dryly.

'O, Good. I like married women. They're so much more experienced. Would you like to sit on my knee for dictation?'

Audrey decided to laugh off his advance.

'No, I wouldn't, they look knobbly! But I must say I find your attitude very offensive.'

'It was you who asked for it, giving me the old "come on" like that.'

'No I didn't. All I did was shake hands.'

'And gaze into my eyes as if you wanted something more than dictation. Most women do.'

'Let's get on with the letters shall we?'

They both sat down on separate chairs, he in his, and she on the hard wooden one at the side of his desk. In an embarrassed fashion, she smoothed her skirt and pulled it well over her knees.

Between smiles and nods he dictated ten letters, all of a similar nature, stating that payment was overdue and threatening to take legal proceedings if the amount owed was not paid by a particular date. She found his dictation slow and boring. She felt uncomfortable, and longed to get out of the room as quickly as possible.

When she returned to her desk and had typed a couple of letters, Miss Drabbal approached to see how she was faring. She peered over Audrey's shoulder and touched the reference with her right index finger.

'Only on your third letter? My goodness, you're slow. The girl next to you is on her eighth. You'll have to quicken up.'

'I'm doing my best, Miss Drabbal. I've been in for dictation for over half an hour!'

'Well, hurry up and get on then,' she snapped.

Again, Audrey didn't like the supervisor's tone.

She felt emotional and wanted to tear the mantle of grandeur and over-importance from the woman's shoulders. She recognised that the job of overseeing the typing pool had gone to the supervisor's head, but she kept her counsel in case she said too much and was reported to the agency for being insolent. She needed to continue working to save money not only for buying their first home, but also for their forthcoming holiday to Brussels in a few weeks' time. So at the end of the day, instead of going home, Audrey went to the agency and told them she didn't want to go back to the finance company again.

'I'm not surprised,' said the receptionist. 'Most girls we send there won't go back after one day. I wonder why?'

'It's the attitude of the staff – the supervisor, and one of the managers who thinks he's God's gift to women – but he got short shrift from me. Can you send me somewhere else tomorrow?'

The only alternative offer of temporary work for the rest of the week was typing envelopes in a nearby factory at the lowest rate of pay. Audrey knew it was only sixpence an hour less that she was earning, so she accepted it, even though she knew it would be a very boring job.

That night she told Rocky about her experiences. His arm was comforting as she told her tale.

'Silly man! How could he interpret your smile as a "come hither" look when you love *me* so much? You'll have to grow a thicker skin and develop a quicker wit. You mustn't let people like that get you down. Everyone is important to themselves. You're important as well as them. Learn to stand up for yourself. Put it down to experience. Our holiday will soon be upon us, so at least you've got something nice to look forward to.'

CHAPTER 16

SCHOOL TRIP

In the first week of the school holidays, shrieking, excited boys ran around the playground with their parents nearby, and suitcases packed. Den was extremely well organised and when he arrived with Lil, they had them under control in no time at all. A forty-nine seater coach arrived five minutes before it was due, and Den read out the list of boys' names in alphabetical order.

Ten more boys than originally planned had indicated they wanted to go on the trip so that had involved him in more paperwork and he'd required another professionally qualified teacher to accompany them. Rob Magistrate, Head of the Junior Evening Institute, had volunteered to pay for himself and his wife to participate in the educational holiday, and would carry the additional responsibility needed to meet the local authority's requirements.

The sun shone brilliantly. Parents helped to see their offspring on to the coach and the boys climbed in, animated and buoyant. They waved goodbye cheerfully as the coach moved forward. A hum of excitement was in the air.

Audrey sat towards the rear of the coach with Rob's wife, Verity. Although they had never met before, they got on well together. Verity explained how she had been a dancer before marrying Rob. She'd trained in tap dancing, got a gold medal, and joined a troupe of professional dancers but now she only danced for pleasure and exercise. It had become a hobby in recent years. She asked Audrey what she'd done for a living.

'I started out as a shorthand-typist in a solicitors' office in York and worked my way up to being a personal secretary in the hospital service. Now I'm doing temporary secretarial work for an employment agency.'

'Oh, how clever! Shorthand's very hard to learn, isn't it?'

'I suppose it is. There are lots of rules to learn, exceptions to rules, short-forms and phrases, but fortunately I had a wonderful teacher. She was so enthusiastic for her subject, it rubbed off on almost everyone in the class.'

'How marvellous to have a teacher like that.'

'Indeed. Mrs Topping was fantastic. She wore callipers on both legs so she couldn't keep jumping up from her desk to write outlines on the blackboard. Instead, she used her index finger and wrote shorthand outlines backwards in the air so that we could read them the right way round.'

'She must have been exceptional.'

'Yes, she was. I remember one example in particular. She was teaching us the rules for writing the sound of aitch upwards, and with her index finger, she drew five outlines in the air and at the same time said the sentence 'I *hide* sweets from my little girl, *Heather*, because she *happily* eats too many, then gets a *horrible headache*. Of course, it wasn't true, it was just an example of how to write the symbol for "upward H", but we found out that she really did have a little girl. It had been a miracle for her. For us, she was a truly inspirational teacher.'

'What a wonderful story.'

'It's true! I hope Rocky's teaching will enthuse his pupils to remember what he's taught them long after they've left school.'

At Victoria they caught a train to Dover docks, where they went as foot passengers to Ostend. From there they boarded a Belgian coach, which Den had booked in advance. It was left-hand drive, and the boys commented that all the traffic was driving on the "wrong" side of the road. They were also surprised to see that Belgian Police were armed. None of them had seen a policeman with a gun before.

They arrived at Brussels late in the evening and were very tired. They registered into their hotel and were allocated bedrooms.

Having checked that all the boys in his group were settled into their rooms before going to the dining room for their evening meal, Rocky went to his own bedroom, where Audrey was asleep on top of a single bed. He quietly walked across the room to another single bed and laid on it. He looked up at the ceiling. It was twice as high as those in the Victorian villa which they'd rented in York. There was no wallpaper; the bedroom walls were colour-washed in an ageing shade of Wedgewood blue, and the twin beds looked lost in the lofty square room.

He gazed at the tall window with window-sashes which allowed the panes to be moved up and down, and wooden shutters which could be closed across it, rather than curtains. At the side of the window there was an antiquated wash-stand with a pale blue bowl in which stood a large ceramic pale blue jug full of cold water.

He turned his head and observed that there was one armchair and one dining chair in the room. On one wall there was an old-fashioned fireplace which had been painted over. There was well-trodden linoleum on the floor, and a light which hung down on a metal chain from the centre of the ceiling. The careworn room felt cold and old, not a bit welcoming for holiday-makers.

Audrey roused. Her voice broke the silence of his survey.

'Where's the bathroom?' she queried.

'Try further down the corridor.'

She wearily went to wash and freshen up her appearance before going down to the restaurant.

The main course was veal with tiny square chips and sauerkraut. The chips were a success, but the sauerkraut wasn't.

Next morning the meal was much better. Continental breakfast foods were available. There was a huge bowl of yoghurt, and fresh fruit for them to dive into and a selection of cereals with full-cream milk. Thick chunks of bread spread with butter and chocolate strands were a winner.

In his preparations before leaving England, Den had planned a schedule of visits and pre-booked a Belgian coach to arrive at their hotel each day of the visit.

The boys' favourite outing was to see Brussels oldest inhabitant, the Mannekin-Pis fountain made out of bronze in 1619. They laughed, howled and pointed as the little boy statue urinated in front of them. They were in their element when a maintenance engineer arrived to clean it. He switched the water off then deliberately switched it on too high, much to their amusement. Water shot out at great speed. The boys revelled in the fun.

Everyone was fascinated with the Atomium, situated in the Heysel Plateau on the Northern outskirts of Brussels. At first sight, it was not as tall as they'd anticipated, but it was eye-catching as the Brussels balls sparkled in the sunlight.

The English-speaking guide told them that originally the planners in the 1950's had intended to build an upside-down model of the Eiffel Tower for the International Expo 58 World Fair, with a ground-level entrance, escalators up a tall tower to an area spread out at the top which would give people a bird's eye view of the City, but after consultation with architects decided that an atomic structure, which would stand for six months, would be more symbolic of the new technological era, so they were very lucky to see it still standing four years after it had been opened by King Baudouin on 17th April 1958. It was not only a vision to be seen, but also to be experienced, and everyone enjoyed exploring everything it had to offer.

Another place which aroused the boys' senses was their canal trip in Bruges. At first they watched Nuns making lace outside in the streets. But the stench of the canals was overpowering, and they were more interested in the Grote Markt than their trip on the foul-smelling water.

Some boys bought locally made woollen gloves and scarves to take home for presents, whilst those with more spending money bought padded tea cosies which opened at the top. They were designed to stand a teapot inside the padded frame, then the sides were lifted up and clasped closed at the top. They were a real novelty, but were quite expensive for the boys to purchase.

Soon the Belgian coach-driver became a figure of fun. His stock phrases, through a hand-held microphone, 'Here now in a moment on the left ...' and 'Here now in a moment on the right ...' were mimicked by some of the pupils, and staff had to stop them from repeating his high-pitched voice, and copying his arm gestures.

Other excursions included a day out to Walcheren Island in the mouth of the River Schelt in Holland, where they enjoyed a ferry ride. In 1944 the British Royal Air Force had dropped bombs to create holes in the dyke surrounding the island in order to force the German invaders out and open up the harbour of Antwerp to allied shipping. Now it was a tourist centre and the boys enjoyed their day there. When they got home they'd be able to say they'd been to Holland as well as to Belgium.

For the penultimate day of the holiday, Den had planned a day at the coast and had booked the coach to take them to Blankenberge beach in the Western province of West Flanders where the inhabitants were Flemings and (a few) Walloons.

Although the pier was long, it was nowhere near as long as the one at Southend which some of them were used to visiting, but there was a sandy beach where the boys played ball games. In the late afternoon it started to drizzle with rain so they took shelter in the town. To save overcrowding the shops, the party broke up into their four groups of ten, with their team leaders to accompany them and agreed to meet back at the coach in time to travel back to their hotel for their evening meal. Every so often the leaders would do a head count.

Near the end of the day, to Den's horror, he found that three of the boys from his group were missing. He gathered the remainder together, identified the names of the absentees, and enquired who'd seen them last, and where. One boy claimed to have last seen them in a stationer's shop looking at postcards and had commented that it was a bit late now to be buying cards to send home, and had left them twizzling the card stand around.

Den took his seven boys back to the coach. They met up with Rocky and his group, then Rob and Lil arrived with their groups. The three pupils hadn't gone back to the coach.

Leaving Lil, Rocky and the two wives to look after the boys in the coach, Den and Rob went back into the town to search for the missing trio.

Den was in a terribly anxious state. His heart thumped loudly in his chest. His blood pressure rose. He puffed and panted as they hurried to the stationer's where the boys were last seen. They couldn't see any of their boys in the shop and asked a shop assistant if they'd seen them. But the assistant couldn't speak English and didn't understand what Den was saying.

Another assistant was called to help, but he didn't understand either, he only spoke Flemish. Rob tried speaking in a limited French tongue, but again, the assistants didn't understand.

A Flemish customer who also spoke a small amount of French, and a little English, tried to help. Eventually he ascertained that the boys had been taken into custody. They had been seen shop-lifting by the owner, who had notified the police. The boys had been searched and each of them was found to have a boxed fountain pen in his pocket, but no receipt for it. Den would have to go to the Police Station. He advised Rob to go back to the coach and instruct the driver to take them back to Brussels, and asked him to say nothing about the incident to the boys, just to tell them to pack their cases after their evening meal.

Den was livid. The shop-keeper had laid charges. The boys had been arrested and the police were not willing to release them. The boys were in cells, and none of the police could speak English, only Flemish and Walloon. Den offered to pay for the pens. He took out a book of travellers' cheques and showed them to the officer. He indicated visually that he would make recompense to the shop-keeper, but it wasn't easy to make anyone understand. Eventually an official police interpreter was summoned and after six hours of questioning and negotiating skills he managed to resolve the situation. There were statements to be made; forms to be filled in; an official letter of apology to be drawn up given to, and accepted by, the flustering, blustering, gesticulating shop-keeper together with a cheque to cover his losses.

Den got the interpreter to hire a taxi to take them all back to their hotel. He was fuming with rage and did his best not to lash out at the boys either physically or verbally. On the way back, one of the boys broke the uncomfortable silence by saying that earlier in the week they'd spent most of their money on purchasing expensive tea cosies for their mothers and had nothing to give to their fathers. They had run out of money and had taken the pens to give as a going home present for their dads.

Den's fury did not abate at the excuse for thieving. He told them in no uncertain words that their actions were despicable, a disgrace to themselves and the school, and nothing less than total, dishonest, theft. He challenged whether their parents would be pleased to accept a gift if they knew it had been stolen, and that they were very lucky to be going home at all. The shop-keeper hadn't wanted to withdraw his charges; the police hadn't wanted to release them; and he'd had a terrible job to obtain their freedom.

Each of the boys sullenly muttered their apologies, but Den remained incandescent with anger and declared he would never, ever, take a school party abroad again as long as he lived.

The next day, on their way home, everyone avoided Den who was still smouldering and smarting from his previous day's experience. Lil knew he would be all right once he had calmed down but until that time arrived it was better to leave him to stew in his own thoughts and work out how he was going to report the incident to the Head when they got back. Would it be in a written report, or should it be a verbal one? The Head would have to know, but would he also have to notify the School Governors and the local authority? Perhaps he would tell the Head before writing a report? What advice would the Head have to offer? As far as Den was concerned, he had taken the responsibility on to his own shoulders, the matter had been dealt with and resolved, and as far as he was aware there should be no further repercussions; but anxiety gnawed at him.

On the coach to Ostend the rumour mill was in full gear. It churned out a tale that one of the boys had been taken ill and the other two had stayed with him; that they'd been taken to hospital and no-one could speak English. Eventually Den had arrived and they'd had treatment before they could be released, and they'd hired a taxi back to their hotel.

Den neither denied nor confirmed the rumours, he just hoped the real truth would never get out. Like the three guilty boys, he stayed shtoom.

After a tedious sea crossing from Ostend to Dover and a train ride to Victoria, the group was glad to climb into the pre-booked coach waiting for them, but the outward journey's hum of excitement was not repeated. Instead, the majority of boys were tired. Many of them slept on their journey back to Romford.

Half-way home, Rob singled out Audrey. Verity moved to a seat at the other side of the aisle as if she was anticipating his arrival, and he sat where she'd been sitting.

'Verity tells me that you're a shorthand writer.'

'Yes, that's right. I do both shorthand and typewriting.'

'As a matter of interest, are you able to write shorthand at a hundred and twenty words a minute?'

'Yes,' she replied, quizzically, wondering why he had this sudden interest.

'Have you got a paper qualification to prove it?'

'Yes, I have. Why do you want to know?'

'You know that I run the Junior Evening Institute at the school?'

'Yes.'

'Well before it was set up we put a questionnaire out asking what sort of activities the youngsters would like to do. The majority wanted indoor sports like table-tennis, snooker, darts, chess, and so on but we had eleven boys who indicated that they wanted to learn how to write shorthand.'

'Surely that's very unusual?'

'Yes, we thought so too! Anyway, we found out it was because we'd had a Careers Guidance Officer in from the local authority and he'd enthused some of the boys to consider preparing for a career in journalism. We looked into the matter and were told that eleven people was insufficient to run classes, but if we could get fourteen or fifteen people interested, that would be a viable number. We thought if we could find a teacher, we could perhaps advertise a course to include some of the pupils from a nearby girls' school. We've run advertisements in the schools' bulletins for the borough every month for five months, but so far we've had no applicants.'

'Really?' Audrey shuffled in her seat and wondered why he was telling her this. She couldn't help. She wasn't a qualified teacher.

'Well, when we were looking into this, we discovered that if a person had a qualification to write shorthand at a hundred and twenty words a minute they could be employed in an evening institute as an instructor, not a qualified teacher, and would be paid a pound an hour by the local authority. I was just wondering, having seen how well you've handled the boys on this trip, whether you'd be interested in doing a two-hour session one night a week, starting next September, providing we can recruit the necessary numbers?'

'Oh, Rob, I don't think so. It's something I've never considered. What if I couldn't cope? What if I couldn't discipline the class?'

'You'd cope. I've watched you with the boys. They respect you. If they want to learn to enhance their future prospects they'll behave, believe me. It's when they don't want to learn that there's trouble.'

'It's very kind of you to consider me, and I appreciate it, but it's so sudden and out of the blue. Can I have time to think about it?'

'Of course. Discuss it with Rocky when you get home and let me know by mid-August so that we can start recruiting and, if you don't want to do it, I've still got time to advertise again for someone to start in September.'

Audrey's heart raced. It was the opportunity of a lifetime. Rob got up, winked at his wife, and walked forward along the coach to where he'd previously been sitting. Verity moved back into her original seat.

'I'm astonished,' Audrey admitted. 'I expect you've had something to do with this.'

'Not really. I just told Rob about your shorthand skills and how enthusiastically you'd spoken about your teacher. He came up with the idea himself.'

'I'll certainly think about it. What an amazing way to end a holiday.'

For the rest of the journey she thought about nothing else.

CHAPTER 17

INSTRUCTION

Safely home again, Audrey asked Rocky if he knew that Rob had asked her to think about instructing Evening Institute pupils in shorthand.

'Of course,' he replied. 'Rob had a word with me first. I told him you'd be approachable, but I couldn't answer for you; you'd have to decide for yourself.'

'I'll certainly do that! In some respects I'd love to do it, but in others I'm frightened that I might not be able to control a class; and what if I taught them something that wasn't right? I'd feel a fool and an idiot, and what if I spoilt things for you? Children can be quite cruel at times and if they found out that I was married to you they might poke fun at you and say that you were the man who had a wife who was a flop and a failure? I couldn't bear it if they did.'

'Stop being negative. When have you been a failure? Never!'

'My mother said I was a failure when I didn't pass my eleven-plus exam and they didn't buy me the bicycle that they'd promised, if I'd passed.'

'That's stupid. Some people are late developers. You might have been one of those. Look at you now! Did your mother pass her eleven-plus when she was young?'

'No. They didn't have eleven-plus exams in her school days. In fact, she didn't go to school at all when she was eleven. Her father was injured when he fell from their pony and trap and died in 1918. Her mother needed her to help in the pub, because Uncle Quilliam was serving in World War I, and Auntie Dorcas was too young and by law she had to go to school.'

'There you are then, she's been trying to live her lost opportunities through you. She's wanted you to achieve what she couldn't. There are loads of women who send their girls to ballet dancing classes because they wanted to do ballet dancing themselves but couldn't. Now's your chance to show her what you can really do. She can't think of you as an educational failure if you go into my line of business. If Rob says you're qualified to do it, that's good enough for me.'

'Oh, Rocky, you are good. You're a really positive thinker.'

Audrey gave him a big hug and he reciprocated her affection by putting his arms around her and rewarded her with a lingering, passionate, kiss.

'You'll need to draw up a scheme of work, and I'll help you to make a lesson plan for the first week. You must know what you want the pupils to learn, and how they're going to achieve it. You must also estimate how long you think you might spend on a topic, and ensure that you have enough material prepared. If you prepare too much, it doesn't matter because you can use it next time. It's better to have too much prepared than too little. Remember, children assimilate information at different speeds. Some will pick things up instantly, others will take longer. You have to aim towards the middle ground, but you're paid to teach them all, so you have to be fair to everyone in the class.'

'I understand. But what about discipline?'

'Be positive at all times. Never weaken. You must be in charge from the moment you step inside the classroom. Once that door is closed, you're on your own, so take an authoritative stance without being offensive. They'll respect you for it; and for goodness sake, keep them working. The busier they are, the less time they have to play up.'

'Rocky, darling, thanks for all your help and advice, but it's still a bit scary when I've never done anything like this before.'

'Well, it's up to you. A pound an hour is excellent money. I don't want it. You can keep it for yourself, to do with whatever you want. I don't want to force you one way or the other. You must think it through for yourself and when you've made up your mind, tell Rob. You know I'll be supportive, whatever you decide to do.'

Later that week she went to the library and borrowed some beginners' shorthand text books. She studied them and, with Rocky's advice, drew up a scheme of work to last a term, then worked out a lesson plan for what she considered would cover a two-hour session.

Feeling much more confident, she decided to accept, and told Rocky of her decision. He was pleased.

'Good. I knew you could do it once you'd put your mind to it. Now, here's another tip. The students only have one name to learn – yours. But you'll have to learn all of their names on the first day. So before the session begins, draw yourself a desk seating plan. You'll be given a register to mark. Ask them to put up their hand when they respond to their name. Call out their names slowly, look at them, and write down their name in the appropriate place on the plan. Later when you ask a question you can name, pause and ask – what we call NPQ, or you can ask a question, pause, then name someone, and that's called QPN. They'll be impressed that you've remembered their name and will respond to you more quickly.'

'Oh, Rocky, you are clever.'

'Not clever, my love, it's basic teacher training. I'll help you as much as I can. You only have to ask.'

So Audrey notified Rob that she would take on the role of Instructor for two hours a week on Tuesday evenings, and asked him to make sure the pupils brought a shorthand notebook and a pencil sharpened at both ends when they started in September. She knew from personal experience it wasn't ideal for students to use a pencil because the lead could snap or go rounded and would need to be sharpened. Pencils also slowed the kinaesthetic skill process down because, when she was learning, her college friends tended to draw outlines slowly rather than write quickly; but at this age few pupils would have fountain pens, let alone shorthand pens so she decided it was the best option in the circumstances.

On her first evening as an instructor, the caretaker opened the classroom door half an hour before the start of the lesson and gave her a key which was to be handed in after she'd locked the door at the end of the session. Audrey drew a sketch of the layout of the room. The desks were squat squares of worn wood carved and scribbled all over with graffiti. On the lid of each desk there was a square hole in the top right-hand corner in which a circular white inkwell was affixed but the ink in them had dried up. The hard, wooden chairs looked most uncomfortable to sit on for two hours so she was glad there was a ten minute break half way through the session. Someone, presumably from the day school, had left the blackboard covered with chalky writing. It didn't have a note saying "please leave" so she found a board wiper and cleaned it all off so that she could use it to demonstrate the three positions of writing outlines above, on, and through lines. She set out her folder of prepared work on the teacher's desk then went to collect her register, locking the door behind her.

When she returned five minutes before the start of the session, there was a queue of fourteen babbling students waiting in the corridor. There were eleven boys whom she didn't recognise because she hadn't seen any of them on the school trip; and three girls from a nearby girls' school to make up the required minimum number. She greeted them smilingly before unlocking the door.

'Good evening everyone.'

The youngsters all politely chanted 'Good evening Miss,' then piled into the room.

Rocky had warned her that the mischievous pupils usually went to the back row of desks while dedicated learners and attention seekers would sit at the front. He was right. In the four columns of desks there were five students on the back and front rows, leaving several empty desks in the middle. She drew the ones on the back row further towards her, and became aware that there were fourteen pairs of eyes looking at her in keen anticipation.

'Good evening, ladies and gentlemen. My name is Mrs Driver. I've come to instruct you in how to write shorthand.'

The pupils had not been called 'ladies and gentlemen' before. The majority of them giggled but the remark brought various other reactions.

'I'm calling you ladies and gentlemen rather than boys and girls because writing shorthand is a very grown-up thing to do. I want you to act, and learn, like adults, not like children, and that way we'll get along together very well.'

Some eyes went up; some sniggers were heard, some shoulders were raised, but by saying something different from the way teachers in day-school spoke to them, she'd got them reacting and from their responses she quickly noted the loud, reactionary students, from the quiet middle-of-the-road ones.

'First, I need to call the register. Please would you put up your hand when I call your name? Tracey Brown?'

'Yes Miss.'

A well-built girl sitting on the seat right in front of her raised her hand. Audrey wrote her name on the desk plan, as advised.

'Deborah Carpenter?'

'Yes Miss, but all my friends call me Debbie.'

'Thank you, Debbie. You can put your hand down now.'

'William Dowell?'

'Yes Miss, but all my friends call me Willie,' he replied jokingly, standing up and cupping his hands around the genital area of his trousers in order to attract the attention of the girls from the nearby girls' school.

Audrey put on a stern voice.

'Thank you, William, that will do,' she scolded, trying not to get drawn into the class's frivolity at his antics.

'You may sit down, now that we know who you are.'

'John Franks?'

'Yes Miss. I'm usually called John, but my parents call me John Willy when I'm naughty.'

Now she put even more authority into her tone.

'Well, John Willy, you'd better not be naughty in my class because your parents aren't here to correct you, but I am, and I can be far stricter than they are, so please sit down and act like a responsible young man who's come to learn and not to play the fool.'

She surprised herself at her response, but she couldn't let them get the better of her. Rocky had insisted that she must be in charge, not the pupils, otherwise they would play her up and she would be putty in their hands.

The boy coloured to the roots of his hair. The class laughed, but when the register was complete, they settled down and got on well with the work planned for them. Audrey showed them how to hold their pencils and how to write small strokes and outlines along the lines in their shorthand pads.

Most of the boys were very good and quick to learn. Two of the girls were rather clumsy in their handwriting style and produced huge outlines instead of small neat ones. She insisted that they wrote much smaller until they had at least thirty strokes across each line of their shorthand pads. She continuously walked up and down the columns of desks, watching the pupils writing outlines to her dictation and correcting their techniques where necessary. That is, until the big girl on the front row took out a paper bag of sweets, unwrapped a toffee, put it into her mouth and started chewing it loudly.

Audrey knew that she had to do something, but what? Rob had told her she needed to treat evening school students like Dresden China. They were coming of their own volition, because they wanted to, not because they had to, and if they were disillusioned or broken in any way they wouldn't come back; and she needed to maintain the numbers to keep the class running.

Audrey tried to think on her feet and said:

'Excuse me, Tracey, but didn't you know it's rude to eat sweets in front of people, without offering them around?'

'Yeah,' the girl observed in a somewhat gauche manner.

'Well, you're eating a sweet and you haven't offered one to anyone else, so perhaps you'd do so now?'

'Wot! Give everyone in the class one of my sweets?'

'Yes, that's right. Either you put yours in the waste bin, and apologise to everyone in the class for your rudeness in eating in front of them or you offer everyone a sweet, including me. It's up to you.'

The girl shook the bag and counted the sweets.

'There's only one each, and if you have one, there won't be any left for me.'

'That's all right. You've got yours now. Everyone else can put their sweet on top of their inkwell and eat it at our half-time break, not in the lesson.'

To Audrey's amazement, Tracey lumbered out of her desk and offered the bag of sweets to each of the eleven boys and the other two girls from her school, and offered her one, too. On principle, Audrey took the last one. The sweets were placed on top of the inkwells and remained there until break, when everyone in the class ate them, except Tracey who'd already eaten hers earlier.

For whatever reason, it did the trick. The children worked hard for the remainder of the lesson. They did their best, and Audrey praised them all. She allocated some work to be completed at home and brought to the next lesson, and before closing the class asked if anyone had any questions.

One effeminate little boy, the smallest in the room, put up his hand. She had noticed during the lesson that all the lads in the class had referred to him as 'Gwen' when, in fact, his name was Gwyn, but she had ignored it earlier because he had taken it all in good part and it hadn't bothered him. One lad shouted out:

'Gwen's got a question for you, Miss.'

'Yes, Gwyn. How can I help?'

'Miss!'

'Yes, Gwyn?'

'Miss, are you married, Miss?'

'Yes, Gwyn,'

'M-i-iss. Are you married to our Mr Driver in the day school, Miss?'

'Yes, Gwyn, I am.'

'Oh, Miss! However can you stand him?'

Everyone laughed. Then one boy shouted out loudly:

'Because she likes lorries, Gwen,'

'Lorry Driver. Got it?' called out another boy.

'That will do,' she chided. 'Now make sure you've got everything. It's time to go home.'

'Smashing lesson, Miss, see you next week' said one pupil as she closed the classroom door and locked it.

Her first lesson was over; she had enjoyed it, so had the pupils.

Arriving home all buoyed up and keen to tell Rocky about her first lesson, she noticed a police car parked in the street near their block of flats.

'Funny time for the police to be here, late at night,' she murmured under her breath. 'There must have been a break-in somewhere. I hope it isn't at our flat.'

She parked her bike in the cycle shed which they'd rented since one became available and mounted the stone steps to their flat. As she put her key in the lock and pushed the door open she could hear voices coming from the lounge.

'Oh, my God, it is here!' she uttered quietly to herself. 'But we've got nothing of value to take.'

She started to shake as she walked along the passage and went in to the lounge. Rocky was standing by the fireplace looking shocked, while a young police constable stood stroking the rim of his helmet with his thumb in a stance that indicated he was just about to leave.

'I'll go now,' he said 'and leave you to tell your wife what's happened. We'll be in touch, but here's our local station number so that you can ring us direct if you need to. You don't have to ring 999.' He handed a printed card to Rocky before taking his leave.

'Evening ma'am.'

Rocky escorted him to the door and she heard the lock click as the door closed. She put her handbag and briefcase on the bed-settee. When Rocky returned to the lounge she hardly gave him time to get back in to the room.

'What ever's wrong? What's happened?' she gasped.

'You'd better sit down, love. Do you want a cup of tea?'

'No, no. Get on with it. Just tell me what's happened.'

'Well, you'd better prepare yourself for a shock. It's Edwynne.'

'Oh dear, what's happened to him?'

'They don't know. He's missing.'

'What do you mean missing?'

'Well apparently this morning the milkman noticed that Edwynne's front door was slightly ajar when he was delivering the milk at about six o'clock. He thought it was very unusual and called out, but there was no response, so he pushed the door open slightly to shout again. The draught excluder screen by the front door was on the floor and he could see cushions, papers, clothes, keys, and so on strewn all over the floor. It looked as if the place had been ransacked. He called out again and, realising Edwynne wasn't downstairs, he went upstairs and he wasn't there either. His bed hadn't been slept in, and the two bedrooms were also in a mess as if someone had been in searching for something.'

'Oh, poor Edwynne. How awful. But a burglar isn't likely to kidnap an old man – so what do you think has happened to him?'

'I don't know, and the police don't know either. Apparently amongst the things they picked up they found an address book. Having ascertained from the milkman that Edwynne's surname was Driver, they searched through it to see if there was another Driver mentioned who might be a relative and they found our name and address. They made enquiries through their systems and contacted our local police station who sent the young constable here to see whether we were related. I told him that Edwynne was my father. He asked quite a few questions; he'd been here for over half an hour before you arrived.

It's awkward us not being on the phone, but they'll contact us again as soon as they get some news.'

'Oh, Rocky, this is terrible. We'll have to go to York and clear up the mess and tidy things up before he gets back.'

'They've been taking finger-prints today, and they've started a search. The constable asked me if I knew where he might have gone, but apart from your parents, or Aunt Matilda's, I just don't know.'

'Oh, dear. It's not like him at all. I can't imagine him going anywhere without leaving a note.'

'I'll have to go and ring the Head. I still have his phone number somewhere. Will you be all right while I go to the phone box?'

'No. I'd rather come with you. I don't want to be on my own.'

'Come on, then, we'll go now. What a thing for you to come home to on your first night as an instructor. You can tell me all about it when we get back from the phone box.'

CHAPTER 18

ANXIOUS FEELINGS

The next morning Audrey and Rocky were up early. Rocky went to the telephone call box and phoned the local constabulary to let them know that he had the Head's permission to go to York to sort things out and search for Edwynne. They travelled by train, arriving at the cottage mid-afternoon. The York police had been contacted and were expecting them, and there was a policeman on duty at the cottage.

'Sorry about all the mess, sir. They've finished taking fingerprints so you can start clearing the items. Later this afternoon someone will come along and give you an incident number so that the old man can make a claim on his insurance.'

'Thanks, officer, but we have to find him first. We'll have to contact the local hospitals and see if he's been admitted to any of them.'

'Good idea, sir. I think you'll find we've already done that yesterday, but there's no harm in trying again.'

'What else have you done to find him?'

'We're in the process of doing a house to house search in the village and asking people when they last saw him, and where. But it's a slow process, sir. Some people are at work and we have to go back again, sometimes two or three times before we get a response.'

'Is there anything we can do to help?'

'You can think of places he might have gone to. We're also contacting everyone named in the address book to see when he last contacted them.'

'I see. What I don't understand is why, in a village where everyone knows everyone else's business, no-one has seen him or anything of any significance.'

'Surprising, isn't it, sir? Sometimes the villagers know something about somebody before they know it themselves.'

'You don't need to tell me that! I was born and brought up in the village myself. I know only too well what you mean. It's happened to our family more times than I can remember. Is it all right for us to clear up the mess?'

'Go ahead, sir. The forensic team have finished here now.'

Rocky and Audrey started to pick up the pieces. It was a soul-destroying task. They piled items on to the table so that they could sort things out before trying to put them away in their rightful places. The trouble was, in many instances they didn't know where the rightful places were.

In their tidying process, Rocky came across an old wooden box that had been broken into. The lid was hanging off. Inside there remained some legal documents – birth and marriage certificates for Cora and Edwynne, Cora's death certificate, and Edwynne's hand-written, self made Will, leaving two gold sovereigns, Cora's wedding ring and a gold chain with locket, to be passed to any grandchildren he may have in the future, in order to keep the gold in the family. Cora's costume jewellery and any other worldly goods were to go to Rocky with his love. Neither Audrey nor Aunt Matilda were mentioned in the Will. He looked at the date. It had been written after Cora's death.

He rooted through old bills, some going back over seven years or more. All had been date-stamped when they'd been paid.

'Might as well get rid of these now. I can't see any point in keeping them,' he fretted to himself. 'But where are the gold items referred to? I would have expected them to be in the box with the paperwork, but they're not there. Perhaps mum had a separate jewellery box?'

They continued to clear the floor and chairs but found nothing of value. Audrey felt despondent. After such a high spot last night, now this. She would remember it for ever.

'Poor Edwynne,' she commented dolefully. 'It looks as if an opportunist thief has seen the door ajar whilst he's been working in the back garden, frantically searched for money and valuables, ransacked the place in a hurry, and taken the family gold.'

'Looks very much like it! Poor Edwynne didn't have much in life and somebody's taken the little he had. I hope they catch him or her and that they get a long sentence for doing this to my dear dad.'

Suddenly Rocky felt hungry. They'd had a very early breakfast and nothing since then. There was very little to eat in the pantry – no bread, cakes or biscuits, just a couple of tins of stewed steak – but there were plenty of fresh vegetables in the garden. He pulled some carrots, washed them, and ate them raw. Still not satisfied, he went back in the garden, picked some peas, and ate them straight from their pods.

Audrey also felt hungry, but she didn't feel like eating.

'The smell and sight of all this has got to me, and the anxiety of not knowing what's happened to Edwynne is terrible. Words can't express my feelings. I think I'll sit down outside in the fresh air for a bit. I feel quite ill. Will you take a chair outside for me?'

'Of course,' Rocky responded. He took one of the painted dining room chairs and put it outside the front window. She sat on it and smoothed her dirty, dishevelled dress. It was filthy across the front. She longed to soak in a lovely warm bath, but she had no intention of getting the old zinc bath down off the wall in the kitchen, carrying water in from the well and heating it up in the old copper wash-boiler. She would have to wait until she got to her parents' house. What ever would they say when they heard about this?

Rocky felt keyed up. He wanted to be on his own for a bit.

'Do you mind if I wander over to the church for half an hour?'

'Not at all, just don't expect me to come with you, I'm all in.'

Audrey felt safe with the constable still keeping guard. Rocky was pleased with her response, not to hear that she was 'all in' but to hear she didn't want to accompany him. He needed time on his own, to think about things in solitude.

As he walked along the drive from the cottage, gravel scrunched underneath his footsteps. He reached a tall beech hedge at the front of the garden and turned left at the ungated opening. It was the first week in September and the sun was sinking in the west. The sky was a glorious shade of orangey-pink. Darkening grey clouds surrounded by golden perimeters impinged on the hue. Apart from an odd bird singing in the treetops the atmosphere was quiet and cool. It seemed strange to him that he never saw anyone in the gardens he passed, nor met anyone, not even in a car or on a bicycle. In other circumstances he would have relished such glorious serenity, but as he walked along the country lanes he was troubled and anxious about what he might find. He'd had a thought while they were clearing up and wanted to investigate.

He'd remembered that Edwynne took fresh flowers to Cora's grave each week and he wondered how fresh they were today. Had Edwynne put fresh flowers there this week? If not, the flowers would be dead with the heat of the summer sun, but if they had been changed they would still be fresh. That could possibly narrow down the time span that his dad had been missing.

He made his way to Cora's grave in a shaded area away from the church and the road. Huge moths fluttered in his stomach. He had a horrible, harrowing, feeling that he might find Edwynne there. He did. It looked as if the old man had tripped and fallen. He was lying face down, blue with cold.

Old, and not so old flowers were strewn around the grave as if he'd dropped them whilst trying to save himself from stumbling over the kerbstone when he was replenishing the spent vaseful. Rocky bent down to touch his beloved father.

'Dad. Dad. Wake up, dad. It's Rocky, your son.'

But it was no use. Edwynne had been there too long and was as cold as the marble headstone.

Rocky ran to the church to see if the Rector was there. He wasn't. The echoey interior was empty, in spite of the fact that the church door was always kept unlocked so that parishioners could go in any time for meditation and private prayer. It was a wonder no-one had seen Edwynne at the grave. There was usually someone about in a village, especially in a churchyard. His pulses raced. His head was spinning. He ran to the vicarage and raised the alarm.

Villagers were shocked when they heard the news. No one had seen or heard anything. It was a complete mystery as to why Edwynne had left his front door ajar. They came up with many different theories as to what might have happened. The police noted them all.

An inquest was opened and adjourned for further investigation. The post mortem revealed the cause of death as myocardial infarction and senility. Edwynne had not tripped and laid until he was dead, as Rocky had originally thought. He'd died of a heart attack whilst changing the flowers on his wife's grave. That would explain why he hadn't called for help. But it didn't explain why his front door was found ajar and his cottage had been ransacked.

Edwynne was buried in the same grave as the wife he'd loved so much. Once more they were together again – for evermore.

* * * * *

Back home, through the late autumn and winter months the Evening Institute pupils kept attending classes. Another two girls joined them, which allowed a little leeway in case anyone missed a class. Audrey loved her job, it was so rewarding to see the pupils achieving week by week and she reaped much pleasure from preparing lessons and refreshing her own knowledge of the theory. She bought a shorthand dictionary, and made handouts and homework sheets.

She decided to write to the local authority and ascertain if there was any way she could become qualified to teach the subject professionally. The staff at the education office were most helpful. They sent leaflets and pamphlets about full-time and part-time teacher training courses, and a correspondence course. She studied them thoroughly and considered the time involved in each undertaking, and the cost. As she perused the information for the third time, weighing up which course to opt for, she felt nauseous. She put the papers on the little table and subconsciously stroked her slightly distended stomach. She got a shock. She couldn't? Or could she? It was true her period was running late, but she'd bled last month albeit only for one day. She could hardly wait for Rocky to come home from school, and when he came through the door, blurted:

'Rocky, darling, I'm not sure, but I think I'm pregnant.'

Her self-diagnosis was confirmed. The couple were over the moon at the news. The thought of God's gift of a child was exhilarating and they were enthralled at the prospect, but what about her instructor's job? She decided that the best thing to do was to discuss it with Rocky, think about the consequences of giving it up when she'd only recently started, and got all the pupils interested, then to talk it over with Rob. She felt fit and well, and wanted to continue. He'd had problems obtaining a shorthand teacher in the first place.

His advice was for her to study for the correspondence course, keep instructing the pupils as long as possible and when the time came for her to have the baby he would try and get a temporary replacement or close the class; he would cross that bridge when he had to, and not before.

In addition to studying at home for the shorthand skills teaching certificate, and submitting weekly coursework, Audrey had to attend a local technical college and give a lesson, in order to be assessed to see if she was a suitable person to teach.

The assessor asked her to give a forty-five minute lesson on the 'shun hook,' and also asked various other questions. At the end of the assessment, he told her she'd passed the practical teaching section, and wished her well in the two written examinations which would come at the end of the course. She was ecstatic and launched into her coursework with even greater resolve. Every day she studied for one or two hours; every week her stomach grew larger; every month Rocky's call upon her body diminished as he respected the growth within her.

* * * * *

That winter was hard and long. Snow and ice arrived in early November and persisted for months. As Christmas approached, stories of babies being born deformed with hands on the ends of their shoulders, or feet attached to their thighs, hit the headlines. Audrey and Rocky were horrified. The cause had been traced to a drug called thalidomide which the mothers had taken in early pregnancy to combat morning sickness. They knew the drug hadn't been prescribed to Audrey because apart from the odd occasion she'd been extremely fit and well and hadn't needed to take drugs.

In the new year Audrey didn't have one baby; she had two. The twins were beautiful. They were perfect. She put her finger into the babies' tiny hands. Even their fingernails were perfect. She scrutinised their feet. Fortunately they had not inherited Edwynne's extra toe. She was overcome with joy, exhilaration, emotion and tiredness. In her opinion throughout the centuries no-one had ever had babies so beautiful and perfect as these. She

190

cuddled each child to her chest and in turn, put them to her nipples; first the boy, then the girl. It was a most glorious and wonderful sensation. She was a mother. Rocky was walking on air. Each day he visited his wife and children in the maternity ward and revelled in their well-being. He was ecstatic. He was a father, twice over.

Leaving the hospital a fortnight later the wind blew cold icy snow into their faces. It had been warm in the ward and Audrey had forgotten about the freezing conditions outside, but Den and Lil were there to take them all home in their car.

Rocky sent a card to Mr and Mrs Small to notify them of the births. In reply, they sent a card of congratulations and said they would come through when the weather improved but realised how difficult it was for them to stay when there was only one bedroom in the flat, and Audrey would have to get up for night feeding.

Choosing a name for the twins was difficult. Any first name starting with L had to be abandoned otherwise the children would be nick-named 'Learner Driver' when they got to school. They also abandoned the idea of names starting with an A. After a lot of deliberation, they selected the names, Ken and Dee in the hope that they couldn't be shortened further.

'We have so much to look forward to, we'll have to leave the past behind us now.' observed Rocky. 'Nevertheless, I'd still like to know why Edwynne's front door was ajar. I can't let go of those memories, I think they'll stay with me for ever.'

He encircled Audrey in his arms.

'Well done, you! Thank you so much for our wonderful little family.'

'Well done, us, you mean. Having one child of each sex is marvellous. What ever we do, we can't improve on it, we can only repeat one or other, or both. At least they've got something that neither of us have had – a brother or a sister!'

* * * * *

One evening towards the end of November that year, while Ken slept soundly in his cot, Dee was kicking her legs in freedom without the restriction of a towelling nappy. Audrey looked at their children with pride and admiration. She was so glad that the mites knew nothing of their grandfather's demise, or the ransacking of his home, or of the Profumo affair, or the Great Train robbery which had taken place earlier that year.

Rocky was at school that evening participating in a parents' evening and wouldn't be home until after ten o'clock, and she was listening to his radio. In the background, Audrey could hear the Beatles' record 'She Loves You' which had sold over a million copies the previous month. Suddenly the music stopped. An announcement came over the air that President Kennedy had been assassinated in America. She was stunned. The consequences of the incident would change world history. She lifted Dee's legs, pinned a warm nappy around her buttocks, caressed her, and drew her close to her chest, more for her own comfort than the baby's.

She was in shock. Dee pushed her away in rejection of her pressurised grip.

'Oh, I'm sorry, darling.'

She immediately loosened her hold.

'I can't believe it. Jack Kennedy was such a good man in America. Oh, I wish your daddy was here with us both. What a shock!'

She cradled the baby gently in her arms, kissed her tenderly, then laid her in her cot. The child didn't object. She didn't cry. She was totally oblivious of all the hateful and historical events that had happened that year and peacefully fell asleep.

Audrey made herself a cup of instant coffee and listened to the news bulletins and commentaries.

Rocky arrived home later than expected. One of the staff had heard the news on the radio and had enlightened his colleagues when the parents' evening concluded.

The next day the newspapers were full of pictures and stories. Within hours Vice President Lyndon Johnson had been sworn in as the new President, with the late President's wife, Jacqueline Kennedy, at his side.

Two days later, Lee Harvey Oswald, suspected of the gunning down, was murdered by Jack Ruby. Not only Americans, but people all over the world were outraged. Everyone wondered what the world was coming to, and there was certainly no way that Audrey and Rocky could possibly envisage what the following years would bring for them.

CHAPTER 19

GOOD AND BAD NEWS

Through Rocky's avid reading of daily newspapers he became aware that the London County Council had made a decision to grant one hundred per cent mortgages to people who lived in their catchment area. He and Audrey knew that they would need larger accommodation now that they had a growing family and decided to take advantage of the facility. They went to many estate agents and were horrified that house prices had increased considerably.

They went out viewing every Sunday and were shocked at the state of some of the houses available at the lower end of the price range. Many of them were in need of considerable costly repair work being done, and others weren't in a suitable locality.

Eventually they found a small semi-detached, on offer at three thousand five hundred pounds. After viewing it, Audrey asked if that was their only price, or whether they would accept an offer. Miss Tiller, the owner, immediately dropped the amount by five per cent and the couple verbally accepted and went to the estate agent to put in a formal offer.

Whilst proceeding with the purchase, quite by chance, they discovered that another agent was also selling the property and they were involved in a contract race. It was a very anxious time but their estate agent made enquiries and discovered that the other purchaser had falsified his income and his Building Society had withdrawn their offer of a mortgage.

Miss Tiller was embarrassed when the estate agent confronted her with the facts and a new purchase price of three thousand pounds was re-negotiated. Rocky made an application to the London County Council and a mortgage offer for that amount was received, with a twenty-five year repayment period of seventeen pounds a month.

Being first-time buyers, the purchase went through quickly. Audrey and Rocky couldn't have been happier. They had a wonderful family and now a home of their own.

The house needed a lot of work doing to it, but they felt they could work at their own pace.

The move went well and they soon settled in to their new abode. Despite everything else that was needed, Audrey's first purchase for the new house was a twin-tub washing machine for coping with the babies' dirty nappies.

As soon as they had moved into the house, Mr and Mrs Small came to visit. They adored the twins and took them out every day. However, Mrs Small was scathing about the house. She criticised how small it was, how much cleaning and re-decoration needed to be done, how there was hardly any furniture in it, no carpets on the floor other than in the front room where their previous carpet square now lay. She also commented on how the front gate was hanging off its hinges, how tall and smelly the privet hedge was in the front garden, and how it would attract insects, how the back garden needed digging over. She went on and on, but her biggest gripe was about the price they'd paid.

She vociferously declared that the young couple had put a millstone around their necks for the next twenty-five years, and had probably bitten off far more than they could chew. In this respect, Larry agreed with her.

Rocky tried to appease his in-laws but they were still aghast at the amount of debt to be repaid. To them, three thousand pounds was a fortune.

He explained they had calculated everything carefully and that they were only paying rent to themselves. Eventually their financial obligation would be at an end, and the house would become theirs, mortgage free. But still Audrey's parents were not convinced that they should have taken on such a huge financial commitment.

The next morning, at breakfast, Mrs Small had a lot to say about Edwynne's demise. She asked questions galore and wanted to know whether the police had caught the intruder.

'Not yet,' Rocky told her. 'But they're still working on the case.'

After almost an hour of interrogation and conjecture about the break-in and related events, Larry decided enough was enough.

'Leave it Suky, darling. The bairns will soon need feeding. I think our lass has enough to cope with. It's time we gave them both a helping hand. They've got so much to do. I'm going to go in the back garden and dig it over. Is that all right, with you, Rocky?'

'That's fine by me. I've done some weeding and clearing, but there's a lot more work to be done to it. Mind yourself on the brambles if you go down the bottom of the garden. They're quite sharp.'

'Right. I'll make a start by digging out the rockery and putting in some fresh plants that will spread, and give a lot of colour.'

'I'll come and help,' offered Mrs Small.

'No, dear, I want to smoke my pipe, so you help in the house.'

For once, Mrs Small did as she was told. She washed and scrubbed as if to save her life. She worked hard and diligently.

The following day she and Larry stripped off the wallpaper in the tiny dining room. In the next couple of days they painted and wallpapered it as a 'welcome to your new home' present. Finally Larry paid for, and laid, some linoleum. The room was fresh and clean and such an improvement on its previous state.

Audrey and Rocky were most appreciative of their efforts, and thanked them profusely.

After Mr and Mrs Small had gone home, it was as if a whirlwind had passed through the Drivers' little house. However, it had helped Audrey and Rocky enormously and, after the first couple of days, they'd got on without any further major discordance. They realised it was probably having the twins that had made such a difference. Audrey's parents idolised them.

When the summer sales were taking place, Pebbles departmental store was offering selected furniture items at considerable reductions. Rocky and Audrey were attracted to a curved four-seater settee in a similar shade of green to their two fireside chairs. They purchased it and put in their front room, and moved the bed-settee into their second bedroom.

While the sale was on, they also bought a drop-leaf table and four dining room chairs and paid for everything by cheque, from their savings. It was a bit extravagant to do that, but they never considered taking out hire purchase because their mortgage commitment was enough to pay each month. Audrey explained to Rocky that there were times when it was hard to make the weekly housekeeping stretch far enough, but because they were on a tight budget, he couldn't raise the allowance any more. Sometimes Audrey had to queue at the Post Office on a Tuesday to collect the eight shillings a week Family Allowance which the Government paid out on the birth of a second child. There was nothing forthcoming on the birth of a first born; but they would never admit this to Mr and Mrs Small in case it gave them the opportunity to say 'we warned you not to buy a house and land yourselves with a mill-stone around your necks.' However tight the financial situation was, Audrey and Rocky knew they had done the right thing and did their best for themselves and their growing family.

* * * * *

Many months after Edwynne's death, routine police searches revealed some interesting information.

The investigating officer had wondered, from the beginning, why an old cottage in a poorer part of the village had been burgled when there were potentially richer pickings in more affluent houses further round the country lanes. They had read the birth and marriage certificates of Cora and Edwynne which were in the wooden box, and had noted Cora's unusual birth name, Cora Angelina Kent.

Fingerprint researches had identified a repeat offender for housebreaking who had escaped from a woman's open prison on the outskirts of York. Her name was Cordelia Leena Bandy, an unmarried mother, whose child was in care whilst she served her latest term inside. Her home address wasn't in Cornwall, but in Leeds. When police checked her home she wasn't there, but they kept it under observation on a regular basis, and made further enquiries. Her ancestry was checked. Her mother was discovered to be a Shirley Bandy, née Kent, the sister of Cora Angelina Driver, Rocky's mother. The offender was, in fact, Rocky's cousin.

Rocky's eyes boggled when he heard the news. Audrey could hardly believe her ears. They begged the policeman to continue.

'Last week we were called to an affray in a public house in Leeds. Those arrested for being drunk and disorderly were put in the cells overnight. One of the group turned out to be Cordelia Bandy, your cousin. She was wearing a wedding ring and a locket on a gold chain. When questioned, she said the locket had been her grandmother's and it had been passed down through her line of the family. It contained a photograph of a pretty young woman, probably taken sometime in the eighteen hundreds.'

'How amazing,' Rocky commented. I had no idea I had a cousin, and I had no idea mum had a locket with a picture of Grandma Kent in it.'

'Well, after further investigation and probing, she finally admitted that she had seen her chance for freedom, taken it, crossed the main road to thumb a lift back to Leeds, but the driver had only been going as far as the Shafto Shoe Inn, and had dropped her off there, which was back on the same side of the road as the prison. She saw a signpost for Bilborough and it rang a bell with her. She melted into the quiet countryside lanes, and sustained herself with whatever food she could pick from people's vegetable gardens. She'd remembered that her mother had sent a Christmas card each year to her sister and husband at an address near Bilborough, and if she could get there, perhaps her they would give her a drink and some food.'

'Surely she knew my mum had died?' Rocky queried.

'Apparently not,' continued the policeman. 'She recalled the address and when she found the cottage there didn't appear to be anyone about. She knocked on the door but there was no reply. She turned the handle and the door opened. She went inside, closing the door behind her. She went into the kitchen to get a drink and was horrified to find there was no running water. She looked in the cupboards and found a large jug of cold water and drank from it. She raided the pantry, eating as much as she could and stuffed more food into a couple of old shopping bags which she found there. But she had no money, so decided to look for some. She had to be quick, before anyone came back. She found an old wooden box upstairs but couldn't open it, so she took it downstairs, and peeped through the window. The coast was still clear. She forced the box open with a knife and broke a hinge off in the process. At the bottom of the box she found forty pounds in notes, some loose change, and some gold jewellery. She grabbed the lot and stuffed it into one of the bags.'

Rocky and Audrey listened intently, without interrupting his flow.

'Suddenly she heard a dog bark. She peeped through the nets again and saw, at the end of the driveway, a dog with its leg cocked against the pillar by the ungated entrance to the drive. She could see a man's head over the top of the beech hedge, and waited until they'd gone. Then she fled with her bags of food and her 'inheritance'. She didn't attempt to close the door properly in case it made a noise, and just made her getaway as fast and as silently as she could. Once she got back to the main road, she thumbed another lift and got as far as Seacroft on the outskirts of Leeds, and laid low in the unlocked garden shed of an empty council house.

The following day she got a bus into Leeds town centre and met up with a friend who took her in and she's lived there ever since and hasn't gone home again. If she hadn't been involved in the incident at the pub, we may never have caught her.'

What a terrible thing to happen. But, if she was going to the cottage for something to eat and drink, knowing it to belong to her relatives, why didn't she wait for them to come home and feed her properly?'

'Who knows? Perhaps panic set in. People do funny things when they're in a tight spot. Perhaps her thieving instincts took over. A person like her would have gone over the premises like a dose of salts. Professional thieves can raid a house within minutes and get away with thousands of pounds worth of assets in next to no time. What we need to know, is whether you intend to press charges against her?'

'Oh, I don't know,' said Audrey. 'She is family after all.'

'I most definitely will,' responded Rocky. 'You're too soft. She's caused us a great deal of anxiety and heartache. She must be charged and serve her time. She means nothing to me. I don't know her, I've never met her, and hope I never will.'

When Edwynne's inquest was re-opened the coroner recorded death by natural causes, but Rocky felt there should have been an addition to "myocardial infarction and senility" on the paperwork. He considered the wording should also have included "loneliness and a broken heart".

CHAPTER 20

VILIFYING REMARKS

With the birth of the twins Audrey gave up the idea of working, other than at home. She had given up her instructor's post at the Junior Evening Institute at the end of the academic year in July, to concentrate on bringing up their family.

Their little house was further away from the school than their rented flat had been and Rocky found travelling times getting longer and more tedious. He obtained a provisional motor bike licence and one Saturday when he wasn't refereeing a football match, he went to Romford town centre on the bus and came back on a brand new small motor cycle. He obtained insurance through the dealer and paid two shillings and sixpence to fill up his half gallon tank with petrol. He quickly learned how to drive the bike, and passed his motor cycle test.

The week after the inquest results were known, Mr and Mrs Small arrived on a Saturday, to stay for a week. It was term time, so Rocky had to work the following week days, but he was able to meet them at Romford station when they arrived.

Audrey stayed at home with the twins. That morning, with Rocky's agreement, she'd made up their double bed for her parents, and she and Rocky would sleep on the bed settee in the front room. In the afternoon she prepared a substantial meal for their arrival.

Mrs Small made a huge fuss of the children but when dinner was over she could hardly wait to finish her food before probing deeply into the results of the inquest and the police findings.

Between them Rocky and Audrey unfolded the whole story. Turning her back on Rocky, Mrs Small turned to her daughter.

'There yer are. I told yer so. I told yer he was no good but yer wouldn't listen to me would yer? I said at the time yer shouldn't've married him. I said yer didn't know anything about his stock. But, no! Yer had to go yer own way. Now look what's happened. We've got a thoroughly bad lot in the family.'

'It's nothing to do with me,' Rocky defended himself. I didn't know the girl, or her family. I've never met them. Didn't know anything about them.'

'There yer are again! Yer just proving what I said. If yer didn't know yer own background, how could Audrey know about it? She should've found out more about yer before yer got tied up together. I've never liked yer from the start. But .....'

'Suky, dear, you've said enough.'

'What've I said now? All I said was .....'

'We don't want to hear what you said,' Larry interjected. 'Have a drink of water and wash your mouth out, you're not only upsetting us, but you're upsetting the kiddies as well.'

Rocky got up from the table and walked out of the dining room into the kitchen. He mustered every bit of self-control he could raise. He couldn't stand the woman's attitude. He mumbled to himself:

'Ye Gods! She relishes in upsetting people. I hope and pray that Audrey never gets like that. Well, she won't. I won't let her.'

At that moment he felt a warm hand on his shoulder. He turned. Audrey was there to comfort him.

'Don't let her get to you, love. She can't help it. She just comes out with these things.'

'She can help it. She's just a venomous virago. She doesn't stop to think before she speaks. Malice comes tumbling out of her mouth and she does nothing to stop it. I bit my tongue and walked away. Otherwise, I could have said too much as well, then where would we have been? She doesn't think of the hurt she causes. Listen. You can hear her still going on from here. I'm surprised your dad puts up with it. Many men would've walked out long ago. I can't believe hearing her talk like this, after the way she was so kind and cleaned and decorated our house for us the last time she was here. I'm going for a walk to cool down. I'll see you later, love.'

Rocky opened the back door of the kitchen, walked down the garden path and disappeared through the back gate.

Audrey went back into the dining room where her dad was looking embarrassed. Her mother had stopped quibbling and was tidying crumbs from the tray of one of the high chairs where the twins were banging with spoons and making a lot of noise.

'Mam, you're really going to have to stop all this criticism, especially in front of the twins. It's not a good example to them. They'll soon be able to pick up what you say and ape your tone of voice, and that's the last thing we want.'

'I don't know what yer going on about. I haven't said anything that isn't true.'

'That's your opinion. You're hypercritical, and we all want it to stop. So please, mother, think before you speak, otherwise you won't be welcome here again.'

Audrey picked up Ken.

'Time for a cuddle, I think.'

Mrs Small lifted Dee from her high chair.

'I agree. It's a long time since I had a little girl on my knee. How about you having her, and I'll have the boy. I like boys much better than girls.'

'That's a terrible thing to say. You shouldn't prefer one sex to the other, mam. They're both human beings. You should love them both equally.'

'Oh, I do love them both. What I meant was, that never having had a son, it'll make a change for me to have a little boy to cuddle.'

Not wanting to give in to her mother too readily after her latest flare-up, Audrey responded:

'Well, I've got him now. You can cuddle him later.'

She jogged the child on her knee while her dad cleared some dirty pots from the table, took them into the kitchen, and came back for more.

'Where's Rocky?'

'He went out for a while, he'll be back later.'

'Is he all right?' Larry enquired.

'He will be by tomorrow. He's not used to people like mam. He was brought up in love and affection in a gentle, quiet, environment and he doesn't know how to deal with outbursts like mam has. I find him very tolerant, and he has endless patience with me and the twins. But we'll have to get through to mam to guard her tongue. I don't want any more scenes like that while you're here. It's bad for all of us, but especially for the children.'

'Don't worry, lass. I'll have a word with her tonight and tell her that if she starts up again we'll go straight back home. She won't want that as we've seen so little of the children. She'll want to stay as long as she can.'

'Good. Let's hope she behaves herself. Perhaps we ought to get a tape recorder and when she starts, record what she says, and play it back to her? I think she'd get a shock.'

'Oh, I don't think so, that might be going a bit too far. Leave it for now.'

Rocky came back home when it was closing time at the local. He didn't usually drink, but a couple of pints of brown ale and a game of darts with some of the chaps had appeased his animosity. He went to bed and slept like a log.

Next day Rocky went to work and the rest of the family went to Hainault Park for a picnic. Everything went well. The sun shone, the children were good, and not a cross word was spoken.

The following day when Rocky came back from school he was elated. One of the teachers was organising an educational trip to Russia on the school ship SS Erudition and had been allocated an additional free place for a qualified teacher to accompany the party, to take responsibility for supervising pupils during the summer holiday period. A dozen teachers had indicated their desire to participate in the project, so by mutual consent all their names had been put into a hat and the Head had pulled out a paper with Rocky's name on it.

Audrey was overjoyed for him. Usually her dad was lucky at winning things; now it looked as if her husband was lucky, too. She considered it was the opportunity of a lifetime and congratulated him sincerely. He explained that the only cost involved would be sixteen pounds to travel to Moscow from Leningrad on the overnight train; the rest of the trip was free.

Mrs Small wasn't at all pleased at the prospect.

'I'm really surprised that yer want to go away for a fortnight and leave yer wife at home with two small children to look after.'

Before she could say any more, or show any bitterness or resentfulness, Larry stopped her and reminded her that he would take her home that very day if she said anything else.

Realising her husband's determination to do what he said, she insisted that if Rocky did go, then Audrey and the children must go to York and stay with them during the time he was away so that she could help look after the children, and that way Audrey would get a holiday as well.

Larry offered to use a privilege ticket from his allocation on the railway so that Mrs Small could come to Romford and help with the children on both of the journeys.

As agreed, their plans went ahead. Rocky accompanied the staff and pupils to Russia and Audrey and children went to York with Mrs Small helping them.

After three days in her parents' home, late in the evening, Audrey was in the front room watching television and the children were in bed. Her parents were in the dining room where Mr Small was eating a meal before going to work for an eleven o'clock night shift. The sound of a raised voice came through the walls. It was so loud, she could hear every word.

Mrs Small was criticising the fact that Rocky had gone off all over the world, enjoying himself, and left Audrey to cope on her own. She didn't like him, and never would. She didn't like the way Audrey was bringing up the children. She didn't like the way they were dressed; she didn't like the scuff marks on Ken's shoes; she didn't like the way their hair was done; she didn't like the twin push-chair – it took up too much room in the passage. The denigration went on and on but Mr Small didn't appear to respond, he just continued to eat his meal. Audrey was furious. She opened the dining room door and burst into the room.

'Just stop it, mother. First thing in the morning I'm going home. The children are asleep now, but I'm not staying here to be insulted. When it's daylight we'll go.'

'Yer can't go back tomorrow. What ever would yer Auntie Dorcas say?'

'I don't care what Auntie Dorcas, or anyone else for that matter, would say. You've hurt me once too often. Tomorrow I'm going home and that's final.'

'Oh no, yer not! Call that a home? It's more like a doll's house, it's so tiny. Spending all that money to buy it, yer absolutely mad.'

'It's more likely that you're mad, shouting and going on like this.'

'And what about him? Clearing off; going half-way round the world; leaving yer to look after two small children on yer own. Call that love? No way! He doesn't love yer, never has, and never will. He's no good. I hope he's gone for ever. Good riddance, I say.'

'He's only gone for two weeks! He hasn't gone for ever.'

'More's the pity. Yer should never've married him in the first place – what with him and his rotten family – the sooner yer get rid of him the better.'

Audrey shook with rage. Her mother's cutting words were preposterous. They were so unkind, and so uncalled for. Her teeth grated at her father's lack of defence.

Larry Small continued eating in silence. He pushed his fork into a plump sausage and sliced it lengthways. He looked at it carefully on his fork, then plonked one end into a mound of tomato ketchup and slowly and meticulously put it into his mouth and chewed it quite precisely as if lost for words, but creating something else to do with his mouth. Audrey turned on him.

'As for you, dad, I'm very surprised at you! You've never said a word in our defence. They're your grandchildren as well as hers; does your silence mean that you agree with every word she says?'

'No, lass, it doesn't,' he said with his mouth still stuffed with food. 'I'm just staying out of it. She'll run out of steam soon. What you've got to realise is that I have to live with her all the time. You're only here for a fortnight. I know she's got a mouthy tongue but she doesn't always mean it.'

'Then she shouldn't say anything. She should think before she speaks.'

Mrs Small, feeling by-passed, stood up and moved her cup and saucer off the table and piled them on top of an empty plate. She took a stance that was both frightening and intimidating.

'So much for yer opinion,' she glowered, and stomped off into the kitchen carrying the crockery noisily.

Audrey didn't wait to hear any more. She slammed the door shut, went upstairs and immediately packed her case. The following morning she was up early. It was only five o'clock but she wanted to be away before her father came back from his night shift and while her mother was still asleep.

She finalised her packing, fed the children, put them both into the twin pushchair and walked to the station pushing the handle with one hand and carrying her case in the other. She sheltered in the waiting room for the first train to Romford and made her way home in a defiant, emotional, mood.

It had been an uncomfortable, fraught journey with two young children to care for en-route, so at Romford station Audrey hired a taxi home which was an extravagance, but worth it. She settled the children down in their beds, made a pot of tea, took a cupful up to her own bedroom and laid on the bed to rest.

Her mind whirled. She thought about Rocky's comments on that day when he was angry and took himself off to the pub. How peculiar, she thought, that so many nasty-meaning words commenced with the letter v. Her mother could be described as a vile, vicious, vindictive, vituperate, vixen. Indeed, he was right! She was a virago. Yet, surely the word virago had a double meaning. On the one hand it meant a loud, overbearing woman; a termagant; on the other hand it meant a woman of great stature, strength and courage. Both sides of the coin could possibly be attributed to her mother. She could be really kind, considerate, loving and giving. She thought about all the hard work her mother had put into cleaning and decorating their house when they moved in. That took real stamina and strength of character to continue until the job was done, and not give up part-way through, so perhaps she did suffer from a split personality. On the other hand perhaps she was just showing two different sides of her character, like Janus' two faces.

The silent voice in her head trailed to a close. Lost in thoughts, she drifted into oblivion.

Just over two hours later she was aware of the front doorbell ringing.

'Oh, go away,' she said to herself. 'I'm tired and soon I'll have two babies to feed.'

But the person didn't go away. The doorbell rang continuously until she made the effort to go downstairs and see who was keeping their finger on the bell-push.

When she opened the door she got the shock of her life to see a sorrowful, tear-stained pathetic-looking little woman standing on her doorstep.

CHAPTER 21

SMALL TALK

'Mother! What ever are you doing here?'

Audrey looked aghast at the pathetic looking image facing her. It seemed no time at all that she had arrived home herself with the children. Now her mother was standing on the doorstep looking subdued and downcast. Audrey's body froze into a block of ice. She caught her breath. Momentarily she was speechless.

Mrs Small shifted from foot to foot. With head down, shoulders low, all sign of vituperation gone, she mumbled:

'Can I come in?'

Audrey hesitated for a moment and stared at the wizened, crestfallen, remorseful figure standing in front of her.

'If you must.'

Audrey's voice was terse and hard. She didn't smile. She didn't know she could be so cold.

'Yer father's sent me to apologise,' Mrs Small blurted, as she eased her way in sheepishly, looking humiliated and dejected, and put a small case down in the entrance hall, then walked into the dining room and sat on a dining chair.

'I can't believe seeing *you* here!' Audrey sat on a chair opposite her, and faced her unexpected parent.

'How did you get here? What's happened?'

Mrs Small ignored the first question but answered the second.

'I heard yer go. I looked out of the window and saw yer shoving the kids down the street in their pushchair.'

'I went because of all the nasty things you said about me, the children and Rocky last night. You were absolutely odious.'

'Well, I'm sorry now. I don't know what got into me. When yer dad got home from work and found yer'd gone, and taken the children with yer, he was furious with me.'

She twisted her handkerchief around her fingers, anxiously.

'For the first time in many a long year he shouted at me. In fact, he was so angry he picked up his cup of tea and threw it at me. It hit me elbow and cut it – look.'

She rolled up her sleeve and revealed a large blood-stained plaster.

'That's terrible.'

Audrey mellowed slightly.

'Did you get scalded as well?'

'No, but I had a big mess to clear up. It's surprising how much liquid there is in a full cup of tea. Anyway, it brought me to me senses.'

She rolled her sleeve back down to cover over the plaster.

'One of the troubles is, that normally yer dad's very weak. Because he's six years younger than me he feels inferior. He's always let me have me own way and I've got used to doing and saying what I want.'

Audrey's anger subsided a little more.

'What hurt me, as much as anything you said, is that he appeared to be agreeing with you. He never said a single word in my defence, or Rocky's.'

'He never disagrees with me, well, not usually, because he knows he's got to live with me. He can't afford to walk out. We haven't had a hum-dinger like this since we had that do when yer were born.'

Mrs Small fidgeted with her wedding ring, twisting it round and round in rebuffed anxiety. For the first time in Audrey's life, her mother looked a pathetic little figure, deflated in domination, possessiveness, dignity and egotism. She'd never seen her look so insecure and in need of support before.

'You were saying that you and dad had an altercation when I was born? I don't know anything about that.'

'Well, I suppose now yer a married woman with children of yer own, I can tell yer. I've always shielded yer from it and said I never would tell yer, but as we're making a clean breast of things..... let's have a cup of tea, or a glass of sherry, if yer've got one.....'

'You can have either. I've got a bottle of sherry left over from last Christmas. It hasn't been started into.'

They went into the kitchen. Audrey took two tumblers from a cupboard. Her mother half-filled one of them with the fortified wine and tossed some down her throat, before topping up the glass, and pouring them both a drink.

'Let's take these into the front room, it's more comfortable in there,' suggested Audrey.

'Now, what's all this about a to-do when I was born?'

Mrs Small sat on the settee and held her wine glass in her lap, taking small sips as she explained:

'Yer were a terrible child to bring up. Yer absolutely ruined our married lives. We'd only been married a few days when I fell for having yer. Once yer dad knew I was pregnant he wouldn't come anywhere near me physically for fear of 'harming the baby'. So there I was, legally married, but absolutely untouchable. Sex was taboo as far he was concerned. I ached for him, but couldn't have him because of yer inside me. Looking back, I suppose I was jealous of yer. Then half way through the pregnancy, he didn't tell me at the time, he lost his job. Instead of admitting it, he went out every day and came back at night as if he'd been to work, but I didn't find that out until yer were three days old. Fortunately for me, yer grandma had come to do some washing for me and while she was there two bailiffs came to take our furniture away. Yer dad hadn't been paying any of the bills, because he hadn't any money coming in.'

She took a huge slug of sherry and gulped.

'They took our dining table and chairs, and a three-piece suite from downstairs, and they wanted me to get out of bed so that they could take it away. I went berserk and screamed, shouted, and cried, and told them I needed the bed because yer'd only been born three days ago. But they got the dressing table down the stairs and attempted to get the wardrobe down, too, but it was so heavy they dropped it. That's why the mirror on the inside of the door is cracked. Anyway, grandma pleaded with them not to take me bed or yer cot and she paid them a lot of money to leave the bedroom suite. If it hadn't been for her, I don't know what I would've done. Believe me, the last thing yer want is to have the bed yer lying in taken from yer when yer still bleeding from childbirth.'

Mrs Small took a huge mouthful of sherry and twirled the remaining contents around before slurping the glass empty. Audrey listened intently to her mother's story.

'When yer dad came home that evening, as if he'd been to work, and discovered what had happened, he was riveted with shame and told us about losing his job several months earlier. He thought it would upset me if I knew, so every day he'd gone out looking for work and would've done anything, but he couldn't find employment anywhere. I was more angry that he hadn't told me. We had a real show down, and he's never been the same since. I took over the money side of our marriage and had a loan from me mother. After a long time yer dad got a job cycling round the streets selling tea.'

'Poor dad, he must have been broken-hearted.'

'What about me? How do yer think I felt? Well, whether yer were affected by our distress or not, I'll never know, but yer developed such a powerful suck that yer took all the skin off me nipples. Me teats were red raw, cracked, bleeding, and painful beyond belief. I had to have a doctor, because me breasts went lumpy. He nearly had a fit when he saw the state I was in. He got some glass shells to put over me nipples. They had a rim around the edge and caught any breast milk that came out, and I had to keep emptying them and putting the milk into a bottle to feed yer. But as if that wasn't enough, yer kept wailing and screaming to be fed. I was in pain. Yer dad was guilt-ridden and disheartened. Grandma was furious that the situation had arisen. After two weeks of unsuccessful breast feeding I had to have some tablets to dry me milk up because I'd formed abscesses. Yer had to go on to powdered baby-milk, which we could hardly afford to buy, so we had to cut down on our food, and eat things like tripe, and liver, which previously we'd only ever given to grandma's dog.'

Audrey was moved to tears. She wiped her eyes and sniffed.

'Why haven't you told me this before? I would've understood, I'm sure I would.'

'Because there's such a thing as pride. Yer don't want people to know these things, especially yer children. There's nothing they can do, and it's in the past now, but that's the reason why yer father won't buy a house. He won't have a mortgage under any circumstances. He absolutely refuses to run the possibility of getting into debt again. It was far too much of a trauma, so we've to make sure we never take on any more hire purchase or loans. If we can't afford something we've to do without it and save up until we can. The trouble is, by the time we've saved enough either it's gone up in price so we still can't afford it, or it's gone.'

'Oh, mother, that's an awful thing to happen and you've been harbouring grudges against him and me ever since, but telling me now helps me to understand his attitude to house purchase and why he was so concerned that we might get into debt by taking out a mortgage. Fortunately Rocky's in a job that isn't likely to sack him, not unless he commits some misdemeanour like robbery or murder, and he certainly won't do that.'

'I'm going to get another glass of sherry. Is that okay?'

'Don't you think you've had enough wine, wouldn't you prefer a cup of tea?'

'We'll have one later, if that's all right. I need something stronger to calm my nerves. I feel absolutely dreadful.'

Now the tables had turned. Audrey felt sorry for her mother. Her iciness was melting and she agreed to her request.

The children were still having their afternoon sleep. Audrey went upstairs to check that they were both all right whilst her mother was pouring herself another drink. They were fine. She came back downstairs and her mother continued her horrendous story.

'Just after yer dad got the job of tea salesman, the war came along. Yer were only a few months old when dad got called up. I couldn't afford to pay the rent on me own, so we went to live with grandma at her house. I got a job at The Eborocum Emporium as a sales assistant, and grandma looked after yer. We managed to get along okay until a bomb landed further up the street. It blew two houses right out of the ground and left a huge crater. Grandma's roof was blown off and we couldn't stay in her house. She went to stay with Auntie Dorcas and I took yer to live with one of the ladies who worked in the shop. She offered us her spare bedroom because we had nowhere else to go. Everyone in the street was evacuated and during that time yer dad came home on leave for forty-eight hours. Imagine his shock when the street was deserted and no-one knew what had happened to us. He saw that grandma's roof had been blown off and thought we'd been killed in the blast. He was devastated. He got a bus to yer Auntie Dorcas's house and found yer grandma there. She told him that I was staying at the other side of York with yer. Eventually he found us. He was so pleased to find us safe and sound, he wept like a baby. But his relief was short-lived. The next day he had to go back.'

'Oh, mam, that's awful.'

'The whole war was awful. Yer hated the sirens, and screamed when they went off. The blackout-man used to be on guard outside and shouted that I had to keep yer quiet. Sometimes in the dark I needed to put the light on to see what I was doing. If there was the slightest crack in the blackout curtains he would shout at us to put the light out. It was one of the worst times of my life.'

'Surely there couldn't have been much worse than that?'

'Oh, there was. Every day there was something to cope with. Anyway, I needed to keep working, so until the war ended I got yer into a day-home and had to take yer there every morning and collect yer every night.'

'You must have been very tired, especially after you'd been standing on your feet all day as a shop assistant.'

'Yes I was, but a customer at the shop told me about a little house that was up for rent quite near to the care-home, at a very low cost, so I took it on until yer dad came back from the war. We couldn't stay in that woman's one bedroom indefinitely, kind as she was to offer it! Then when yer dad came home after the war, yer didn't know who he was. Yer kept saying "Who's that man? Send him away. I don't like him." Yer made life very difficult for him. I hated yer for it because he loved yer from the moment he knew yer were conceived. He was so thrilled that I was having a baby, and he guarded yer within me body and wouldn't do anything that might cause a miscarriage or damage yer in any way.'

'Oh mam, I'm so terribly sorry. I had no idea of any of this.' Audrey snuffled into her handkerchief and blew her nose. 'I feel absolutely awful.'

Mrs Small put the tumbler to her mouth again and drank the amontillado as if it was water.

'Well, I used to get so angry and het up and sometimes I used to hear meself saying things I didn't mean. They just came out, and afterwards I felt sorry I'd said them.'

'But that doesn't explain why you hated Rocky so much. He's never done anything to hurt you, so why are you so hostile towards him?'

'I suppose it's fear. As yer know, yer grandpa Ferry was a publican, and one day in 1918 when I was only 11, he fell out of our horse and trap when he was coming home from collecting some hay for the two horses that we stabled for a couple of customers. Yer grandma took over the licence, and I had to help her even more – cleaning spittoons, scrubbing floors, washing glasses, serving drinks – and when I was fourteen, doing the books as well. That's why I'm so quick at adding up. It was part of me job. Uncle Quilliam couldn't help – he was serving in the first World War – and Auntie Dorcas was younger than me so she had to go to school otherwise the School Board man would've come looking for her. Anyway, to cut a long story short, when I was eighteen I got engaged to one of the regulars, Bill Boyd. He was six years older than me, and grandma started me off with a bottom drawer.'

'What on earth's a bottom drawer?'

'It wasn't a drawer at all; it was a term used to describe a collection of items which yer put together towards yer forthcoming marriage.'

Mrs Small took a more genteel sip from the tumbler and continued. 'Sometimes people used to give yer things for birthday or Christmas presents, like towels, or pillowcases, and sometimes yer'd see things in a sale that took yer eye, and yer'd buy them, like sheets and so on, and that gave yer a good start when yer got married.'

'Oh, I see, like tea towels and things?'

'That's right. Well, yer grandma gave me some beautiful linen tablecloths and some sheets. One day when there was a sale on, I bought a blanket and when I went to put it in the ottoman where the other items were kept, they'd gone. No-one knew what had happened to them. Then several weeks later, yer grandma noticed that her best tablecloth was missing, so she set a trap. One of her regulars saw Bill go upstairs, and he told me mother. They caught him in the act of taking a large bath towel from a cupboard. It turned out that he was engaged to someone else as well as me and was stealing things to set up a home with the other woman. When they were married, he was going to ditch me. Well, yer grandma was beside herself with rage and reported the matter to the police. She laid charges and he served time and, of course, she forced me to break off the engagement. I never went out with anyone else until I was twenty-seven, when I met yer father through Uncle Quilliam and Auntie Jen. They were on holiday in Filey and invited me to go there for a day out with them. Yer father was staying at the same boarding house. I thought he was about the same age, or older than me, but by the time we got married I was thirty-one and he was only twenty-five.'

'That's incredible, mam! But what's all this got to do with Rocky?'

'Well, Rocky's the spitting image of Bill Boyd. In fact, from his appearance I'm convinced he's Bill Boyd's son.'

Audrey's blood ran hot and cold.

'Oh, mother! No way! It's not possible. I've seen Cora and Edwynne's photographs of him from his birth. There's no way he could be your ex-fiancé's son.'

'I'm glad to hear it. But he brings back all those horrible memories every time I look at him. I get creepy feelings running up and down me spine whenever I see him. I've hated him since the first time I saw him and tried to put you off him because he reminded me too much of me past.'

With that comment she drained the remainder of the cheap cooking sherry down her throat and licked her lips.

'Mam, you can't blame a person for looking like someone else. They say we all have a double somewhere in the world. Rocky's not like that. He's kind and considerate, and very patient. Please get to like him for my sake and for the sake of your grandchildren.'

'I'll try, but it won't be easy. Are yer sure he's not adopted?'

'Absolutely certain. His parents were definitely Cora and Edwynne. In fact, I've got his birth certificate in an envelope upstairs together with mine and the children's, and our marriage lines. I'll go and get it and you can see the evidence for yourself.'

Audrey brought the envelope down and her mother pored over the document. She heaved a great sigh of relief and the tension within her visibly dissipated.

'Well, I feel a lot better knowing that.'

'Isn't it amazing what upsets us and worries us? Children don't ask to be born. They don't know they cause problems. I'm so sorry I caused you problems with my feeding. No wonder I screamed and carried on. Blood-flavoured milk couldn't have tasted very nice for me, as well as being so painful for you. Perhaps we can both put the past behind us and start afresh. What do you say?'

'I'll try from now on. I've drunk two-thirds of what was in yer sherry bottle. Let's put the kettle on.'

Audrey mentally acknowledged that at last her mother had admitted her problems. For over a quarter of a century she'd been jealous of her own daughter and, ever since she'd met him, she'd been afraid of her son-in-law's possible relationship to her ex-fiancé without checking the facts, and had drawn the wrong conclusion.

Audrey was sensitive, and felt she must take the problem on to her own shoulders. But how could she help? What could she do to alleviate the situation? Perhaps she had already helped by listening and offering tea and sympathy? Perhaps her mother's pent-up feelings would dissipate now she'd talked about it, instead of bottling it all up? Would her hatred and resentment dispel quickly, slowly, or not at all?

The questions went round and round in her head like the sails of a windmill churning corn into flour. As they drank their tea, Dee awoke and roused Ken and they wanted to play. Attending to the twins eased the tension. Her mother's confessions were over and she'd calmed down. They spent the rest of the afternoon and evening occupied with the children.

Audrey hardly slept a wink of sleep that night. She hoped that the next day would bring a new start. Her attitude would be different. Would her mother's attitude be different as well?

She drifted into thoughts about how she liked to be different. She didn't like to wear the uniform of fashion, not like the young Mary Quant, who encouraged young girls to wear mini skirts to be different from their mothers. She'd been put off in the early sixties when Matron Doughty had sacked three nurses for wearing topless dresses at a nurses' ball even though they were the height of fashion at that time. Suddenly, she roused.

'Yes! That's it! That's the answer! Instead of me being different from my mother, as I've always tried to be, I'll attempt to change her to be more like me. But will she change?' she asked herself. 'Can she stop being resentful, jealous and intimidating after all these years? Only time will tell, but at least I'll try and change her attitude to be a more positive one.'

At breakfast the next day, Audrey suggested that they all went to the local park.

'The flowers are beautiful at this time of year. We can take a picnic and relax. I take it you're going to stay until Rocky gets back?'

'I could do, but I'll have to write to yer father and let him know, that I'm staying longer than a couple of days.'

'Good,' Audrey encouraged. 'On the way there we'll call in at the discount furniture shop in North Street and you can help me to choose a double bed. That bed-settee we moved upstairs isn't very comfortable now. With a bit of luck, they'll deliver one tomorrow.'

For once, her mother didn't disagree. Audrey suspected that following the shock of Larry standing up to her, and her pent-up feelings being released yesterday, a new attitude had already begun.

'It's time to build a better relationship between us,' she encouraged. 'I bet Rocky will be surprised when he comes home and finds you here.'

'I expect he will,' Mrs Small replied. 'But I'll probably go home the day before he gets back. I'm sure yer'll both have plenty to talk about, with his holiday, and all I told yer yesterday.'

Mrs Small stayed with Audrey and the children for eight days. Her attitude improved. She was far less hostile and domineering. It had been a shock that her husband had stood up to her and taken the lead in making her catch a train to Romford and apologise, but once she'd done that, she felt so much better, and also benefited from the change of environment. She said it was her intention to turn over a new leaf and put the past behind her, but she avoided meeting Rocky on his return by going home the day before he was due to arrive back.

Audrey and the children accompanied her to Romford station. Mrs Small departed in a much more stable state of mind than when she'd arrived, and Audrey hoped her mother's new attitude would be permanent.

CHAPTER 22

BEGGING QUESTIONS

During the summer holidays whilst Rocky was at home to look after the children, Audrey took, and passed, the written papers for the correspondence course teacher's diploma in shorthand. Although she had given up her job as an instructor to look after the family, she knew that all the studying throughout her pregnancy and child-rearing had been worthwhile. The certificate would be evidence of her new-found status as a teacher if ever she wanted to apply for a commercial teaching post in the future. She was overjoyed at her successful outcome and experienced a great sense of achievement.

The following year there was a major inspection at the school and some staff worked hard to impress the Inspectorate. Rocky had never experienced an inspection before and no-one had mentioned them during his teacher training. He couldn't understand why so much zealous activity occurred before the visit, and he carried on as usual.

The school attained an excellent report and afterwards the Head suggested to Rocky it was time he started to look for a Science Department Headship of his own. It wasn't that he didn't want him at the school but his present Head of Science was settled for the duration and Rocky needed to spread his wings and enhance his career.

'What a funny thing to say,' Audrey observed when he told her. 'You'd think he'd want to keep good staff once he'd appointed them.'

'Apparently the Inspectorate said that young teachers weren't advised to stay too long in one place. Five years is plenty, they'd told the Head. At seven years in their first job they're stale. It's too late! They need to move on, like a bee, fertilising new ideas. Their ideas might be old to them, but they may be new to a different administration. What do you think to that, my love?'

'I'm astounded, actually. I would have thought stability was all-important.'

'So would I, but I can see his point. Some families have a lot of children and when you get four or five brothers in a school, in different years, you can keep meeting similar problems. Anyway, it might be worth moving on before our own children have to start school so that they don't have to move if and when I do.'

'Are you thinking of moving out of the area, then? Can't you get a job here so that we can stay in our little house?'

'It all depends whether a suitable job comes up locally, and if it does, if I'd be appointed or not. I think we have to be open-minded and, as your dad says, move to where the work is, if necessary.'

After a couple of applications and interviews, Rocky was offered, and accepted, a Head of Science Department post at a school in the Midlands. They put their house on the market and found it incredible that its value had increased by over a thousand pounds. They accepted an offer of four thousand two hundred and fifty pounds and were overjoyed.

For the same price they chose a three-bedroomed semi-detached house with a large garden just outside the catchment area of the school where Rocky would be teaching in the quiet small Cathedral City of Lichfield.

They paid off the balance of their LCC mortgage and took out a new, larger one, with a building society to give them some leeway for buying new carpets and furnishings.

When Mrs Small heard about the profit they made, she was envious.

'How can they make so much money in such a relatively small space of time, Larry? It's more than two years' of yer wages!'

Her old green eye glinted again. Once more she nagged her husband about buying a house of their own but, again, he didn't want to know.

A fortnight later, when Larry came home from work, there was a letter from his father's neighbour, to say Mr Small Senior was not well. He'd contracted pneumonia and had been taken into hospital, and she thought Larry ought to be informed.

Because he couldn't take time off work, Mrs Small went alone to see him. She liked Larry's father, and always called him Pa. He had come from good stock, which she thought was important. He'd been a First Class Engineer in the Merchant Service. He was a good man, a lovely man in every way. She didn't want him to die.

She took the spare key which they kept for him, and went to his house before visiting him in the hospital.

The accommodation was tidy, but there were some dirty pots in the sink so she washed them and put them away.

Upstairs, she looked in his bedrooms. The sheets on his unmade bed were creased and she could see dried stains of sputum on the pillowcase and bottom sheet. She stripped the bed and took clean ones from the airing cupboard. When she was tucking the bottom sheet in, she noticed something under the mattress and pulled it out. It was a thin, soft leather document holder. She opened it and found it housed his private papers. Mrs Small sat on the bed and perused the items with curiosity.

There were his birth and marriage certificates, his wife's birth and death certificates, an examination certificate issued by the Board of Trade in 1908, an identity and service certificate as a member of the Mercantile Marine, a testimonial issued by the Ministry of Shipping Coasting Trade Office, his service record signed by every Captain he'd ever served with, a wedding photograph, an insurance policy and three savings bank books.

Mrs Small had never seen any of these before, and was intrigued. She couldn't resist looking at everything. There was an insurance policy for one thousand pounds plus profits, payable on his death, a Co-operative Building Society savings passbook showing another thousand pounds invested and years of interest added to it; a Friendly Society savings book with eight hundred and fifty pounds, and a Post Office savings book which looked as if it was used as a current account to pay bills and buy Christmas presents.

'My goodness me!' she said out loud. 'I never knew he had all this money. He's rich beyond compare.' Her heart pounded as she calculated the totals. 'All that money, and he's never mentioned it. What we could do with some of that! We could buy a house outright without having a mortgage. He could've had a car, or nice holidays. What a waste, just saving it up and getting no benefit from it. What good is it going to do him now, if he's dying? It would come to Larry, and we could still get a house. But what if he doesn't die, and gets better?'

Then she had another thought.

'But where's his pension book? He must have an old age pension. And surely he would've had some cash in the house.'

Her fingers trembled as she put everything back in the document holder and slid it back under the mattress. She finished making up the bed, and went downstairs to look for his pension book and cash.

In a sideboard drawer she found various receipts, his pension and rent books, five one pound notes and two ten shilling notes in a wallet and some loose change in a purse. She looked through other drawers. Everything seemed to be in order.

When she visited old Mr Small later that day, he was in a bad way. Compared with his own father, who'd reached the ripe old age of ninety-nine, Pa was not so old, but he thought he was dying.

To cheer him, Mrs Small talked about his great-grandchildren and told him of Audrey and Rocky's good fortune in making over a thousand pounds profit on their proceeding house sale which they were going to use towards the purchase of their next property.

'I wish we could buy a house of our own, but Larry won't entertain the idea,' she told him.

'Well, you've got a nice little home, why do you want to buy one?'

'Because it's dead money, Pa. We keep paying rent and over the years it continuously rises. There was a time when we used to pay seven and six a week, and it's kept creeping up and up ever since. Now we're having to pay twenty-two and six a week. We can't keep going on like this. God knows how much it will be when Larry retires in ten years' time and we don't have a wage coming in, only his state pension. I wish we had the money now to buy a little place outright.'

'Would Larry move if you did?'

'I think so. It's having a mortgage that puts him off. For the past twenty-five years I've been paying one and sixpence a week into an insurance policy, intending it to be a little pension for us. It's due to mature this year, with profits, so I reckon we should get over nine hundred pounds back. It would go a long way towards buying a house, but it's still not enough to buy outright. I feel so frustrated. I don't suppose yer could help us could yer?'

'How much more money do you need?'

'At least as much again, because buying a house isn't the end of it. There's solicitors fees and removal fees to pay. Then our carpets and curtains may not fit, but I do wish we could get one before he retires.'

'If I get better from this, I'll see what I can do to help. If I die it'll come to Larry anyway. Like you, I don't have a house to sell either, I also rent mine, but I've got a bit put away for a rainy day.'

'Oh, Pa, do yer mean it? Yer not just saying it because yer ill?'

'No. When your money comes through, you and Larry look for a house and if you find one that suits you at a reasonable cost, I'll give you and Larry a thousand pounds towards it.'

She grinned and clasped his hand.

'Oh, thank yer, Pa. Thank yer ever so much.'

He adjusted the oxygen tube in his nostrils and closed his eyes.

'Keep going, Pa. We need to get yer offer down in writing and witnessed.'

'He opened his eyes. I'd like to rest now. I can hardly breathe. Come back again tomorrow.'

The following day when she visited, Mrs Small took a pad of paper, a ball-point pen, and a clean envelope. On the top sheet of the pad she had written:

I promise to pay my son, Larry Small, and his wife Suky Small, the sum of one thousand pounds for the specific purpose of them buying their own house.

When she got to his bedside he looked much the same as the previous day.

'How do yer feel today, Pa?'

'Not so good. Not so good. I think my time's up.'

'Not before yer've signed this piece of paper. I've written down the promise yer made me yesterday. I'll ask the ward sister to witness it.'

Pa shakily signed the paper in front of the sister, who signed and dated it. Mrs Small folded it, put it in the envelope, and carefully zipped it inside a pocket in her handbag. She never said that she'd found his private papers under the mattress.

'Thank yer, Pa. Now yer need to concentrate on getting better so that yer can see what we buy. Yer can come and stay with us when yer better. I don't think yer'll be well enough to go home and live on yer own again.'

'Let's wait and see what happens, shall we? I'm so tired now. I'd like to go to sleep. I feel exhausted.'

Mrs Small left the old man weak and washed out. But modern medicine was a wonderful thing. Each day for three weeks he got better and stronger. When he was discharged he went to convalesce with Larry and his wife.

When Mrs Small told Larry about the promise he'd made, he was extremely angry at her gall.

'How dare you go and tap Pa for money when he was so ill and vulnerable? It's a wicked thing to do.'

'No it isn't. He might have died and it would have come to yer anyway.'

'But he didn't die, did he? He's got better. And we can't spend the money on anything else. You've specified it's to be used on a house purchase.'

'Exactly. That's my point. All my life I've wanted a home of me own. When me insurance money comes through we'll have enough money to get one. It'll be small, I know, but it'll be ours. We won't have to go on paying twenty-two and six a week rent. That can go towards things like paint and wallpaper. We'll still have to pay bills like rates, electricity, gas, and so on, but we pay them anyway. How are yer going to afford to pay rent when yer on a pension in just over ten years' time? It'll be even more then.'

Larry was exasperated. He found it very difficult to argue with her; she always got her own way in the end. He took himself off to his allotment, tended his vegetables, smoked his pipe, and cogitated. As he did so, another allotment holder arrived. He took a couple of old chairs from his shed and they sat and chatted until the evening clouds obliterated the light.

'Better go home,' Larry declared.

'Good job you've got one to go to. I'm going to doss down in the shed tonight.'

'Why's that?' asked Larry in a horrified tone.

'Got behind with the rent. The landlord's evicted us. The wife and kids've gone to stay with her sister but there's no room for me. There's plenty to eat here, and we've got running water in the stand-pipes. I'll be okay here for a couple of nights. We'll go to the Council offices tomorrow and see if they'll put us on their housing list. We'll find something, somewhere, I hope.'

Larry walked home in sombre silence. The man's plight made him think deeply. He felt incredibly sorry for him, but he couldn't offer the fellow a bed because Pa was staying with them.

In the time it took him to walk home he decided that they would view houses in their price range and make a cash purchase if they found one, once all the money was in place.

Mrs Small was over the moon with his decision. She scanned the papers ardently. They viewed a dozen houses or more. It wasn't as easy as it had seemed. There wasn't a lot of choice at the lower end of the market.

Audrey and Rocky's house moving procedures progressed slowly. They got caught up in a chain of sales and purchases and Rocky had to take up his duties in April before the house sale was finalised. He lived in rented accommodation near the new school for a whole term, and every Friday he rode home to Romford on his little motorcycle, and every Sunday evening he drove back to the Midlands to complete the next week's work.

It was an anxious time waiting to get contracts exchanged; but eventually they were, and the family moved to their new home during the last week of the summer holidays.

In addition to being bigger and better in every respect, the new house had a telephone installed in the front room. It was a novelty for the children, who'd never seen one before.

The day after they moved in, while they were still in bed, they heard a letter plop through the letter box. The envelope bore a York postmark and was addressed in Mrs Small's backhand spidery writing.

'I expect it's a letter congratulating us on our move. It's some time since they saw our brochure, they'll probably want to come through and see what we've bought this time.'

Audrey opened the letter and read it. Her mouth fell open.

'You won't believe this, Rock! They've bought a house!'

'What? Let me see!'

'Well I never!'

'They've never squeaked a word.'

'Let me read it again.' She quoted from the letter:

'Dear Audrey,

You'll be very surprised to hear that dad and I have bought a house. It's very old and dirty. It needs a lot doing to it, but at least it's ours. We didn't dare tell you before in case our purchase fell through, but now we've moved in.

When we saw that you'd made over a thousand pounds profit in such a short space of time, it motivated me to do something before your dad retires. I asked Grandpa Small to help us and he did. An old man has lived in it on his own for over ten years since his wife died. He'd done nothing to it in all that time, so we put in an offer and got it cheaper. Auntie Dorcas has been up and helped us to clean the kitchen. She's used five cans of scouring powder trying to get the grease and dirt off the walls. That's all for now, just thought you'd like to know.

Love, Mam and Dad.'

'That's absolutely mind-boggling! I'm astounded at their news. I'm so pleased for them. All her life mam's craved to have a home of her own. Perhaps, at last, she'll feel fulfilled. We must go through and help them.'

'Remember I start a new term next week and I've got a lot of preparation to do. You take the twins to York for a few days to see what you can do to help. I can't come with you just now.'

'Okay! I wonder if they've got a phone? They don't give a number, only their new address.'

'Best to write back and say you'll go up. I'll be all right here.'

When she got there, Audrey was shocked at the state of the house. The window ledges were rotten; many of the slates on the roof were cracked; a down pipe was shattered; the guttering needed to be replaced; there was a huge hole in the rendering at the front; the back door didn't close properly, it kept sticking at one corner; but it was a 1920's semi-detached. It had three large bedrooms and a bathroom with separate toilet upstairs. Downstairs there was a large front room, a small dining room and a large kitchen with walk-in pantry. The garden at the rear was long and narrow, untidy and seriously overgrown, but Larry would have pleasure clearing it.

'Where do you want me to begin?' she enquired.

'In a bedroom,' came the reply. 'We're aiming to make the kitchen hygienic first, then do one room to live in and one room to sleep in. We'll clip away at the back garden as and when we can, but as yer can see, we need a new bath and toilet. The old man has never cleaned them for years. I put endless bottles of bleach down the toilet before we could use it.'

So the renovation began. The work gave Mrs Small a new interest in life and, between shift work, Larry made new window sills and painted them, fixed the back door, paid a roofer to do the necessary work and put up new guttering.

After helping her parents to get two rooms into reasonable order, Audrey returned home with the twins. Rocky was glad to have all his family back and they had much to talk about.

'We're going to have to make new friends here in the Midlands. Leaving Den and Lil will be a terrible wrench. They've been superb friends. We'll also miss Vic and Candy but they've all promised to keep in touch, even if it's only a card at Christmastime.'

'That's true. It isn't easy making new friends in a new area. But we managed when we moved to Romford. I'm sure we will again, especially when the twins go to school. I'll meet lots of mums taking and collecting their children.'

In many respects the move to the Midlands was a good one. It was only a hundred and twenty miles to York instead of three hundred, so they were able to travel up and down to see Audrey's parents in their new home much more frequently, and catch up with friends from the past whilst they were there.

By the Spring of the following year the house was like a new pin. It was the turning point in their lives and, being mortgage-free, Larry never begrudged a penny spent on the property. Mrs Small was over the moon to achieve her lifetime ambition of owning her own home.

Pa was delighted to see what his money had helped to buy. He said he'd rather see what they'd spent his money on in his lifetime, than leave the money to them in a Will and never know what they'd spent it on after his death. It gave all three of them a new lease of life.

CHAPTER 23

COPING WITH CHANGES

Once both children had settled into their first school, Audrey decided to look for a part-time job. She saw an advertisement for a shorthand teacher needed for four hours a day, two days a week at a private secretarial college.

'That would fit in beautifully with the children's school hours. I could take them there on a morning and be there to collect them when they finish at three o'clock. They'd have to stay for school dinners. What do you think? I'd like to try for it, Rocky.'

'Far be it from me to stop you. You'll have to ask the twins whether they'd like to stay at school at lunch-time.'

Ken was keen to stay. He said he'd be able to play football and do other games. Dee was not so sure, but said she'd give it a try. So Audrey applied and was appointed.

For a year everything worked out satisfactorily but when, during her second year, heating, lighting, staff wages and the lease became too expensive for the management to make a profit, the Principal served notice on all the staff.

It was an anxious time. Some of the older, more experienced teachers were offered jobs in the London branch, but didn't want to move house at their time of lives, and if they didn't transfer, would lose any redundancy money to which they were entitled. Two of the younger staff got better jobs as trainers in the business world and the other teachers' timetables, including Audrey's, were altered to include teaching typewriting skills as well as shorthand until the college closed at the end of the academic year.

One of the teachers was a member of an Association of Pedagogues and she invited Audrey to accompany her on one of their six-monthly outings. Keen to make new friends, Audrey accepted and Rocky looked after the children for the day.

An elderly teacher on the coach, sitting in a nearby seat to Audrey and her friend, overheard their conversation about the college closing down and turned to them.

'What ever are you going to do financially?' she queried.

'I've accepted a full-time job, in Crewe,' the friend replied, 'and I'm going to move and live there.'

'I don't know,' replied Audrey. 'I only work part-time, so I haven't thought about it in any seriousness yet.'

'Oh, my dear, I think it's dreadful that a college of that calibre is closing down. The staff have no jobs, no money, no redundancy money either! Would you like to come and work at the college where I work? I do part-time day classes but they also want me to do three evenings a week next September. I don't want to do three evenings because I've a disabled husband at home. I don't mind doing one evening a week, but not three! If you give me your name, address, phone number and a list of your qualifications I'll pass your name forward. Perhaps they'll interview you, and you could do one or two of the evenings for me?'

'That's very kind of you, Mrs Brock, but I've never heard of your college and don't know where, or how far away it is. I don't know whether I could get there, even if something was offered.'

'Don't you worry about things, I don't,' she fabricated, and produced a piece of paper and a pencil for Audrey to write down her personal details.

A fortnight later Audrey received a printed postcard with infilled hand-written details. It read:

Dear Madam,

You have been appointed as a visiting lecturer to teach shorthand from 7-9 pm one evening a week on Tuesdays commencing with effect from 1st September. Please confirm your acceptance of this position as soon as possible.

Yours faithfully.

It was signed personally by the Head of Department.

Audrey couldn't believe her eyes. How could they offer her a job without even interviewing her? They must be really desperate for staff or, Mrs Brock must have given her a glowing reference, or badgered the Head of Department to have her hours reduced to two evenings a week and offer the work to a qualified substitute to take her third evening's class.

Clutterbuck Technical College was situated in an area of the Black Country. Audrey had no knowledge of its whereabouts or reputation, so before accepting the offer she went to find it, looked around the area, and checked that there was a suitable bus service to get there and back. She went home and wrote a letter of acceptance.

On her first evening's attendance she went to the college office to report for duty. She was given a register into which several blank forms had been slotted – there was a record of work sheet to be completed at the end of the lesson, a marks sheet for classwork and homework, and a salary claim form to be completed once a month. She was given a key to the classroom door and was told to return everything to the office before leaving the premises.

The Registrar also told her that the Head of Department was not a good face-to-face communicator so she would find it necessary to read the notice boards in the corridor outside his office, and in the staff room.

'How very odd.' she observed. The Registrar explained:

'About twenty years ago he had a problem with one of his staff and since then he's done everything by the book. He puts everything into writing, and keeps copies of replies. I don't think you'll see him very much, if at all. He goes home at four o'clock every day and leaves a senior lecturer in charge over the evening staff.'

'If he had problems twenty years ago, he must have been here a long time?'

'Yes, he has. He's been here over thirty years. Apart from the Principal, I think he's the longest serving member on our staff.'

Audrey thanked her, and went to look for her classroom. She unlocked the door, found the light switch, cleaned the black board and set out her preparation on the teacher's desk in readiness for her students' arrival.

By seven o'clock almost everyone named on the register was present. There were twenty-four students, whose faces ranged in colour from straw to sienna. Most of them spoke in a dialect based on diphthongs and triphones.

'Ease these the riot roo-um for beginners' shorthand?' she was asked.

'Yes. Come in. Welcome. Have a seat.'

'Can uz sit dow-un anywayer?'

'Of course.'

Audrey wasn't familiar with the Black Country burr and had problems making the students understand her slight Yorkshire accent. When she pronounced the vowel sound ay, as in pay and bay, the students corrected her and pronounced the vowel sound as oy, as in poy and boy.

She battled on as best as she could.

After an hour had passed, a senior lecturer entered her classroom and officially welcomed the students to the college. He counted heads and checked that the number tallied with the marked register. This was a new experience from teaching junior evening institute pupils or private students in the last college where she'd worked; no-one had ever entered her class and checked student numbers. Before leaving, he asked the students if everything was all right. One student lilted:

'Er torks diffrunt frum un.'

Another asked:

'Duz uz 'av ter riot shorthand in 'er langwidge or can uz use ower owen?'

Fortunately, the lecturer smoothed things over. Differences in accents and dialects was something Audrey hadn't anticipated.

* * * * *

Rocky was coping in his day-school and was pleased he'd moved on to his new job there, but it seemed to rain a lot more in the Midlands than it did down South. One particularly wet day, when he arrived at school drenched, a colleague told him that if he had a full motorcycle licence he could use it to drive a three-wheeled car-style motorbike which would keep him dryer than his Honda. He'd never heard of that loophole in the law, made enquiries, and discovered the fact to be true. He also found out that if Audrey applied for a provisional car licence she would be allowed to drive the three-wheeler on her own, but if a front seat passenger accompanied her, that person must hold a full driving licence.

They considered the news seriously. It would be wonderful to take the children to see their grandparents in a car-style three-wheeled vehicle instead of having to go by train. It would be so much cheaper, and more convenient going from door to door. They calculated their financial position, traded in the motorbike and bought a bright red "Reliant Robin".

Audrey and the children travelled home on the bus. She was petrified Rocky would have an accident on the way home. He'd never driven a car before and coping with an accelerator, brake pedal and gear lever would be a new experience, plus judging the length and width of the vehicle. Her heart was in her mouth all the way home; but when they turned into their street, there was the pristine vehicle on the driveway. The salesman had taken him to a quiet area, showed him how to operate the pedals and gears, and let him drive it around some of the back streets, before he'd set off for home.

The colleague who'd recommended purchasing the vehicle, had a full car-driving licence and every Sunday for several months he sat in the passenger seat and taught Rocky how to drive it proficiently.

Not only did Rocky pass his test at the first attempt, but he also made a friend for life.

Audrey obtained a provisional licence and took car driving lessons with a driving school, but it took her three attempts before she passed her test.

On one occasion when they were visiting Audrey's parents, Mrs Small started to query the amount of money having a vehicle would cost them; then she remembered the promise she'd made to Audrey to turn over a new leaf, and kept that promise when she realised that she would be able to see her grandchildren more frequently and Audrey would be able to share in the driving.

* * * * *

After her disastrous start at Clutterbuck Technical College Audrey completed three years of teaching shorthand in the evenings there, then gave it up to enrol at a polytechnic to take a one-year, one-evening a week, teacher's diploma course in office practice.

To familiarise herself with modern office equipment, she took a part-time clerical job at a nearby university, working twenty hours a week as a part-time secretarial administrator.

She was astounded at the progress which had been made in the development of electric typewriters.

On her first day in the new job she was allocated a bright red typewriter with a golf-ball head. She'd never seen a *red* typewriter before – nor a box full of interchangeable golf-ball heads in different fonts and pitches. She had difficulty using the machine, and had to be shown by one of the young office girls.

There was no carriage-return lever, and she felt stupid when she automatically raised her left hand and hit the air. The carriage didn't move. The golf-ball head did. It rotated and pivoted at great speed as she struck the typewriter keys. A very clear imprint appeared on the paper because the typewriter used a carbon film ribbon instead of one of the previous cloth ones which went backwards and forwards and lasted until the ink was pale. These carbon ribbons could only be used once, and mustn't be put into a waste bin, otherwise by using a mirror, the imprint could be read, and confidentiality would be lost.

The young girl deftly showed Audrey how to remove the golf-ball head and insert another when a different style of print was required within a piece of work. The typewriter was no longer called an electric, it was called a Selectric because of a typist's ability to select different type faces, and have work produced in ten, or twelve pitch. There was even a golf-ball with mathematical symbols.

The Professor's secretary had a blue typewriter, called a Selectric II. That machine was capable of squeezing corrected material into a smaller space, by using a half-space facility; and it had two ribbons – one black, and one white – the latter being a lift-off tape for correcting errors by overtyping the mistake with the white ribbon, then retyping the correct version in black.

Audrey felt so behind the times with the new technology and despite working at the university each day, she never missed attending any of her evening classes, while Rocky stayed home and looked after the children.

Punched card systems were becoming obsolete and being replaced by mainframe computer systems, and a new memory typewriter was invented which could store words and sentences and reproduce them at the touch of a button. That was a real boon because standard paragraphs could be stored and churned out to create personalised letters effortlessly. With out realising it, Audrey had passed into the rapidly developing business world of Information Technology.

CHAPTER 24

CANDID CANDIDATES

Having passed the practical and written examinations for which she'd been studying during the evenings, Audrey became qualified to teach office practice.

One day, while perusing the newspaper, she saw a job advertisement for a full-time assistant lecturer to teach shorthand, typing and office practice at Clutterbuck Technical College where she'd taught shorthand in the evening for three years prior to working at the university. She applied and was invited to attend for interview.

The interview panel comprised five people, including the Head of Department but she didn't know him, and he gave no sign of recognising her.

Three other applicants had been invited to attend and one by one they were called into the committee room, in alphabetical order.

A Mrs Arbuttnott went in first. When she came out from her interview she left the building saying she had decided to withdraw her application.

The next person to be called in was Audrey. The interview went well and the Principal asked her to wait outside and not to discuss the questions she'd been asked with any other candidates waiting to be called in.

The next two candidates were interviewed and also asked to wait. More than an hour went by and it was difficult to sit in silence. They talked generally, not specifically about their interviews.

Audrey ascertained that none of the candidates were Ministry qualified but one candidate had a good degree and the eldest had taught at the college on part-time day release courses for two years.

'The panel must have some serious deliberations to make,' the older woman said.

'Surely they aren't drinking tea all this time!'

Finally the door opened and Audrey was invited to go back into the room to meet the interview panel again. The Principal asked:

'If the job was offered, would you accept it or not?'

'Definitely,' she responded enthusiastically. 'It's a lovely college. It's fairly near to home and I don't have a problem with transport.'

Two panel members smiled. One asked:

'What about your family?'

'I have a very supportive husband who has helped and encouraged me to get this far. I can't envisage him withdrawing his support now.'

Some eyebrows went up. One panel member removed his spectacles and said:

'And what about your children? What do they think about their mother going out to work?'

'My children are fit and healthy. They both go to school and they're wise enough to know that their lives, and holidays, will be enhanced by the additional finance my job will bring in to our home.'

Panel members looked at each other again. One member, a college governor, nodded approval. The Principal said:

'Well, Mrs Driver, I think you've answered our questions satisfactorily. I would like to offer you the position of assistant lecturer to teach shorthand, typing and office practice in the office skills department, to commence in September this year. Do I take it that you will accept?'

'Yes, sir. Thank you very much.'

'We will, of course, put this formally to you, in writing. Welcome to the staff of the college.'

They all shook her hand and she emerged from the committee room grinning like a Cheshire cat. The other two candidates were thanked for attending, and dismissed.

As the applicants walked to the car park together the graduate asked:

'Did they ask you how many children you had?'

'I don't remember,' Audrey replied, still walking on cloud nine. 'I don't think so.'

The eldest replied:

'They didn't ask as a direct question, but by their interview techniques I told them quite a lot of personal things including telling them I had five.'

'You fool,' commented the graduate in a scathing tone. 'They asked me and I told them it was none of their business.'

'You didn't!' the eldest applicant exclaimed, in a shocked tone.

'I bloody did. When all's said and done, the Equal Pay Act passed a couple of years ago makes conditions of employment on the basis of sex illegal in three years' time, so they're going to have to pull their fingers out and stop asking impertinent questions. I told them they shouldn't be concerning themselves with information like that. They don't ask men if they're married, single or divorced. They don't ask men how many children they have and what arrangements they make for childcare while they're at work, so why ask women? It's not right. What arrangements we make is up to us. We're not going to jeopardise our jobs by making inadequate arrangements so that we have to take time off work to look after them. What do they think grandparents are for? To sit at home all day and twiddle their thumbs? Not mine! My mother loves looking after my kids. And I told 'em to keep their noses out of my personal life and stick to matters concerning my professional capabilities and experiences.'

Audrey felt shattered. Her colour rose. Her cheeks went bright red. She felt her armpits emit body odour through the anti-perspiration spray she'd used that morning. Her hands felt clammy. Some vague reference had been made to children the first time she was in the room, but she couldn't remember what she'd said, then when they invited her to go back in a second time, she'd unwittingly referred to 'both' children going to school – thus informing them that she had two. Had that answer clinched the interview rather than her own teaching skills and qualifications?

She was embarrassed at her naivety and lack of knowledge about the political implications of the Act.

She drove home carefully to her family who greeted her warmly. She kissed and hugged them, aware that the twins may have been the reason why she'd been offered the job. She had less than half the children of the older woman, so may be less likely to take time off work to look after them if they were ill, and the graduate had been arrogant in her interview and spoken her mind vociferously, which might have upset some of the panel members.

Whether she'd been offered the job on her own merits, or on the downfall of the other candidates, she thought she'd never know, but she was delighted when the offer arrived in writing and she'd confirmed her acceptance.

It was with great misgivings that she handed in her notice at the university; she had loved working there, but she'd passed her teacher's certificate in office practice and her objective of being qualified to teach another subject had been achieved. She still wasn't a Ministry qualified teacher like Rocky, but she'd taken another step towards it.

CHAPTER 25

RED RAG

Although two years ago Audrey had worked at Clutterbuck Technical College for three years, teaching shorthand one evening a week, she didn't know the Head of Department. Her only contact with senior management had been the senior lecturer, Dudley Gornall, a local man. She'd heard rumours from evening school staff that the Head was an uncommunicative dour Manxman who had no sense of humour, and no people skills, and she'd been used to reading the notice board because that was his main method of communicating with staff.

On arrival the first morning in her new job she was surprised to find a memo pinned to the board calling a meeting for herself, and another new member of staff starting that day.

Audrey was the first to arrive at his office for the time stated. When she knocked on the door, she heard the Yale latch being released, and the door opened. Without smiling or showing any form of acknowledgement of seeing her at her interview, he gestured with his arm for her to be seated. She greeted him with a cheerful 'Good morning, Mr. Burke,' but as he stared at her blankly and made no response, she sat in silence, assessing his character from his outward appearance.

He was a short miserable looking man with a grey wrinkled face. His round bald head looked as if it had been polished, apart from a semicircle of fine white hair which spread from ear to ear above his collar line. He looked as if he was in his dotage, but she realised he couldn't be, otherwise he would have retired long ago. He wore a brown tweed suit, out of which he took a half-hunter from his top pocket, looked at the time, said 'Um!' and replaced it.

He shuffled some papers in silence. Audrey gazed around the room. It was sparse of furniture but had six grey filing cabinets, and he sat at a wide desk positioned in front of a window. He opened the top drawer, manoeuvred something inside it, then closed the drawer again.

Within a few minutes a young woman arrived. She greeted them both brightly, apologised for being late because she'd got lost, and gave a huge smile. Without looking at her his only words were:

'Be seated, Miss Jordan.'

Audrey returned the young woman's smile and immediately took to her. She was of a similar age and appearance. It was uncanny; apart from the colour of their hair they could have been sisters. Miss Jordan had dark hair, whereas hers was fair.

Mr Burke opened the drawer again. It sounded as if he had switched on a light, but no lights came on. He left the drawer slightly ajar and adjusted his spectacles, before explaining the procedures for enrolling students onto part-time day and evening courses offered by his department. He gave instruction sheets for the duties that the two new staff would be responsible for carrying out throughout the whole of the academic year. He didn't introduce them to each other; they only ascertained each other's surnames when they were included in an instruction.

'Here are the syllabuses which you will work from this year. You must draw up your own schemes of work and let me have a copy before the end of the week. And here are your timetables.'

Audrey looked at the top sheet of paper. It was covered with squares. The left-hand vertical column listed the days of the week. The other eight columns were headed with hourly periods from 9 am to 5 pm. She counted 24½ squares filled in with the letters SH TY and OP all of which were fairly evenly spread over the week. In the top left-hand corner of each square was a course number and in the bottom right, a room number. But in the first double period on a Tuesday were the letters GOD.

Ruby also perused her timetable. She saw that 20½ squares were filled with French. She was indignant.

'Why have I got nothing but French on my timetable? At my interview you said I would be teaching Spanish and German as well. Why I haven't got either of those? I told you I preferred Spanish.'

'Because they weren't offered in the prospectus before you were appointed, it's up to you to organise suitable courses for next year. Then you can teach them. I never said *when* you would be teaching them.'

'That's not fair. You gave the impression that I would be teaching them this year.'

'What I suggest is that you organise courses to be offered as evening classes. I'll offer them at enrolment and providing we get sufficient numbers you can teach them in the evenings.'

'I suppose that's better than no Spanish at all. But I'm very disappointed. That hasn't got us off to a good start has it? And what's this GOD the first two periods on my timetable on a Friday? Surely we don't have to teach religion do we? Because if we do, I'm not doing it.'

'No, no. In my department every full-time member of staff has to do a weekly routine task such as checking that all the textbooks are in the cupboards; counting up handouts and making them back up to full sets if any are missing; cleaning typewriters; making sure past exam papers are in order and so on. So the GOD slot on the timetable indicates General Office Duties. Mrs Driver, you will check the tape recorders each week, and all the shorthand speed tapes. Make sure they are in working order. If not, I need to know. You can record any problems here and put the sheet in my in-tray.'

He passed her a sheet of lined paper drawn into a table with columns headed 'make of recorder', 'place of location', 'fault' and 'tape/cassette number'.

'Thank you,' said Audrey meekly and put the sheet on top of her timetable.

'And you, Miss Jordan, will have to physically check that every classroom has an overhead projector in it, and that the light bulb in it is in working order.'

'I'm not going to check OHP's,' retorted Miss Jordan. 'I came here to teach language skills, not to count overhead projectors and their light bulbs.'

'Stay behind, Miss Jordan,' he said curtly, 'and we'll sort this out when Mrs Driver's gone.'

He dismissed Audrey and she went into the staff-room.

'Good morning, everyone, I'm Audrey Driver and I've just joined your full-time staff today.'

'Is it Miss or Mrs?' one member of staff asked. 'We don't use first names here.'

'It's Mrs, but I'd prefer to be called Audrey if that's all right. Surely between ourselves in the staff room we can call each other by our first names?'

'We can, as far as I'm concerned. I'm Paul Freeman.'

Another man responded:

'I don't think we should be so hasty. I'll stick to being called Mr Christian for the time being, if you don't mind.' He turned to Audrey.

'What subject have you come to teach?'

'Shorthand, typing and office practice.'

'Oh, coming to pass on your practical skills to other people?'

'Yes, I hope so.'

'Don't suppose you've got a degree then?'

'No, but I'm qualified to teach shorthand and office practice and I've taught typing in a private college before.'

'You don't need to justify your existence to me. You've been appointed, and that's good enough for me.'

At that moment a corpulent woman came in to the room. She was flamboyant in her attire and wore a ginger coloured wig that was held on above each ear with a row of five or six hair grips. The back of the wig had curled up and layers of mesh could be seen, making sections of it appear to be inside out. She held her head high above her buxom chest, shoulders back and gestured with her arms as if she was playing a leading lady in the theatre. She spoke in a precise manner, enunciating her words with clear diction. Turning to Audrey she said:

'Good morning.' I am Miss Toddy, Mr Burke's senior mistress. May I have your name for my staff register?'

'I'm Audrey Driver.'

'Oh, yes, you're the *assistant* lecturer, aren't you? Your new colleague is a lecturer!'

Audrey wasn't quick enough to think of an appropriate reply before the obese woman continued:

'Where is Miss Jordan? Has anyone seen her?'

'She's in with Mr Burke. They're talking about checking overhead projectors.'

'Have you physically seen her here today?'

'Yes.'

'I'll tick her off then.'

She opened her register and the two names were already typed into alphabetical order amongst the other staff names on the page.

'No need to tick her off,' Audrey muttered under her breath. 'The Head of Department's doing that already.'

True enough, the conflict of personalities was still taking place in Mr Burke's room. He was adamant that Miss Jordan would check, every week, that all the OHP's were in every classroom in his department, and she was equally adamant that she wouldn't.

'I wasn't appointed as a technician,' she argued. 'You appointed me to be a lecturer in charge of language skills, not a labourer, counting teaching aids. I'm not going to do it.'

'Oh, I think you will,' he answered firmly. 'I haven't been running this department for over thirty years to be told by one of my staff they're not going to comply with my instructions. I can get lecturers much more easily than I can get technicians. You *will* do it! Good day, Miss Jordan. That's all.'

'That's not all,' she stormed. 'I'll take it up with the Union.'

'Suit yourself, but you *will* check OHP's.'

Ruby Jordan left his office in a fury. She had been to university, got an excellent degree, spoke five languages fluently, had taught in schools and colleges both in this country and abroad and had never, ever, been instructed to check educational equipment on a weekly basis. She went into the staff room in a rebellious frame of mind.

'He's not going to get away with it,' she said to Audrey as she sat at the available desk next to her.

'Perhaps other departments' staff come and borrow them and forget to bring them back, or bring them back and they don't work.'

'That's not my problem! I shouldn't be doing that. I came here as a lecturer, with part-time staff to organise, courses to prepare, students to teach, not as a technician to check OHP's. I'm not going to do it.'

Audrey didn't know what else to say or do. She was so inexperienced. She left it to other staff in the room who were intrigued to ascertain what had happened.

That night Audrey related the incident to Rocky.

'You were right to stay out of it,' he advised. 'It's her concern, not yours. As for the dramatic Miss Toddy, do be careful. It sounds as if she could become your bête noir if you're not careful. Whatever you do, don't let her take over your mother's former frictional role now that you've brought her round and you're on a much smoother footing.'

'I'll try not to,' she said. 'Let's see what tomorrow brings.'

The remainder of the week ran fairly smoothly, everyone was engaged in enrolment procedures, and Audrey hardly saw her new colleague. However, very soon there was more trouble for Ruby Jordan.

One afternoon, in the first teaching week after enrolment, she arrived at her classroom and found sixty students waiting in the corridor for her arrival. She unlocked the classroom door and they could hardly get inside. They had to stand anywhere they could fit in. They had all come to learn various aspects of French.

A French man, called Monsieur D'Sainz, and a Spaniard called Señor Santana, both members of the part-time staff, had been timetabled for the same room as herself and were also present.

The three registers were labelled "French A-G"; "French H-P" and "French Q-Z" instead of "French Beginners" "French 'O' Level" and "French 'A' Level". Ruby was horrified. Surely the Head didn't expect each of them to teach all three levels in one room simultaneously?

She divided the students into three groups; those who had never done any French before; those who had done some French and wanted to study for 'O' level; and those who had passed 'O' level and wanted to progress to 'A' level. She assigned the complete beginners to Señor Santana and asked him to take his group to the college library and work quietly in there until she could be allocated another room for them. She left the 'O' level students with Monsieur D'Sainz in the room, and took the 'A' level students to the first empty classroom she could find. She made lists of names of people in the different groups, then went to the Head of Department's room to tell him what she'd done. But the door was locked and he didn't open it. She went to the staff room, angry and frustrated. One of the staff on general duties there told her that she would have to make an appointment to see him because he tape recorded all meetings, and he carried a miniature tape recorder in his pocket so that if anyone spoke to him outside of his room, he could activate it and record the conversation. He kept a record of everything.

'The man's mad,' she retorted. 'He's not just aloof, he's a recluse.'

'You're right,' said the colleague. He lives in a former woodcutter's cottage on the edge of Cannock Chase, miles away from everyone. There isn't another house anywhere near his. He likes complete privacy.'

Ruby was livid. She telephoned his secretary and made an appointment to see him later in the day. When she told him what she'd organised, and gave him the lists of groups of students, he was not at all pleased.

'Oh, no! You can't do that,' he objected.

'I've already done it.'

'Well you'll just have to undo it. We can't have that.'

'Why ever not?'

'Because we have to alphabetise them.'

'I don't understand. What do you mean?'

'When you're teaching a subject and there's more students than will fit on to one register you have to continue on another one, putting all the surnames into alphabetical order. It just happens that with your French students you need three registers.'

In horror, she exclaimed:

'That's ridiculous!' You can't homogenise language groups like that. You have to keep similar levels together. You can't teach conversation, 'O' and 'A' levels all together in three different groups with three different lecturers. Each level must be kept separate. The syllabuses and learning techniques are different at each level. You wouldn't put beginners, intermediate and advanced level typing students together in one classroom all at the same time.'

'Oh, I don't know! So long as they've got a typewriter each, and a textbook or past exam paper to work from, and a teacher to answer any questions, why not?'

'Because people need to be taught. A teacher needs to teach, to demonstrate, to guide, to explain, to encourage and to help. We don't all open a textbook and tell our students to read it for themselves.'

'Ah, but students need to learn. Their learning should be student-centred, not teacher-centred. You and your French team will just have to learn how to cope. My arrangements stay the way they are.'

'That's ridiculous!'

Ruby Jordan saw red. She was incensed by this man's lack of understanding and attitude and demanded to see the Principal.

'By all means,' said the Head in an inflexible tone. 'There's the phone. Pick it up and make an appointment.'

To add insult to injury, he quoted the internal number to be dialled to contact the Principal's secretary.

Ruby was shocked at his confidence to let her go over his head. He had the reputation of lacking social and people skills, so why was he agreeing to her demand? What was his game? What was he trying to do? He must be in the Principal's pocket, knowing that he would back him to the hilt. She hesitated slightly. Whilst she did so, he added:

'On your first day here I told you that if you had anything to say to me you had to put it in writing.

All these locked filing cabinets are full of memos from my staff, and my dated replies, so that I know what's been said for future reference. I'd be glad if you'd follow my instructions.'

'I haven't the time or the inclination to be a Paper God. I believe in sorting things out face to face.'

'That's your problem. You haven't any evidence of what we've said, but I have. I've got it all on tape, and my secretary will type it up tomorrow.'

Ruby's mouth fell open but before she could say anything he continued:

'Oh, and, by the way, that evening class in Spanish that you organised – I've appointed Señor Santana to take it.'

'But I wanted to take that class! I organised it for myself. Spanish is my speciality.'

'Well, it's too late now. I've offered the work to a member of my staff who's taught here for years. Spanish is his native language so he's the best person for the job.'

Ruby was furious. She grabbed the telephone receiver off its cradle.

'What did you say the Principal's secretary's number was?'

He repeated it, and she made an appointment for three days' time. That was the earliest appointment she could get.

CHAPTER 26

BLACK OUTCOMES

Ruby expected the Principal to be sympathetic and understanding to her problems. But he wasn't. He listened to her complaints in silence.

'I'm very sorry to hear you're unhappy. Mr Burke is my longest serving Head of Department. He is fully autonomous and I have complete confidence, faith and trust in the way he runs things in his department. I wouldn't like to add to your unhappiness by forcing you to stay, so if you are sure that you and he can't sort the problem out amicably together, then perhaps you'd like to consider offering your resignation?'

Ruby was appalled at his lack of conciliation and his blindness to see that the Office Skills Department wasn't running efficiently. On the spur of the moment she retorted:

'Don't worry. You've got it. Right now. I'll leave immediately.'

'You can't do that,' he replied. 'You have a contract. You must give a term's notice. The earliest you can leave is Christmas.'

'It can't come too soon,' she replied hostilely. She stormed back to the staff room and told everyone about her interview. Without hesitation she wrote out her resignation and handed it in to his secretary the same day.

In the weeks that followed Ruby applied for every modern languages lecturing post which was advertised nationally, irrespective of where it was in the country. She was invited to attend many interviews but wasn't successful. Every interview panel queried why she was leaving so soon after being appointed, and she kept saying it was because there was a personality conflict between herself and the Head of Department. They were all wary, and didn't offer her a job.

In the week preceding Christmas, Mr Burke asked her to reconsider her position.

'You haven't got a job to go to, and I haven't got anyone in charge of the modern languages section. Can't we call a truce? Are you prepared to withdraw your resignation and stay?'

'Are you prepared to withdraw your instruction for me to count OHP's?'

'Oh, no. I couldn't possibly do that.'

'Well, in that case, I couldn't possibly stay. I'm going.'

Ruby knew she was going anyway. She had no intention of staying. She couldn't understand some of his philosophies and would never have got on with him in a million years. She left at the end of the term without another job to go to.

Audrey felt sorry to see her colleague leave with such hatred in her heart. She had a bright, bubbly character, was full of fun and very amusing. Audrey and Ruby had got on very well during their term together. Each lunchtime they went to a local café for coffee and a cream cake and caught up with each other's classroom experiences.

Ruby had told stories in the staff room that made everyone roll with laughter at her antics. The problem was, that she was the exact opposite of the Head of Department. He lacked communication skills and put notices on a notice board rather than speak to staff directly; she was a good communicator, ebullient, and outgoing. It was such a pity that they didn't get on.

With the departure of Ruby Jordan things changed considerably. There were no applicants for the full-time vacancy so the Head of Department appointed a part-time lecturer to teach French. She'd been born in Paris to a French mother and an Italian father, and had been brought up in France. In her early twenties she had married a 'Black Country' man and settled in Wolverhampton where they had run their own small private language and translation school until her husband's death five years ago. She had since sold the business, re-married, and after her second husband's death, lived alone.

Vesuvius Franks had been named after the volcano in the country where her father had been born, but her name didn't describe her nature. She was delightful, charming, captivating, elegant, tall, slender, chic. Her appearance belied her age. Her charisma and appearance gave the impression she was in her mid forties, but she told some staff she was sixty-nine. Because there was a college rule that visiting tutors could only work there until their seventieth birthday, her time in the department was limited. All the staff and students who encountered her were captivated by her charm elegance, and élan.

One class of twenty teenage police cadets recruited on a part-time day-release course from the local constabulary idolised her.

When she entered the room they stood up and cheered. She would smile and gesture for them to sit down, as she greeted them in French.

'Bonjour mes amis. Asseyes-vous s'il vous plait,' to which they would respond:

'Bonjour Madame, merci beaucoup' or 'merci bien.'

They worked like Trojans to please her, and competed for top marks in their class and homework exercises. She had a talent for knowing how to handle people and get the best out of them. Her students adored her and achieved well.

On the days when Vesuvius came to college she sat in the vacant desk next to Audrey, which Ruby had occupied. She was also a fantastic cook and occasionally, for lunch, she would bring a spinach and cheese flan which she'd made at home, and offer a slice to her colleagues in the room. It was delicious, and so different from the squashy cream cakes which Audrey and Ruby had devoured in their lunch hours, in the false hope that comfort eating would help to alleviate Ruby's hatred of the Head.

One lunch time when they were enjoying a slice of cottage cheese pie as only the French can make them, Vesuvius asked:

'Why don't you apply for part-time day release with full pay, to go on a teacher training course to become Ministry qualified?'

'I didn't know such a thing was possible.'

'Of course it is. The Head won't tell anyone about it because he'll have to find substitute lecturers for the days his staff are on the course, and it will cost him money to pay them. But it's your right. You're entitled to go if you want to. We put quite a few people through to Ministry qualified status when we ran our school and we, and our students, benefited as well as our teachers.'

She smiled in such a charming and encouraging manner that Audrey knew she would enquire at a later date whether she'd taken up her suggestion.

'I don't know how to go about applying.'

'I'll help you. First of all you approach the training college of your choice and ascertain whether they'll accept you. If they will, you write a letter to the Chairman of the Board of Governors with a copy to your Head of Department, and ask him to present your case for you. That way you are involving him, and he can hardly refuse as it will enhance the qualifications of his staff and look good in the prospectus. If the governors agree, you're on your way to becoming a Ministry qualified teacher.'

So Audrey applied.

In due course her application was considered, and approved, to commence in September of the following year.

In the last week of the academic year Dudley Gornall, the senior lecturer, called a staff meeting at which he announced that he had been appointed to a Head of Department post at a nearby college. Everyone congratulated him. He was a nice man and they would be sorry to see him go.

He also announced that Vesuvius's part-time contract had drawn to an end and she wouldn't be able to come back because of her age. A full-time replacement lecturer had been found to replace her. He thanked everyone for their work in the department and proposed that the staff should hold an end of year celebration one lunch hour in a nearby pub. Miss Toddy was aghast at the suggestion. Mr Burke had not attended the meeting but she felt sure he would not approve and swayed the staff to oppose the idea.

Audrey decided that if the staff weren't going to celebrate Dudley's promotion, she'd do something herself. Both he, and Vesuvius, had been helpful to her. She decided to buy a bouquet of flowers for Vesuvius, but felt she could hardly give a man flowers. Then she had a thought. That night she looked in her pantry and took out a couple of bags of flour – plain, and self-raising; and a packet of cornflour. She put them in a basket and decided that on their last day of service she would buy a cauliflower to add to the items when she bought the flowers for Vesuvius. She knew that Dudley had a sweet tooth, so she would also buy a tin of toffees and hide them under a congratulatory leaving card.

They were surprised, but pleased when she gave them their flowers/flours and they said their goodbyes over a cup of tea in the staff room. She was sad to think she may never see either of them again.

The replacement senior lecturer, Guy Stirrer, was a slick, quick Londoner; an opportunist. He was ruthless. He was rude. He trod on many people's toes. He was disliked by the department's existing staff, two-thirds of whom were nearing the end of their working lives and were set in their ways. He ran circles around Mr Burke who put up many fights, but wasn't always supported by the Principal, as he had been in the past. It seemed as if the Principal was time-serving until his retirement, and wanted a quiet life, so he gave in to the new man's energetic efforts to lift the department out of its moribund state.

New and ambitious courses were offered. The complement of staff doubled and another staff room had to be found to accommodate the increased numbers, but there was no modern technology in the department. Students were still learning comptometer operating skills, and how to touch-type on antiquated typewriters with the letters on the keyboards painted out with black gloss paint.

Miss Toddy, the Head of Department's Senior Mistress, as she called herself, refused to authorise the purchase of new equipment or new textbooks. She said that the ones the department had used over the years were perfectly satisfactory and there was no point in wasting public money when it wasn't necessary.

Audrey argued that it was necessary; the college was behind the times as far as new technology was concerned. There were now Varitypewriters which could justify right-hand margins, and technology was improving at an exponential rate every day. She won her case. Guy Stirrer overruled Miss Toddy and the college acquired a roomful of new, up-to-date *manual* typewriters, and a new set of the old out-of-date typing textbooks. Audrey was furious. To her, *that* was a waste of public money. She was even more angry when Mr Burke instructed Miss Toddy to paint out the letters on the new keyboards. His argument was that if letters of the alphabet, and numbers could be seen, students would look at the keyboard, and not touch-type. Audrey argued that their students were being disadvantaged because every other college in the country would have letters on their keyboards, and now that a figure 1 was included on the top row, instead of using a lower-case L to represent the figure one, and a capital letter o to represent the figure nought, some of the characters, such as a pound sign and a question mark, were above different figure keys.

Audrey's argument carried no weight. Mr Burke was adamant. Miss Toddy stayed late one evening, and put her artistic flair to her paintbrush strokes and blackened out all the keys on the new typewriters.

CHAPTER 27

ENHANCEMENTS

The following academic year was a momentous one for Audrey. First of all, it was the year she entered teacher training college, and was allocated a Ministry number. Secondly, it was the year of the Houghton Report which recommended new salary scales for further education staff. When decimalisation came in, during 1971, prices in the shops had doubled over night. The Government had decided that something needed to be done about teaching and lecturing salaries to keep abreast of rising prices.

Taking into consideration all her previous business employment and part-time teaching experience, Audrey had been appointed as an assistant lecturer two years earlier on a salary scale of £1,315, rising to £2,242 per annum over a period of sixteen years. That was far higher than Rocky had anticipated earning at the height of his career. Now Houghton recommended abolishing that scale and assimilating the salaries into the lecturers' gradation. Assistant lecturers would move up two rungs on their existing scale, and be moved across to the nearest incremental point above it on the lecturer's grade.

That meant a huge rise on to point two for Audrey, giving her a new recommended salary of

£2,121 per annum. The report was ratified by the Burnham Committee; thus she was converted into a fully fledged lecturer.

The start of the following September also brought educational changes to the whole of the Driver family. Rocky had been studying on a part-time evening course concomitantly with his full-time teaching job, and was awarded a BEd(Hons) degree. His efforts were rewarded when he moved to another boys' school, still in the Midlands, as Head of a larger science department, on a higher salaried post. The twins were also allocated places in grammar schools.

One evening at the start of the new term, Audrey answered the telephone at home and was surprised to hear the voice of Ruby Jordan. She was phoning to say that at long last she had secured another teaching post – in Wales – teaching 'A' level Spanish full-time, and was loving every minute of it. The college had a young, progressive Head of the Modern Languages Department with whom she got on very well, a superb language lab with up-to-date equipment and facilities and not one, but two technicians to service it. Their duties also included checking that OHP's were in working order! She was ecstatic.

They spoke for over an hour. Audrey obtained Ruby's new address and telephone number, and they promised to keep in touch for ever.

That Christmas, Audrey and Rocky received a typed letter in a Christmas card from Den and Lil. It related how Den had retired and they had bought a large old house with three acres of land, in Hampshsire. Lil had resigned from her post at Chestnut Grove School and they had converted the house into a private languages school and called it Barbey Lodge for Learners of the English Language. They had converted six of the rooms into classrooms, and were in the process of extending a large car park in the grounds.

The school had been running for one term and had been successful so far. Den was the Principal and specialised in teaching 'O' and 'A' level English courses and Lil was the Deputy Head in charge of running the establishment and teaching English as a Second Language. The latter courses were much in demand from people who came from the Continent.

Rocky and Audrey were delighted to receive their news, and wrote back congratulating them on their successful venture.

Later that week they received a large Christmas card postmarked New Zealand. Candy's huge handwriting covered virtually the whole of the inside, and the back of it. Vic had resigned and they had emigrated earlier in the year, with their three boys. Audrey and Rocky had already sent a card to their old address in England, so in case it wasn't forwarded, Audrey wrote a letter and enclosed it in another card and posted it to their new address half way around the world.

* * * * *

Day-release sessions at the teacher training college were very interesting and informative, but the one day's attendance came and went so rapidly that the part-time two-year course slipped by practically unnoticed in the Driver household.

At the end of it, Audrey was awarded a Certificate of Education with a Distinction in practical teaching ability. Guy Stirrer congratulated her and said it would be nice to put the letters Cert.Ed. after her name in the prospectus. She told him that she already had the letters P.S.Dip. after her name but they were never included because they indicated a secretarial qualification rather than a teaching one. He became interested in what those letters stood for and how she had achieved them.

A few days later she received a memo from the Head of Department making an appointment for her to see him. When she got there, Guy Stirrer was already in the room with him. As a result of that meeting, she was asked to set up, organise, and run a Private Secretary's Diploma course for two evenings a week, on a one year basis for the following academic year.

She felt she needed to be loyal to the college that had paid for her training, and agreed to take on the work of being the course tutor and teach three of the subjects in three one-hour sessions from 6-9 pm on one evening a week, if they would agree to appoint another member of staff to teach English, and Management Appreciation, on another evening. Mr Burke and Guy Stirrer agreed to her request.

So started the most interesting job she'd ever had. She went into industry recruiting students from leading organisations, creaming off their top secretaries on to the course and because it was top level work, she was allowed to run the sessions with twelve students.

The course was a great success and all the participants passed their examinations at the end of their studies.

Audrey felt proud of everyone's magnificent achievements. Without exception, it had been a very rewarding era of her life. To go from being a shorthand-typist, to becoming a lecturer, successfully teaching top secretaries and seeing them achieve so well, raised her confidence and self-esteem. She felt as if she was at the height of her career. And all this had stemmed from marrying Rocky.

At the end of the course Audrey received a letter from the local authority stating that she had been promoted from a lecturer grade I, to a lecturer grade I. She didn't understand, and thought there must be a typing error. She made an appointment to see the Head of Department about it.

'That's quite right,' he confirmed. 'Previously you were a "converted" lecturer through the Houghton Report. Since your success this year with the Private Secretary's Diploma course I'm promoting you to be an "appointed" lecturer, so you'll go up two rungs on the same salary scale.'

Audrey thought that going up on the same scale was a very odd thing to do but gratefully accepted the promotion. With the additional money, she and her family were able to go to York to visit her parents much more regularly. She kept an eye on their health and they looked forward to her visits.

Since moving into their own home Mrs Small had become more content and her former outbursts had stopped. Everything in the garden was lovely.

* * * * *

The sweet smell of success with the Private Secretary's Diploma course was short-lived. Audrey thought that the senior managers would be pleased with the results, and they were, but she hadn't realised it would bring jealousy from other members of staff. The next course to be offered was entered in the prospectus with Miss Toddy as the course administrator.

Audrey requested the Head of Department to clarify where she stood. He granted her an interview and explained that some people had complained that a basic lecturer should not be heading such a prestigious course. They considered it should have the support of a top manager. So in the prospectus he had named Miss Toddy as the course administrator but had instructed her to delegate all the work and running of the course to Audrey. Things would remain exactly as they were as far as he was concerned and he hoped she would have another successful year.

Audrey was disenchanted with his explanation. *She* wanted to be named as the course administrator. She had done all the donkey work and wanted to be acknowledged for it, not the theatrical Miss Toddy. She was very angry and felt miffed.

Mr Burke was adamant. He pointed out that she had already been promoted from being a "converted" lecturer to the higher grade scale so he couldn't upgrade her again and the entry in the prospectus must stand. Either she could do the work, or he would appoint another lecturer to do it. Audrey asked for a day or two to think about it.

When she got home and discussed the matter with Rocky, his advice was not to cut off her nose to spite her face. As she loved teaching the higher grade work he thought she should continue with it and bear no antipathy towards Miss Toddy; it wasn't her fault that she'd been named the course administrator, and Audrey must not resent her authority – she must be thoroughly professional. So Audrey recruited more secretaries from industry and ran the course for a second year, but with even more aversion to her melodramatic senior than before.

Some of the top secretaries said that Audrey should be acknowledged for running the course and all the hard work she'd put into it. In industry there were such things as appraisal schemes and her expertise would be recognised; but she'd never heard of one occurring in the college.

Towards the end of the summer holidays when the examination results were issued, once more Audrey's Private Secretary's Diploma candidates had achieved 100% pass rate. Miss Toddy, in her role of course administrator was benevolent with goodwill. She decided to go out and buy a congratulations card and post it to Audrey to show there was no animosity on her part.

In her flamboyant and irrepressible way, that lunchtime, she went to the shops to make her purchase. Coming back to her parked car, she had to wait to cross the road because there was a long flow of traffic. She was hungry, and wanted to get home to feed her cats.

'Come on, come on, or I'll be late,' she shouted at the car drivers, and flailed her arms at the line of traffic, urging slow-moving vehicles to hurry along.

When she saw a gap between two oncoming cars that was big enough for her to cross the road she darted between them, only to fall over a tow-rope that was joining the two cars together. The second car driver braked hard. The tow-rope snapped. Miss Toddy, clutching the card she'd just bought, really was late home to feed her cats that day! She became the late Miss Toddy.

When word got around the college, everyone was stunned. Photographs and articles about her life appeared in the local papers. It was a very sudden and bizarre ending to the dramatic role she'd played in life. People couldn't understand why she hadn't seen the notice "Towing" in the windscreen, but in all her face-powder, make-up and wig, she probably hadn't been wearing her glasses in the street.

Guy Stirrer took on all her administrative duties and in so doing, got himself upgraded to Deputy Head of Department. It was his name that replaced Miss Toddy's as the course administrator in the next prospectus.

CHAPTER 28

FUTILE ATTEMPTS

Audrey came in for a lot of flak after Miss Toddy's demise. Some people said if it hadn't been for the Private Secretaries' successful results, Miss Toddy would still be alive. Others said it was a pity that Audrey and Miss Toddy hadn't got on better over the years; and Mr Burke instructed Guy Stirrer not to offer the course again, despite it having been advertised in the prospectus.

Audrey was devastated and felt guilt-ridden. Rocky assured her that it was not her fault the accident had occurred; but she was distressed at the loss of a colleague, even if she didn't particularly like her, but more at the loss of her prestigious secretarial course.

With extra time on her hands in the evenings, Audrey decided to follow in Rocky's shoes and embarked on a similar BEd(Hons) course to the one he had undertaken and passed. Instead of doing science as supplementary subjects to Education, she undertook to do English language and English literature instead.

One evening when she was attending the course, one of her peer group told her about an advertisement in a national newspaper and asked if she was going to apply for it. Audrey knew nothing about it. Her friend explained that it was for a lecturer grade II at Clutterbuck Technical College, to organise and run secretarial courses in the department.

'That's odd,' she said. 'I've never seen anything on the notice board, or heard anything about it.'

'Well, go to the college office and ask for details. They can hardly refuse you. If they do, I'll go and get one for you.'

'No need for that. I'll go myself.'

The next day she obtained an information pack and was interested to read that the job was for a lecturer grade II to be in charge over all the secretarial courses in the department, to develop and create new courses, and to be involved in the appointment of new staff to the secretarial section.

The application form had to be completed in black ink or typed. After carefully drafting an application she decided to type it on her portable typewriter at home but as she inserted the printed form between the rollers, it was so thick with double-sided pages being folded over, it caught on the paper bails and ripped. The next day Audrey went to the college office and asked for another application form, saying that she'd ruined the previous one. She was given another pack. When she got home, she discovered that the job specification was totally different from the first. She compared the two job specs side by side.

The second was to assist another lecturer grade II with the running of the secretarial section and to order goods, and maintain departmental records. Quite clearly there were two separate jobs, but only one had been advertised. Being confused, she didn't complete the form, and got an appointment to see the Head of Department the following morning.

'Is there one job, or two?' she asked.

'There's only one job.'

'So why are there two entirely different job specifications?'

'The first was an error. It was a draft of what I thought we wanted, but it had to be re-typed.'

'So all the people that apply for the first one are applying for the wrong job? Surely it will affect how they present their experience?'

'Not necessarily. We'll consider all the applications on their merits.'

'But some people may not know about there being two different job specifications. It takes a long time to complete an application, and decide how best to present your experience. There's a vast difference between leading and assisting. That's not fair.'

'Nothing is fair in this world, Mrs Driver. If it was, we'd all be born at the same time, live in the same type of houses, drive the same type of car, and die at the same time. Life isn't like that. Anyway, it's not up to me, it's up to the interview panel.'

'But you'll be on the interview panel, and the other panellists are likely to be influenced by what you say because you're the Head of Department.'

'That's enough, Mrs Driver. Apply if you want to, but there's no guarantee that you'll even be called for an interview. I've already promoted you once; you're not likely to be promoted a second time.'

Audrey felt as if she'd been slapped in the face.

Mr Burke had already made up his mind that she had no chance of even being invited to attend for an interview. However, she decided to stand up to him and put in an application anyway, but she could understand why Ruby Jordan had felt so exasperated in coping with his inflexibility.

Six applicants were interviewed but no-one on the existing staff was included. Two men were appointed to bring fresh blood and new ideas into the department, to commence their duties the following Easter.

Audrey felt dejected. She knew in her heart of hearts that she didn't have a chance, otherwise the jobs would have been advertised internally so that she, and other colleagues, could also have had an opportunity to apply. But the jobs had been kept secret from existing staff.

A few months later Audrey saw an advertisement in an evening paper for a lecturer grade II required to be in charge of office skills, in the secretarial section of a large technical college in the region.

'That's interesting,' she said to Rocky. 'I think I'd like to apply for that job. Will you go with me, and we'll have a look at the area?'

The teenagers stayed at home to do their homework while Rocky drove Audrey to a seriously deprived region of the Midlands.

'Wait here while I go in and ask if I can have a look around. I don't want to waste my time, or theirs, in applying for a job I couldn't do or didn't want.'

The young woman in the reception office seemed to be impressed that Audrey had taken the time and trouble to find out what she could about the college and escorted her around the office skills section and let her peep through the windows of the locked doors so that she could peer into the classrooms and see the equipment in them.

For all its age, and its Victoriana, which she hated, it seemed a clean and a reasonable environment in which to work. She returned to the car.

'I think I will apply,' she said. 'Hopefully there won't be the same type of fiasco as there was in last job I applied for. There's no guarantee that I'll get an interview here either, but as that Inspector said years ago, it's not good for a teacher to stay too long in one establishment. *I* feel stale now. It's time to move on, so at least I'll have a try.'

At her current college, educational changes were taking place at a rapid pace. Audrey found herself faced with a new challenge.

She was given a timetable which had no shorthand on it at all. Guy Stirrer said shorthand was becoming outdated and audio was the 'in' subject. Office practice was re-named as 'secretarial duties' and her timetable included teaching three periods of IMPENG each week. She looked at the timetable in amazement. No-one in the staff room knew anything about the subject, so once more, she approached the Head of Department with a query.

'It's a new idea' he explained. 'It came up at Academic Board when we were discussing ways of raising college finances. It's a short course backed by the Government to help non-English speakers to settle in Britain. If it's successful we'll run end-on courses, both in term time and all through the summer holidays. The idea is that foreign students learn English using a typewriter. As they tap the keys, they say the letter out loud and that will help the sound and position of the key to sink in. Your job will be to teach them the alphabet, and devise some very simple exercises for them to practise. As you're doing English on your degree course, and you teach touch-typing, I thought you were the best person for the job.'

'If they're all foreigners and they can't speak English how am I going to make them understand what I'm saying?'

'The course tutor is called Mr Prakesh Vishuaremi. He has been timetabled to be in the room with you. He speaks six different Indian languages as well as English and he will introduce you and translate everything you say.'

'Is there a syllabus for this?'

'No. You just have to do the best you can. With all your experience, I think you'll make a good job of it and it will be a change from anything you've ever done before.'

'So what does IMPENG mean?'

'It's just the abbreviation I've used. The course is called Impressive English. IMP for IMPressive and ENG for ENGlish.'

'And what about the typewriter keys that had their letters painted out by Miss Toddy? *These* students will have to see where to put their fingers if they're to learn the alphabet first, rather than the usual method of teaching home row keys. They'll have enough to cope with without facing blank keyboards!'

'Perhaps you could make some sticky labels and stick them on at the start of each lesson, and remove them at the end?'

Audrey found it incredible that after being in his job for over thirty years, he still lacked understanding of teaching skills subjects, and held such antiquated ideas.

Thus Audrey found herself faced with a class of fourteen students of different races. The majority were from the Indian sub-continent, but there were two Chinese girls, one of whom spoke English fluently but wanted to learn to type and asked if she could join the class. The other girl could speak a little English but because she'd read books in English, she could understand more things if they were written down and there was a little Bangladeshi boy who looked as if he was only nine or ten years old, yet he had to be sixteen to be admitted to the college.

The Indian boys were recalcitrant. They didn't want to be taught by a woman, and made little effort to learn. Together with the help of the course tutor, discipline was maintained, but Audrey didn't make much progress educationally. She thought about Lil. If she enjoyed teaching English as a Second Language courses, it couldn't be so bad; she'd just have to change tactics.

At her next lesson, the little Bangladeshi boy was difficult to cope with. He didn't understand anything she said.

She pointed to the first key on the left-hand side of the home row on the typewriter keyboard.

'That is A' she said clearly and distinctly 'You say A.'

Prakesh instructed him in a foreign tongue, to which the boy replied:

'Iz Ay.'

'Excellent. Now tap the key and say A again.'

'Iz Ay.'

'Well done.'

She pointed to a key on the bottom row.

'This is the letter B,' she said slowly.

'Iz Ay.'

'No, that was A. This is the letter B. Say the word "bee" to me.'

'Iz Ay.'

Prakesh explained to the boy again, but his efforts were futile. Audrey thought that after teaching top flight secretaries for two years, this was hard work.

One of the Chinese girls, Tang Li An, put up her hand, then spoke to the other Chinese girl in her own language and seemed to be satisfied with the answer given. Audrey didn't understand a word they said to each other, so she could see how difficult it was for the students to understand her.

At the next lesson, again, the Indian boys made little effort to progress.

That night Audrey discussed her problem with Rocky. He'd had experience of teaching several nationalities in his work. He said that in his opinion, a lot of Indian men had no respect for women.

They treated them as second-class citizens and she may have found herself teaching boys with similar attitudes. She needed to make them work very hard indeed, because the Indian race was known to produce diligent workers and those who came to this country usually worked hard and long hours in business enterprises. His advice was to allocate them twice as much work as anyone else in the class and expect it to be completed in the same amount of time.

'Driver by name, driver by nature. Crack the whip and keep them working. They'll respect you for it in the end.'

'I do hope that I can get that other job to go to,' she sighed. 'I feel so inadequate when I can't get through to these students. Standards of admission seem to have dropped to an all-time low when the students we accept can't even speak our English language. Teaching shorthand, typing and secretarial duties is an absolute doddle compared to this.'

'Remember, love, that a lot of money is riding on the admissions. The college has to prove that their courses are full in order to justify keeping the government finance that comes in, otherwise they might get less money in the future.'

'Well, I hope that things will improve because I hate taking this class. There's no wonder you hear of teachers leaving the profession. It isn't worth thinking about.'

CHAPTER 29

A NEW CHALLENGE

On the first day as a lecturer grade II in her new job at Stellar Technical College, Audrey got a shock. She couldn't park her car outside the college – the streets were already full of parked vehicles – and there was no car park nearby. After driving twenty miles to work she had to drive around rows of terraced properties looking for a vacant kerbside space. She eventually found one four streets away. As she walked back to the college she observed pats of catarrh glistening on the old, uneven, paving slabs and had to be careful where she put her feet. She asked herself:

'What *have* I done?'

She hadn't noticed these when Rocky had taken her to see whether she wanted to apply for the job or not, because he'd parked his car right outside the entrance to the building in the evening when all the day students and staff had gone home.

Once inside, the atmosphere was warm. She was welcomed, shown to the staff room and introduced to everyone. She was given so much work to do, she didn't have time to think about the environment outside.

Gloria Greene, the Senior Lecturer in charge of the secretarial section was beautiful. Her dark hair was sleek and coiffured. She dressed immaculately and ran her section with aplomb. She was cute, and sometimes devious, but all her staff respected her.

Gloria was a forthright character who didn't suffer fools gladly. In her mid-fifties, she looked a good ten years younger. She knew what she wanted for her section, and achieved it. There was no forcing lecturers to use old-fashioned typing textbooks because they'd always used them. She was progressive, outgoing and keen for all her students and staff to achieve well.

Jemima Welsh, normally referred to as Jemma, The Head of the Maths, English, General And Secretarial Department over her was another caring, capable manager. She had authority, dignity and bearing, and was affectionately referred to by male members of staff as a 'Mega Star' while her department was frequently referred to as the MEGAS department, an acronym from the initial letters of all the sections under her. She was a good listener, sensitive to the needs of people, and a very successful entrepreneur and negotiator.

At the interview, Audrey had been impressed by both Jemma and Gloria, and although she knew that if she was offered the job she'd be moving into a more deprived area than her present post, she knew it was the right time to move.

After her successful interview she appreciated being given the opportunity to work with a different set of people who had a more positive approach to education.

Stellar Technical College had an excellent reputation and at enrolment time people of all ages over sixteen queued at the door to be admitted on to one of the many full-time and part-time courses offered.

Over the years, Gloria had devised an entrance test in English to ensure that prospective candidates for her subject areas could understand the English language adequately, and they had to achieve a high pass mark before they could be offered a place on a full-time shorthand-typing course.

Once a month Gloria changed the questions so that people who'd already taken a test couldn't pass on information to later interviewees.

At ten o'clock on her first morning Audrey was given twelve test papers containing twenty multiple choice questions for the English exam and was asked to take a group of teenagers into a classroom, conduct the test, mark the answers, and retain those applicants who had passed, to wait for a personal interview. She looked at the list of names accompanying the papers. It read as follows: Merlyn Ambrose, Pauline Hall, Jaswinder Kaur (5 times) Jayshree Patel (twice) Violet Marshall, Pansy Walsh, and Xia Zhang.

'How do you identify the five Jaswinder Kaur's and the two Jayshree Patels? she asked. Do you number them or give them letters of the alphabet after their names?'

'Neither,' came the reply. 'You have to get them to tell you their family name. They won't admit they have one, but they do, and we have to ascertain it for our records, otherwise it would be impossible to know which test paper belonged to which girl.'

'And what if they are related and their family names are the same?'

'Then you have to ask them to write their date of birth as well and make a note of it on your attendance sheet. It's unlikely that two applicants with the same first, family, and surname, will have been born on exactly the same date.'

Gloria peered over the top of her half-lens reading glasses. Her penetratingly green eyes questioned Audrey's naïvety. She frowned and continued:

'Most of the applicants are second or third generation British, and speak good English, but we have to be sure. Even the West Indians, like Violet and Pansy, were probably born here. I've no idea about the Chinese girl, although her writing on the application form is neat and legible, and she gives an address in the Midlands, so she won't have to pay the fees that a foreign student would incur.'

Audrey gathered up a few pencils in case anyone forgot to bring one and went to a small waiting room where the applicants were seated. She smiled at the girls.

'Good morning, everyone. My name is Mrs Driver. Please come with me to a classroom where it will be more comfortable for you to write.'

She glanced around the waiting room. Among the faces there, she immediately recognised the Chinese girl, Tang Li An, whom she had taught on the IMPENG course at her last college and who was the only one in that group who had been able to speak reasonably fluent English.

'Hello, Li An,' she said in a surprised tone. 'Fancy seeing you here.' The girl shook.

'Oh, Mrs Driver! What are you doing here?' Her lips quivered and she looked startled.

'It's my first day in a new job. I've just started here this morning. What are you doing here? Have you come to take a test for a place on one of our courses?'

'I not know.' The girl looked agitated and distressed. Audrey checked her list of names again.

'Well, you're not on my list, perhaps you're on Mrs Greene's. She's testing some applicants tomorrow. Perhaps you've got the date wrong?'

The girl gulped noisily, shrugged her shoulders, looked embarrassed, and repeated:

'I not know.'

'I'll just let Mrs Greene know you're here.'

'It okay. I come back later.' The girl got up and pushed past her, then Audrey heard footsteps running down the corridor.

'What an amazing coincidence,' she thought, but didn't have time to follow her.

Audrey took the remainder of the group to a nearby classroom. When they were seated she called their names from the typed list and made a note of the relevant details requested by Gloria. There was one absentee, Xia Zhang.

Half an hour later, Gloria came into the room to see how the candidates were progressing. Most girls had finished, and were sitting quietly, but one girl was still writing. Audrey passed the papers to her that she'd already marked. Gloria glanced at the results as she flicked through them.

'These are all right,' she commented. 'Please stop writing now.' She turned to Audrey and said:

'Mark this last paper please, Mrs Driver, then bring it to my office. Girls, you all come with me.'

She took the prospective students with her and Audrey followed them a few minutes later.

After short interviews, successful applicants were offered places on courses to commence the following September.

After everyone had gone, Audrey commented about the coincidence of meeting an ex-student from her last college, and how surprised the girl had been to see her there, and had fled.

'I have no application from anyone called Tang Li An so I can't contact her, but I'll write to Xia Zhang at the address given on her application form and ask why she didn't come to take the test. In the meanwhile we've plenty of other work to get on with. We've just time to have a cup of tea and a sandwich before going to a meeting with Jemma Welsh this afternoon.'

Audrey's previous Head of Department had been autonomous and ran his department like an autocrat. In comparison, this Head of Department had a reputation for delegating responsibilities to her staff, and supporting them in their endeavours. If they did the job to her satisfaction they were praised and encouraged to keep up the good work; if they needed help she guided them along the right path; and if they displeased her in their work she discussed the problem with them privately in her room.

Jemma Welsh's personality was lively and bright. She explained how she and Gloria were looking into the purchase of a new piece of equipment called a dedicated word processor. Audrey had never heard of it. She was shown pictures of a large machine with a television-type screen called a visual display unit or VDU for short, a typewriter-looking keyboard with two additional banks of keys on it and a wide row of function keys across the top. On the right-hand side, underneath the work surface, there was a huge cupboard with two slots in the front, into which two eight-inch floppy disks were inserted and she was told it also contained the 'works' which were referred to technically as a central processing unit, or CPU. On the surface above the CPU where the VDU stood there was also a printer which was capable of printing in black and red ink. Everything was plugged together with electric leads and the machine had to be plugged into a wall socket and switched on.

The word processor cost £9,000. Audrey could hardly believe it – the piece of equipment cost about the same price as two semi-detached houses in the area!

Jemma explained that the Principal had managed to raise funding for £8,500 so they were going to try and get one by asking for a substantial educational discount. She was convinced it was a tool of the future and wanted to give her students the best possible job opportunities when they completed their courses by saying that they could operate one when they went for interviews. She wanted Gloria and Audrey to go and assess the machine and if they approved it, she intended having one at the back of the typing classroom. If they bought one, it would be Audrey's job to teach students and some of the staff how to operate it.

Arrangements were made for Gloria and Audrey to go the following week and see one demonstrated.

Although they had television sets at home, neither of them had seen a visual display unit linked to a typewriter keyboard, nor a flashing cursor showing the position of the next character to be input, and they were amazed to see that when a file was opened the margins were already pre-set and it was ready for immediate use.

At first word wrap-around was unusual to get to grips with because it was a natural reaction to lift the left hand off the keyboard to strike a carriage return lever on a manual typewriter, but on this machine, the computer automatically put the text on to the next line. So, being touch typists, they found the typing technique very much quicker.

Typing errors were easy to correct. If they realised they'd made a mistake they could obliterate it immediately by striking the backspace key. If they found the mistake later, the cursor could be taken back to the error by using the compass rose keys to locate it. A delete key could be tapped to remove an error to the right, and the backspace key could be used to remove errors to the left of the cursor position. There was no rubbing out to be done, or using correcting fluid to paint out the mistake.

Cut and paste techniques were innovative, as was the decimal tab facility, mailmerge, tracing editing changes, centring, printing in italics, bold, red, and so many other operations. They were overwhelmed with the machine's capabilities.

'Will this word processor work all day long, once it is set up, because we want to use it in night-school as well as in the day time?'

'Yes, if you don't switch the machine off. But you'll have to take great care of the disks when you change them. They're very fragile and they mustn't get bent, or wet, and you mustn't put them near anything magnetic.'

As Gloria had been given the authority to purchase the word processor if they approved it, she decided to place an order for one there and then.

'Bring the price down to eight thousand pounds or less, and we'll have one,' she said, allowing herself £500 manoeuvrability.

'We can't bring it down that much, because it costs so much to produce,' said the salesman.

'Oh, yes you can!' she exclaimed. I want a substantial educational discount.'

'I'll have to get the manager's approval.'

'Fine. Get the highest amount off it that you can, otherwise there's no sale. Our maximum price is £8,000.'

The manager joined the group and after lengthy discussion and a calculation of prices, the sum of £8,000 was agreed.

When the demonstrator explained what she was doing, Audrey had taken notes in shorthand,

and when she got back to college, she typed her transcription on to wax stencils and duplicated sufficient copies for all the staff because eventually they would all be teaching students how to use the new equipment.

When the word processor arrived Audrey was given the immediate task of teaching the Deputy Head of Department the various processing techniques. He took to the new technology like a duck to water and taught members of the entire department's staff how to use it.

Gloria decided to double-timetable staff so that while one lecturer was teaching typing skills, Audrey would be teaching word processing in the same room at the same time.

The new venture was time-tabled to commence with a group of mature adult students who were of West Indian and Caribbean ancestry. Gloria thought that it would be a good idea to teach two students at a time, allocating them half an hour per pair; that way Audrey could repeat the session three more times in a double period. But because the students had just started on a beginners' typing course none of them had learnt how to touch-type and they were not familiar with the position of the letters on the keyboard, so the first lesson was an introduction to word processing to familiarise them with the equipment and some of the very simple functions.

For the second lesson Audrey had already keyed in a short paragraph with ten typing errors in it, and saved several copies of it on to the disk. She decided that in addition to calling up the exercise, the next objective would be to practise screen-reading, cursor movement, and correcting errors. Then they would learn how to save their work and print out a copy of their corrected text.

She explained to the students what she wanted them to do, and gave a demonstration. They listened and watched in awe. But even that preparation didn't bring the success she intended.

'We're not washer-women,' the students said. 'Our grandmothers took in other people's dirty washing. Not us. We're not going to do someone else's dirty work for them.'

Audrey didn't understand what they meant, and asked for an explanation.

'We're not going to put right someone else's mistakes. We were born here. We went to school here. We're as English as you are. We're not slaves to do other people's work for them. Who ever made the mistakes, must mend them themselves.'

Audrey was horrified at their reaction. She had no notion that they carried a chip on their shoulders about their ancestry and once more explained that she had typed the exercise to include deliberate mistakes so that they could find and locate them on the visual display unit by reading the screen and moving the cursor up and down, left, and right. They would also learn how to use the delete and backspace keys, insert text, check it on screen, and print out their work. But the students didn't want to know.

'If you made the mistakes, then you must correct them, not us,' they objected.

So Audrey changed tactics. She suggested that they typed their name and a few words, while the other read the text as it appeared on the screen; then they would change places and repeat the tasks. Of course, their names were not initially capitalised, so that caused another problem and she had to show them how to hold down the "Shift" key to get a capital letter. But some of the students had problems in holding the shift key down with one hand whilst looking for the initial letter of their name, so she showed them how to press down the "Shift Lock" key, then the whole of their name came out in block capitals.

The students were slow at finding the letters on the keyboard, and made many typing mistakes, but eventually they saved and printed out their work and put it into a folder, together with the word processing handouts she'd made for them. They enjoyed doing that and felt that they were now really word processing because they were using the keyboard, seeing their work on the screen, and printing it out.

Over the forthcoming year as the students learnt how to touch-type in their typing lessons, they progressed on the word processor more quickly and became skilled in its applications. Eventually they were thirsting for their turn to use the equipment, mastered the machine, and enjoyed using it. Other lecturers also taught their students word processing skills. It was a very innovative time in education.

Alongside her progressive day-time activities, Audrey was still attending two evenings per week for her BEd(Hons) degree.

One of the projects on the course was to take an educational problem, attempt to solve it, and write a report on the processes used to achieve a successful outcome. She discussed the project with Gloria, and Jemma. They suggested that she told her degree course tutor about the problems she'd had in teaching word processing to students who hadn't learnt keyboarding skills; how she'd overcome their problems, and written exercises for them to practise with.

The following week her course tutor agreed that she could include the exercises she'd written as an Appendix to her submission, but her project would have to be assessed by Lou Rocket, the Head of Computer Studies at the university.

Audrey was awarded a high mark. Lou Rocket suggested that as there was a dearth of information about word processing, she should submit the exercises to a publisher, but she felt diffident about doing so, and continued her day job with increased enthusiasm, knowing she was on the right lines.

CHAPTER 30

TWO NEW VENTURES

A few months after she'd been awarded an honours degree, Audrey unexpectedly bumped into Lou Rocket in a local market area and they stopped to exchange festive greetings.

'Had those exercises published yet?' he enquired.

'No way!' she exclaimed. 'Writing them for my own students is one thing, submitting them for publication on an open market is something else. I only did them to help my students.'

'You're contemptible,' he sniped. 'You're not fit to call yourself a teacher.'

'Whatever do you mean?'

Audrey was shocked at his sharp words. They reminded him of her mother's scathing tones in years gone by.

'You wrote those excellent exercises for your students, but you're not prepared to share them with anyone else. You've bought books to help you with your course work. You've used our library and borrowed many of our books to help you in your studies. You've benefited from other people's work in other libraries as well as ours, but you're not prepared to publish your own book to do the same for other people. I'm disgusted with you.'

Audrey was gob-smacked.

'I never thought about it like that. I just didn't think the exercises were good enough for publication.'

'Well, in my opinion they *are* good enough and with such a dearth of word processing books to help people with the new technology yours could be the first book of practical exercises available. Just because someone publishes a book doesn't mean other people have to buy it, borrow it, read it, or use it. But it does provide them with the opportunity to do so, if they wish. If they can do better, then let them prove it. You think about it, and if we meet again, I'll ask you once more whether you intend to continue to be an introverted, possessive, cowardly creature, or whether you've become a positive, professional teacher. I wish your family a very Happy Christmas, and you, a New Year of published material. See you!'

He stomped off, and disappeared into the throng of Christmas shoppers.

Audrey was stunned. Her eyeballs scalded. She felt embarrassed. She'd never been shamed into taking action before. She'd always fought against her mother's idiosyncrasies and her father's obstinacies. She'd been helped and encouraged by her loving husband, and twins, and given a leg up by many different people, but she'd never been humiliated and reproached before – especially for something she hadn't done. His words were sharp and they cut to the quick.

When she got home, she told Rocky about her experience.

'Perhaps you should listen to him and do something about it. Even if you put all your exercises together in a book format, it doesn't mean that a publisher will take them up. It might be worth writing to some publishers first and see what they have to say.'

So early in the new year, Audrey wrote letters to six publishers and asked if they would be interested in reading her work with a view to publishing it, and enclosed a stamped addressed envelope with each one.

One publisher replied by return of post. She waited three weeks and no further replies were received, so she forwarded a copy of her exercises to him. Eight weeks later two more publishers replied and both offered to read her work, but by then the first publisher had taken an active interest and offered a contract, which she'd accepted.

Her expectations were high. She thought because of the shortage of practical word processing exercise books, it would take only a few months to produce, but it took over a year.

During its course of production, one of the major Examining Boards brought out a new syllabus for Information Technology at a higher level than they currently offered. The publishers asked her to write more exercises to meet the requirements of the new syllabus. They also asked her to write an answer book for the exercises.

The Publisher was pleased with her final submission and started to proceed with production. To her surprise, the company involved her in the design and presentation of the finished books. She hadn't realised that she would be asked to provide a book title, she thought the publishers would do that, so she suggested calling it "Typing with IT (Information Technology)". Also, she didn't realise that they would ask her to indicate where her markets lie, or be invited to choose the colour and design of the front cover. This was a totally new venture and she hadn't thought about any of these things.

In addition to bringing out a new syllabus, the Examining Board also advertised for assistant examiners to help with marking scripts during the summer holidays. To stay at the forefront of examination requirements for the new technology, she applied and was appointed as one of them.

She marked many exam scripts, some of them extremely well answered; some not so good; and some absolutely impossible to read.

A few months after her books were published, a letter plopped through the letterbox at home. It was from the Examining Board. It said they had read her IT books with interest and, as she was already an assistant examiner with them, they wondered whether she would be interested in becoming their chief examiner at the new higher level. If so, would she telephone the Director's Secretary to make an appointment for an interview.

Audrey read the letter over and over again. She could hardly believe her eyes. She showed it, first to Rocky, then to Gloria and Jemma.

Jemma Welsh's rounded figure almost burst with pride. She loved achievers, and glowed.

'Oh, my dear, you must accept. Offers like this don't come to many people. Very well done. When you're appointed it will bring great kudos to my department, and to the college in particular. It will open all sorts of doors for you; places you wouldn't normally be able to get into. Go ahead and say you'll go for an interview. If they offer you the accolade accept it with my blessing. I'm absolutely delighted for you.'

So Audrey made an appointment to see the Director and his working party, and discuss what would be required of her.

She travelled to their offices by train, and was welcomed warmly. The Director explained that the job was not full-time, nor even part-time. It was occasional, and would run concomitantly with her full-time job at her current college. They had tentatively approached her Principal to advise him that they were thinking of inviting her, and he had welcomed their consideration and would support her in the role if she accepted.

Her main tasks would be to adhere strictly to the examination syllabus, prepare a set number of examination questions based on it, with model answers and marking schemes, for the working party's consideration. One of the questions would be compulsory and should always follow the same format but she would have a free choice of topics from the syllabus for the remainder of the paper. She would also have to provide at least three additional questions and answers with marking schemes in case the Board didn't like any of the ones she offered them for their consideration. She would have to attend working party meetings once a term to answer any questions they may wish to ask; proofread examination papers when they came back from the printer's; and lead a small team of markers. Also, in order to keep up to date with the advancing techniques of IT in business and industry she would be required to visit leading information technology bureaux during her college holidays.

At lunchtime a trolley of hot food was brought into the committee room and everyone helped themselves. The main course was liver and onions, and vegetables. Audrey thought that was an unusual dish to serve, but took some because by that time she was hungry. She poured some of the rich liver gravy over her potatoes and sat down to enjoy her meal, but was somewhat surprised to discover, when she bit into them, that the croquet potatoes were not potatoes after all. They were fish batons, offered as an alternative to the meat dish! Liver gravy on fish did not appeal to her but the new venture as a chief examiner did.

After lunch the working party went into details about how to assess the scripts marked by assistant examiners and the meeting lasted until late afternoon. Finally she accepted their prestigious invitation with great delight.

Going home on the train she sat back in her seat and wondered what her mother would think of her now. Surely she couldn't still regard her as an educational failure. She reflected on how she had progressed from being a shorthand-typist to secretary, wife, instructor, mother, qualified teacher, lecturer, graduate, author, and now a chief examiner. Once more, she felt that she was at the pinnacle of her career.

CHAPTER 31

SURPRISE INVITATIONS

Through Audrey's new position as a chief examiner in information technology, she visited many IT agencies in London and the Midlands and saw their specialist training centres operating at first hand. She watched IT grow at an exponential rate.

Microsoft disc operating system (MS-DOS) became a standard program throughout the computer industry and after drop-down menus were invented she saw them being used in Britain for the first time. Personal computers (PC's) with a built-in hard disk were produced, and in 1983 the Apple computer company in America invented a 'mouse' control which was quicker than using the compass rose keys.

Computer prices were falling daily. Companies were vying with each other for sales; and the college bought many different types of microcomputers with different word processing packages which Audrey and Gloria had to assess, including Alan Sugar's Amstrad PCW which he marketed in Britain for £399. No longer did students have to operate one word processor two at a time; all students in every department of the college had hands-on computer training.

When the new Easter term commenced in 1984, a couple of members of staff were reading a newly posted notice on the staff notice board. It was an invitation to all lecturers over the age of fifty-five to apply for early retirement with up to five years' enhancement on their pension.

Gloria Greene was attracted to the prospect, went home that evening, did her sums, and decided to apply. Her application was successful. Her service to the local authority was to be terminated at the end of the summer term. Her post of senior lecturer over the secretarial section was advertised both internally and externally, and along with other members of staff, Audrey applied for her job.

On the morning of the interviews, Audrey was in a lavatory cubicle in the ladies' room on the ground floor. She heard the outer door open and footsteps approach. Gloria was talking to a colleague as they entered the room, and her voice could be heard quite clearly.

'She has high hopes of getting the job after all the work she's done leading the way forward in information technology but she's not going to get it. You wait and see!'

'I'll be very surprised if she doesn't! What do you mean?'

Audrey didn't know whether to cough, to let them know she was in the cubicle; to shout out, to let them know she was in earshot, or to keep quiet.

'Eavesdroppers never hear well of themselves,' her dad had once told her. Nevertheless curiosity got the better of her and she decided to keep quiet and listen.

'For God's sake, don't tell anyone I told you, but Jemma Welsh is going to retire at the end of this term. She told me in the strictest confidence that the Principal fancies appointing John, her Deputy Head, into her role because he's excellent at handling people and he's a fantastic administrator. Of course, it will be up to the interview panel, but he's done so much to train all the staff in the use of the new technology, not only in her department, but in other departments throughout the college as well. If Audrey got my job, and John got Jemma's, it would look like nepotism. Of course, neither of them might get the jobs! It's just a lot of "Ifs" at the moment. They'll both have to prove themselves better than any of the other candidates.'

'I see,' the colleague replied slowly. 'But isn't that always the case? All candidates have to prove they're the best person for the job. Anyway, I've finished my fag now, I'll just pop in here.'

'Okay, I'll go in this one,' Gloria replied.

While the two members of staff were preoccupied Audrey fled the ladies' room as quietly as she could, not stopping to wash her hands. She ran upstairs to another ladies' room on the first floor and washed her hands there.

'Well, now I know I've got a real fight on my hands. What do I do? Do I tell them what I've heard said in the toilets, or do I fight a losing battle? What would Rocky's advice be? He'd probably say be professional throughout. But what would a true professional do?' she asked herself. She checked her watch, then her appearance in the mirror, and refreshed her make-up. She went downstairs for her interview with the

Principal, Head of Department and Deputy Head. This time only one Governor was present, plus the regional Inspector for Further Education.

There were five interviewees for the post – three external and two internal. After lengthy deliberations, the position was offered to a lecturer from a rival college in the area.

The next day Jemma asked to see both of the internal candidates separately. She said to Audrey:

'This isn't a post-mortem, it's just to say I'm sorry you didn't get the job after everything you've done to help and support my department. You may have administrative skills in hospital work, but you've no experience in obtaining funding, and that's vital in our line of work. Also, you've never worked out timetables for staff, and that's another vital role in the work of a section leader. However, you're a good teacher, and we value your services highly, so don't be despondent. There'll be other jobs, other opportunities in the future, perhaps even bigger posts to apply for, we'll just have to see that you get some staff development to help you further up the ladder.'

'Well, I knew I wasn't going to get the job,' she blurted.

'How did you know?'

Quickly Audrey thought on her feet.

'I just knew it in my heart of hearts,' she lied. 'I felt it in my bones.'

Audrey kept her counsel. She could have told Jemma about the conversation that she'd heard in the toilets the previous morning, but she didn't.

'I know senior lecturer posts don't grow on trees, and especially not for women, but the Principal is thinking about re-organising the departments in the college and creating a new one in computer studies. As you know, all the computing and word processing is being done in my department at the moment but when Gloria retires it could be moved into a new computer department and, if it materialises, there could be an opportunity for you there. It's quite possible that you could become a senior lecturer in information technology skills. Who knows? We'll just have to wait and see. And if you do go up in the world you're going to have to take plenty of knocks, so perhaps this disappointment may turn out to be some kind of preparation for you in the future.'

Jemma's words seemed to float over Audrey's head in disbelief. There were too many 'possibles' for her to comprehend. Perhaps John would become the new Head of the Computer Studies Department? But surely that would smack of nepotism even more! Lost for appropriate words, she merely thanked her for all the help and support she'd provided over the past five years, and left the room wondering how she would settle down with a new senior lecturer over her.

The following week there was even a bigger shock. Word got round that the Principal had been appointed to a larger Principalship down South and would be leaving at the end of term, to take up his new job on 1st September. That meant that three of the senior managers would be leaving together.

Audrey knew in her heart of hearts that she would miss them all dreadfully. The prospect wasn't worth thinking about.

Her mind turned to the time when she was a child and Grandma Ferry accidentally flicked her wedding ring into the coal fire whilst throwing out a piece of paper. She tried to retrieve it with a poker, but couldn't, so she used a pair of tongs to remove a hot coal from the fire and put it on the hearth while she reached further into the heat with the poker before her ring melted. When the hot coal was placed on the hearth, it lost its fusion, cooled down, and became a useless piece of clinker on its own. And wasn't that same analogy happening to her at work now? Without her helpful colleagues to support her, she was likely to cool down and lose heart like that piece of coal on the hearth. The magnetism that had drawn her to the college five years ago seemed to have lost its attraction. It was as if a magnetic coil had been switched off.

During the summer holidays she received a batch of IT scripts to mark for the Examining Board. She launched into the task wholeheartedly to take her mind off her smarting disappointment.

One paper which she marked, was of such a high standard, that Audrey wished she could meet the candidate. She turned to Rocky and said:

'He, or she, must be an information technology teacher to have so much specific knowledge, or this person must be very high up in the information technology business. I'd love to meet him or her.'

'I don't see why not. It won't be too long before you get an invitation to attend the Prize Giving ceremony in November. Why don't you go, and watch out for where he or she stands up when their name is called.'

So when the invitation arrived, Audrey had no hesitation in accepting it.

She travelled to London by train and when the candidate's name was called to receive the prize, she watched the recipient, probably in her early twenties, arise from her seat and collect her award. Her eyes followed the young woman back to the seat where she sat down, next to her proud parents. When the proceedings were over, Audrey made her way to the prize winner.

'I'm the Chief Examiner in Information Technology, and I'd like to offer my sincere congratulations to you personally. You did an excellent paper. Very well done.'

'You're the Chief Examiner?' The prize-winner's eyes widened and her mouth fell open.

'My goodness, aren't you ordinary?' she gasped.

Audrey was taken aback by the remark, and reeled slightly at this knowledgeable young woman's perception of her.

'Do you think so?'

'Quite definitely. I imagined the examiner would be a man. And I never expected anyone to come up to me and congratulate me personally. Thank you very much.'

They exchanged a few words, then Audrey left to return home.

Sitting back in the compartment on the train, it dawned on her that everything in life was a matter of perception. How one person saw a situation was not necessarily the way another person saw it. Some people she'd grown up with, and others she'd worked with, may have seen things very differently from their points of view.

That day she completed a huge learning curve. She thought about Grandpa Small, who had died of natural causes twelve months ago, but she still had both of her parents, and had resolved her problems with her mother when Rocky went to Russia. She was travelling back to her wonderful husband, and fantastic twins who were adults now, and led their own independent lives.

The words of that young woman, and the noise made by the wheels of the train, echoed in her ears. She could hear them repetitiously saying:

'Aren't you ordinary, ordinary, ordinary? Aren't you ordinary, ordinary, ordinary?'

'Perhaps I am,' she thought. 'Perhaps I'm not. Surely it's all a matter of personal perception.'

She thought about the latest events at college. Times had changed. It was the end of an era. Things would never be the same again.

Her reverie was broken as the train pulled into a station. She twizzled her 'platinum, not gold, not married' (as her mother had called it) wedding ring around on her finger. It had certainly brought her a happy marriage and a career she could never have contemplated when she'd been deemed an educational failure for not passing her eleven plus exam and didn't get the bicycle she'd been promised.

Despite not being promoted to senior lecturer last term, Rocky and her family loved her very much and were proud of her achievements. Even her mother was proud of her now.

She counted the blessings that meeting and marrying Rocky had brought. Without him, she would never have achieved any of this. Life was wonderful. He was wonderful. The twins were wonderful. What more could anyone want? Another job? Possibly. That would depend on what was advertised and when, and where.

When she alighted from the train and was just about to cross to another platform to catch a local train home, she was very surprised to see Rocky on the platform waving frantically as he rushed towards her.

CHAPTER 32

THINKING ABOUT THINGS

'Whatever's wrong? You don't usually come to meet me when I come back from meetings in London. Are you all right? You look dreadful.'

Rocky wasn't his usual outgoing self. His large brown eyes looked sad and he seemed distant. His welcoming kiss wasn't as ardent as usual 'What's wrong, love? Aren't you feeling well today? Have you missed me?'

'Of course I've missed you, I always do when you're not here. But I've got some bad news that I didn't want to tell you over the phone at the Exam Board.'

Audrey's heart sank.

'What's the matter? Is it one of the twins?'

'No, they're both all right, as far as I know. I've been racking my brains to see how gently I can put this to you. I'm afraid it's your mam and dad.'

'What's wrong? What's happened to them?'

'I'm afraid they're both in hospital. There's been a terrible incident.'

'Oh, Rocky, no! When? Where? How? They don't drive a car!'

Her body trembled with shock. She went rigid.

'I didn't say accident, I said incident. It's all the noise here on the platform. Let's go and sit in that empty waiting room for a while. You're trembling, and this isn't doing me much good either.'

Rocky took her briefcase, slid his arm under hers, and led the way into the room. They sat down and he explained:

'About three o'clock this afternoon I had a phone call from Mr Prober, your mam and dad's next-door neighbour. He wanted to speak to you but I told him you were out for the day and wouldn't be back until this evening. There didn't seem any point in phoning the Exam Board at that time of day because the event would probably be over within the hour, and I didn't want you worrying all the way home.'

'You should've phoned the Board, what ever time it was. I'd have come home on the very next train, even if it meant leaving the ceremony.'

'I know you would. That's why I didn't phone. There was nothing you could've done, and I know how much you were looking forward to the Prize Giving and meeting your high-achieving candidate.'

'Do, go on. Tell me what's happened. Don't keep me in suspense.'

'Mr Prober told me that about eight o'clock this morning he was coming back from the shops with his daily newspaper and, as he put the key into his lock, he heard the sound of breaking glass. There appeared to be nothing untoward at his house, so he didn't think too much of it. Anyway, when he went inside to hang his coat and cap on the peg in his hall, he could hear lots of bumping noises coming from your parents' house. He said he thought it was odd because since your dad retired your parents don't get up very early; sometimes they sleep in until half past nine or ten o'clock. So he went to investigate. He peered in through the front window and everything appeared to be normal in the front room. He tried to see through the frosted glass panels in the front door and thought he could hear a faint cry for help. He could see movements, as if someone was at the bottom of the stairs. He called out, but got no reply. Then a man's shape appeared to go from the hall into the kitchen, but it was too thin and agile for your dad. He called out again. There was still no reply, so he walked down the side of their house to look through the kitchen window at the rear, and discovered it was broken. He called out several times, but there was no reply, and no sign of any activity, but he thought he heard a groan. He went home and phoned the police and told them that he thought whoever was in the house was still there.'

'How terrible. What happened next?'

'In the hope that the intruder was still in the house, he took the metal lid off his dustbin to use as a shield, and went back to see if anyone came out. He hoped he might be able to get a good look at him and give a description to the police when they arrived.'

'What a brave thing to do. But what if the housebreaker had a gun? He could've shot him and probably killed him.'

'The chances are, that if he'd had a gun he'd have used it already, and there'd been no shotgun sounds.'

'But he could have knifed him! There must have been a carving knife and plenty of other sharp knives in the kitchen. The invader could have used one of those to attack him.'

'Fortunately he didn't.'

'Go on.'

'Well, Mrs Prober was very frightened for her husband's safety, so she telephoned as many of her neighbours as she could and asked them to take their dustbin lids, and a stick, or something to protect themselves with, and surround your parents' house in the hope that if anyone came out, someone would be able to get an accurate description of them. About half a dozen people gathered around the house quietly and watched and waited. But nothing happened. They were concerned about your mam and dad so they decided to force the person out. One man ran home, got a supply of tablespoons, and the group caused a rumpus by banging their metal dustbin lids with the spoons to make a cacophony of sound to scare the trespasser. They thought that he would probably rush out and they would be able to see his face. But he didn't come out. He was still inside the house when the police and the first ambulance arrived.'

'What an incredible thing for them all to do! If it had to happen, it's a good job it was a Saturday, otherwise most of the men would have been at work. But what about poor mam and dad? What happened to them?'

'Mr Prober thinks that when your dad heard the sound of breaking glass in the kitchen he probably went to the top of the stairs to investigate. He must have tripped, and fallen all the way down them. He thinks your mam must have gone down to attend to him and as she bent over him, the crook hit her over her head with something, such as an umbrella or walking-stick out of the hall stand.'

'That's absolutely terrible. But are they both all right now?'

'No. I'm afraid they're not. Your dad's come round, but they think he's broken his right hip, and he's very badly bruised so they can't operate until all the swelling's gone down and they're able to X-ray him, and your mam has serious concussion and is in a coma. She hasn't come round yet.'

'This is an appalling thing to have happened. We must go there straight away. But what happened about the attacker? Did they find him?'

'Yes, they did. A constable found a youth hiding in the roof space. The ceiling hatch to the loft was hanging down and he was cowering in a corner, behind some polystyrene packaging which your dad had collected from the local shops. Mr Prober said your dad had been collecting it for months, and had been putting it between the rafters to act as loft insulation. Anyway, the offender was arrested and they took him away.'

'What I don't understand is, why did it take so long for us to be informed if all this happened at eight o'clock this morning?'

'I suppose these things take time. Everyone will have done their best. Their first concern would've been for your parents. Then forensic teams would've been working on the house for evidence and I don't suppose Mr Prober would have been able to go in to get our telephone number. Perhaps he had to wait until he could find out if any of the neighbours knew it.'

'I want to go and see what's happened for myself. Is their house locked up? I can't wait to get there. I can buy a train ticket while we're here in the station and get the next train to York. There's usually a train every two hours.'

'But you've only just got back from the Exam Board. It's not very wise. You're upset and tired and in shock. You'd be better waiting until the morning, and anyway, my car is parked outside, we can't leave it there, there's only a limited parking time allowed, plus the fact that you haven't got your parents' spare front door key with you, so you'll have to come home and collect it.'

'All right, but I'm not waiting until tomorrow. I want to go tonight. Late in the evening the roads will be clear of traffic, so we'll go home, have a cup of tea and then go.'

Rocky agreed to her decision. Less than three hours later they arrived at her parents' home. The rooms felt cold and eerie. But to her surprise, Audrey didn't cry. She experienced an inexplicable coolness; a frigidity. A mantle of iciness fell over her shoulders, shrouded her body, and froze her senses from the evilness of the event. She felt numb.

The kitchen window had already been boarded up by someone – presumably at the request of the police.

They went to let Mr and Mrs Prober know they had arrived and would be staying in the house for at least a couple of nights. Mr Prober explained that her parents had been taken to the new District Hospital, opened eight years ago. He found the hospital telephone number for them and Audrey telephoned immediately. Her dad was badly bruised and his hip and legs were so swollen they were unable to X-ray him yet; and Mrs Small was still unconscious. They were advised of visiting hours and had to wait until the next day before they could attend.

Larry Small was still in shock and pain, but was very glad to see them. He was on pain killers, and responding to treatment. They stayed with him for an hour before going to the women's ward. Mrs Small looked tiny in the sheets. She was ashen, and unresponsive; the nurses said she would probably get well, but it would take time. Audrey felt sure they were right to be optimistic because in normal circumstances her mother was a very strong character and, if she came out of the coma, sheer determination would pull her through. When the bell rang to indicate the end of visiting hour, Audrey and Rocky went back to her parents' empty house.

Audrey's mother always kept her home immaculate, like a new pin; there was very little to do, and the garden was in good shape for the time of year. Audrey looked in her dad's book-case for something to read. There were very few modern books but on the top shelf there were several small, linen-backed, Readers' Library, minute-print classics such as Jane Eyre and Robinson Crusoe. Their pages were coarse and yellowed by the passage of time. She recognised them as having once belonged to grandpa Small. Her dad must have inherited them when he'd died. There were also a few other old books, some of which had grandma Small's name inside them. One really tatty old book caught her eye. It was slightly larger than the rest.

'Look at this! Here's that lovely old book of Alice in Wonderland. I haven't seen it for years. Very occasionally, dad would read bits from it to me after he came back from the war.'

She pulled it out, and with it came a small thin handbook that she hadn't noticed when running her eyes across the titles. It was a brief guide to Infant Feeding and Management, priced at one shilling. She started to browse through it and continued:

'My goodness, look at this! Do you remember I told you, when you came back from Russia on that school trip years ago, that mam had told me about her problems in breast feeding me when I was a baby. She must have bought it, or had it given, and she's kept it all these years.'

Rocky acknowledged that he did remember – it was the time that Audrey and her mam had solved their conflict of personality problems; Mrs Small had confessed what had been tormenting her for years – and had turned over a new leaf.

Audrey flicked over the pages and a small photograph fell out of it. She picked it up and looked at it in amazement. It was a photograph of Rocky as a young man.

'What on earth was mam doing with this photograph of you? I don't remember you giving her this.'

'Let's have a look!'

Audrey passed the photograph to Rocky.

'That's not me.'

'Yes, it is.'

'No it isn't. I've never worn clothes like that. I don't remember this being taken.'

He turned the photograph over. On the back in Mrs Small's spidery back-hand writing were the words "Bill Boyd 1924".

'Good gracious! It's a photograph of mam's ex-fiancé, that she was engaged to before she married dad. No wonder she asked if you were adopted. You look the spitting image of him.'

'I can assure you, that's definitely not me. I wasn't born in 1924. And I know for certain that Cora and Edwynne were my parents. Both of their names are on my birth certificate.'

'No wonder mam didn't want me to marry you. She must have been really frightened to think you might have been some kind of blood relation to him. Seeing you for the first time must have really unsettled her. Now I can understand why she caused problems for us when we were courting.'

'Well, there's nothing you or I can do about it now. But it does help us to understand what she must have been going through. Throw it away. It's not going to do you, me, or the twins any good. That relationship was over many years ago. We don't want it.'

'No, I'm not going to throw it away. It's not mine to do so. If mam pulls through and comes home, she may remember it and want to look at it again, but the chances are, she's forgotten it was there. I can't understand why she kept it because it's caused her a lot of bitter memories in the past. However, it's no good being bitter and resentful about it now; she's had enough sadness to cope with. What's past, is past.'

Audrey put the photograph back in the handbook and slotted it back on to the bookshelf.

Rocky turned to her and said:

'I don't know about you, but I feel absolutely empty and bereft. What can we do that will give us a lift and be positive?'

'Well, love, next year it will be our Silver Wedding anniversary. How about making some plans to celebrate it? We could, perhaps, have a party and invite some of our colleagues from work. I don't know whether Lil and Den would be able to come from Hampshire, and I don't suppose for a minute that Vic and Candy will come all the way from New Zealand. But we could invite them. I could make a celebration cake, and send them some through the post if they can't come; and I'd love to invite Ruby Jordan. Perhaps she'd come and stay with us for a week. And if mam and dad are better by then, it would be lovely for them to come to a party, too. It would prove to them that our marriage wasn't a flash in the pan and that we've had a happy and successful union all these years. As for the twins,

I'm sure they would love it, and be able to bring some of their friends too.'

'Now that *is* a good idea. At least it will be something positive, and something to look forward to.'

'And I think I'll do something else as well.'

'Oh, what's that?'

'We've had so much happen in our lives, I think I'll write a story about our love, our life, and our love for life. I'll start with IT meaning sex and finish with IT meaning information technology, and you can help me to recall some of the events which have affected our lives, and if it ever gets published we can give a copy to each the twins, one to my parents, and one to all of our friends at the party.'

And she did.

This is it.